WINNAWARRA

Red Skies – Book One

ELIZABETH M. DARCY

LUMINOSITY
PUBLISHING

LUMINOSITY PUBLISHING LLP

WINNAWARRA
Red Skies – Book One
Copyright © December 2017 ELIZABETH M. DARCY

Paperback ISBN: 978-0-9956898-8-6

Cover Art by Poppy Designs

DEDICATION

To Gary, for his encouragement and with special thanks to Antoinette F Turner for her words of wisdom.

Heart pounding suspense and feel good romance set in the Australian Outback

CHAPTER ONE

Perth, Australia.

"I beg your pardon?"

Emily Perkins stared at the bead of sweat trickling down the solicitor's balding head to disappear into the bush of neatly trimmed hair above one ear. To her annoyance, Mr. Cedric Biggs remained silent with his head bowed over the stack of documents on his polished mahogany leather-topped desk. Above him, the slow rumble from an inadequate air conditioner was the only sound in the suffocating, humid office. *Why did I come here?*

She knew little about Jock Macgregor apart from what her mother had told her before she passed away. The wealthy cattleman had died six months previously, and at first, she believed the letter from Mr. Biggs had been a joke. The idea of a stranger leaving her a substantial inheritance had intrigued and excited her. She had travelled seventeen thousand miles to discover why he had picked her.

The room reminded her of a friend's house she visited in Oxford the previous year and had no idea Victorian style houses existed in Australia. In fact, her impression of koalas in every tree and kangaroos bounding down the main street was way off mark. Her arrival in Perth with its modern glass front buildings had pushed that particular image of the country well and truly from her mind. Impatient, she contained the urge to drum her fingernails on the desk and heaved a sigh.

The chair made a piercing squeak, and Mr. Biggs lifted his head then wiped his brow with a clean folded white handkerchief before peering over his spectacles at her.

"As I explained in our previous correspondence, the conditions of Mr. Macgregor's will are quite specific. To meet the requirements, you must reside at Winnawarra Station for a period of one year. During that time, you will be required to use your business skills to assist the manager. Mr. Macgregor discussed your role in detail with me. He was not confident with his accountant and wanted a fresh pair of eyes to look over the Winnawarra accounts." He turned the page in his pudgy hands and sighing gave her a look of indulgent patience. "Then as I have already explained, Miss Perkins, you have the choice, to sell your portion of the estate to the Macgregor brothers or remain. If you agree to the latter, you will receive a ten percent share in Winnawarra and your share of any accrued profits. We, of course, will pay for your return ticket to London." He raised both eyebrows. "However, you are required to sign a statement to the effect you will never sell the mining rights or allow anyone to destroy Winnawarra."

She leant forwards in the chair, catching a whiff of stale sweat and wrinkled her nose. "I see. What salary will I be paid during this period?"

"Not one cent." He raised his eyes and gave her a tight smile. "You will not require funds, Miss Perkins. Should you need anything, you only have to ask one of the Macgregor brothers. I can assure you at the end of the year, you will receive adequate compensation by either selling your portion or by the profit share. Winnawarra Station covers some twenty thousand square kilometres and runs over seventy thousand head of cattle."

Although she'd thought long and hard before considering the offer and making the journey to Australia, the thought of being stranded in the middle of nowhere without any chance of escape sounded more like a horror movie plot than an idyllic getaway. Having watched movies about worse case scenarios, she gripped the arms of the captain's chair and gaped at him in disbelief. "You dragged me all the way from London on an old man's whim to send me into the wilderness with three men I've never met? Have you lost your mind?"

"Not a whim, Miss Perkins." His mouth twitched into a small smile. "He mentioned your mother was a close friend and decided to honour her memory by offering you this opportunity."

Uncertain why the lure of a free trip to Australia and the offer of a share in a multi-million-dollar cattle ranch had seemed so enticing *before* she stepped into his office, she glared at him. "Can you guarantee my safety?"

"It is the Outback, Miss Perkins, and there are dangers, snakes for instance. No, I cannot guarantee your absolute safety from such things."

Oh, how wonderful. She had watched enough television to know the dangers of the Australian Outback. Heavens above, kangaroos alone could disembowel a person with their back legs. If she added venomous snakes and spiders to the list, her time at Winnawarra Station would be just peachy, not to mention she might be walking into a den of serial killers. She schooled her expression in an effort to cover the rush of terror marching up her spine with the determination of a stampeding herd of elephants and clasped her hands together. "*I see,* and *who* are the men I'm required to live with for one, long year?"

"Ah, well not only men, my dear. Winnawarra has a large staff. There are the three brothers, the cook, kitchen hands, and the stockmen. You will not be alone. No, far from it, Miss Perkins, and I can assure you, the Macgregor brothers are of good standing in the community. Indeed, one is a doctor and is an important part of the Royal Flying Doctor Service." He pressed his fingers into a tower and smiled. "If you agree to the terms of my client's will, I'll have you on a flight to Broome in two hours. Dougal Macgregor will meet you at the airport and escort you to Winnawarra Station."

She swallowed the lump in her throat. *Make a decision, Perkins.* She had already taken three months to make up her mind to leave the UK, and might just as well give it the old college try.

After all, he had offered her an out clause, and she could walk away from the deal at any time. "Very well, I'll go."

"Splendid." Mr. Biggs pushed a wad of papers towards her and offered her a pen. "If you'll sign where I've placed the crosses, I'll finalise the arrangements. In the meantime, my secretary will arrange a meal and have your luggage collected from the hotel."

Not comfortable to sign without reading the details, she sat down and waved a hand at him. "Fine, my bags are in the outer office. Your secretary told me to bring them with me." She flicked him a glance. "I would like time to read these papers before I sign my life away — if you don't mind?"

He gave her a pinched annoyed expression and reached for the phone.

"Miss Davenport, will you go down to the café and bring a selection of sandwiches and cake for my client then contact Dougal Macgregor and inform him Miss Perkins is on her way?"

* * * *

The small plane landed in Broome and Emily followed the procession of people to the exit. The moment she stepped outside, heat seeped through her clothes as if she had stepped in front of a blazing fire. She paused in the entrance to stare up at the endless blue sky and wondered how much higher the temperature would rise in summer. The tarmac shimmered in a heat mirage, and the hand railings to the steps burned her palms. She glanced around the small airport, taking in the scattering of planes neatly parked in a line, and a helicopter pad at the far end of the runway.

In the distance, she made out a car park, but Broome resembled the Australia she had first expected. Rough grass peeked out from rich red soil, and an abundance of palm trees surrounded the terminal.

Inside the small white building, she waited for the trolley with her baggage then dragged her bags awkwardly behind her, moved towards the exit. She glanced around looking for Dougal

Macgregor, although she had no idea what he looked like or even his age. Had she thought to ask Mr. Biggs more questions about the elusive man this would not have been an issue. Moving with the crowd of travellers, she searched the line of people in the Arrivals Lounge in the hope Mr. Macgregor would hold up a card with her name on or something. As passengers left the building and no one came forward, a tingle of unease gripped her.

After moving through the electric glass doors and into a wall of humidity, she waited on the footpath as the other passengers climbed into cars and drove away. Perspiration trickled between her breasts and ran down her stomach to soak the waistband of her white skirt. She batted away a group of persistent flies peppering her blouse and making every effort to climb up her nose. Deciding inside had to be better than becoming an insect snack bar, she turned and dragged her bags back into the terminal. At least inside, she would be out of the sauna-like conditions and enjoy the small comfort of the inadequate air conditioning.

The stark emptiness of the building unnerved her, not one person remained. She moved towards a drink dispenser and dropping her bags in a heap by her feet, searched her purse for change. She selected a bottle of water and waited for it to thump into the collection slot. Nothing happened. The next moment the machine shook violently and the plastic bottle shot from the front opening. As she bent to secure her purchase, a dark shadow fell across her path.

She staggered backwards and tripped over her bags. Someone grabbed her around the waist, and she gaped up at a tall man wearing a battered cowboy hat. Embarrassed, she straightened, intending to move past him to recover her drink. "Thank you."

"No worries."

His deep voice settled her nerves, but the sight of him fascinated her. Her gaze moved over shoulders wide enough to carry a piano, encased in a pale blue tee shirt stretched across a muscular chest, then down to worn jeans and dusty boots. He scooped the bottle up in one suntanned hand and held it out to her. The deepest blue eyes she had ever seen in her life scanned her features. She stared back at his handsome face taking in his long straight nose and determined chin. The ragged pink scar along his jaw gave him a roguish appearance but did not detract from the animal magnetism given off by the stranger. A lock of raven hair had fallen over one eye, and she had the sudden need to tuck the curl under the brim of his hat. *Oh my God! You are gorgeous.* Dragging her attention back to reality, she took the water from him and smiled. "Thank you, again."

"You'd be Emily, right?" He straightened to a good six-five, and one dark eyebrow rose in question. "The English girl my grandfather sent to straighten out us blokes."

She held out her hand. "Yes, I'm Emily Perkins. I'll be happy to help out any way I can."

"I'm not sure why he sent for you. I can see you're having problems with the heat and it's only going to get worse." He had not taken her hand but rubbed his chin eyeing her critically. "I'm sorry, love, but you won't last a week at Winnawarra."

Her hackles rose in defence before she noticed the amusement in his eyes. Was he laughing at her? Fine, agreed she did look a bit frazzled from the flight with her hair in an air travel-induced mess and her shirt was stuck to her with perspiration, but that was no excuse. She lifted her chin and glared at him. "Really?" She gave him an exaggerated once-over. "Tell me, are all the 'blokes' in this part of the world so condescending or is rudeness some type of an Australian, alpha male come on?"

A wide grin slashed across his bronzed face, and he stuck out one hand.

"You'll do." He closed one calloused palm around her fingers then dropped her hand like a hot coal. "Doug Macgregor and trust me, sweetheart, if I came on to you, you'd know." He waved a hand towards her bags. "Are they packed with fancy clothes or did you have the sense to bring a few pairs of jeans, a hat, and a pair of boots?"

Her face heated. She had packed for a warm climate, but obviously, her few pairs of cotton slacks and shorts would not do. "Ah, no none of the above, I'm afraid." She cleared her throat at his frown, needing to explain. "I had no idea what to pack. Not until I spoke to the solicitor in Perth and by then it was too late to go shopping." She pushed an errant strand of hair behind one ear and swallowed the nervous lump in her throat. "The documents I signed inferred I would be helping the manager so I assumed my business skills would keep me inside. I'm not sure why I'll be needing jeans or boots, Mr. Macgregor."

"It's Doug." He folded his arms across a wide chest and stared down at her from a towering height. "Winnawarra is a cattle station, and I'm the manager. Trust me, I do not sit in an office all day. There are cattle to muster, fences to mend, stock to feed, and if I get the time, I manage to give the paperwork a once-over at night. I will expect you to do your bit around the place like everyone else, and yeah, you'll need suitable clothing. I can't believe old Biggsy didn't fill you in with the requirements. He should have known better than to send you out here without so much as a hat."

She gaped at him and tried to grasp the situation. Clothes she could purchase *if* he would give her time to visit the local shops. "I'm prepared to buy anything you deem necessary before we leave for Winnawarra. Does this town have any shops that take credit cards?"

"Yeah, but don't worry about paying for your gear now. We have accounts in most of the shops here and settle up quarterly." He glanced at his watch. "I'll drop your bags in the Ute and take you into town. I suggest you buy anything you'll need for at least a month including medication" — he glanced away into the distance and shuffled his feet uncomfortably — "and any feminine products you might need as we don't have a corner shop."

Relieved to see the human side of him, she offered him a tentative smile. He overwhelmed her to the sixth degree and the rich musky aftershave he used made her knees weak. *Pull yourself together, Perkins.* "Thank you. I really appreciate your thoughtfulness."

He bent to collect her bags, groaned dramatically under the weight then gave her a crooked smile.

"No worries." He led the way through the main doors, strolled across the car park, and stopped beside a dusty old Ford. "Pull back the tarp, and I'll shove your stuff in the back. The Produce Supplies has boots, hats, and jeans." He indicated with his chin towards a wide main street with shops each side. "The chemist is down that way, and when you're done, we'll grab a bite to eat at the pub before we leave. How does that sound?"

Trying not to make him aware of her discomfort, she pulled at the front of her shirt in an effort to catch the breeze and cool her damp flesh. Giving him her best "happiest girl in the world" smile, she moved to the back of the vehicle. "Wonderful."

She attacked the dark cover attached with metal snaps stretched over the rear of the Ute with gusto and pulled it open wide enough for her bags to slide inside. An unbelievable stench singed her nostrils, and she jumped back glaring at him. "Phew, do you carry dead bodies in there or something?"

"You townies are all the same." Doug grinned and tipped back his hat, eyeing her with amusement. "It's a few bags of chook food and some fertilizer for the veggie garden." To her horror, he slung her prized white leather luggage inside the filthy hole and attached the cover. He waved a hand towards the passenger door. "Jump in, love, we haven't got all day."

Doug slid a glance over the girl sitting beside him and shook his head. She looked too damn delicate to be working on a cattle station and the way sweat soaked through her clothes, she would not make it through summer without suffering heatstroke. He turned the air conditioner to high, and her honeysuckle scent wafted over him turning his brain to mush. The circulating air lifted the long blonde hair from her shoulders, and when she turned her deep blue eyes towards him, he realised just how long it had been since he'd had a woman in his life. Biting down hard on the inside of his cheek to keep his mind well and truly centred on driving and not on the long-toned thighs peeking out from her short skirt, he pulled to the curb outside the Produce Supplies then shot her a glance. "Do you have any idea why Pop included you in his will?"

Her blue eyes narrowed, and she frowned.

"Who is Pop?"

"My grandfather. You know — the one who died and spent a fortune bringing you out from the UK — John Hamish Macgregor, does the name ring a bell?" He turned and stared at her in amazement. "You didn't *know* him?"

"No, not personally but my mother told me stories about him. She called him 'Johnny'. I believe they were friends for years and kept in touch. She said he carved Winnawarra out of the Outback with his bare hands. I gather from the solicitor, Mr. Macgregor was aware of my business qualifications and marital status. I think he's been keeping tabs on me for some time." She shrugged and wet her bottom lip. "Kind of creepy don't you think?"

"Nah, you're climbing up the wrong tree, love. Jock was not a letch, he was a good bloke, and helped everyone. The only thing he ever did for himself was to take a trip after my grandmother died. They planned to go to London and then visit New York and never made it, but he promised to take her ashes back to England. She was the kind of woman who wanted to see him remarry straight away but he had other ideas." He pushed back his hat and scratched his damp head. His grandfather had described his romp around the world and the countless women he met but had never mentioned Emily's mother.

He glanced at her again. She could not be a relative and not know the connection. Why would he leave her a portion of his estate? *I wish he'd told me about his plans before he died.* "I guess he had his reasons to bring you here. You're not a relative, are you?"

She turned in her seat and stared at him huffing with annoyance.

"I hope you're not inferring I'm your grandfather's love child because it's not possible. I have my father's colouring."

Fiery little thing. "Hey, don't get your knickers in a twist. I didn't say anything of the sort. It was a question plain and simple. I think you are too young anyway. I'm talking twenty-five years ago."

Her eyes flashed with anger.

"Mr. Macgregor, if you're ins—"

Oh shit, he could swallow his tongue. She looked about twenty-five and could easily be the result of Jock's overseas jaunt. He rushed on forcing the words out in his best soothing tone. "I thought you might be a relative from way back on my mum's side and I asked because we can't imagine why Jock took it into his head to add a stranger to his will the day before he died. He never mentioned his plans, and we are a close-knit family. We grew up on Winnawarra and Jock was a big part of our lives." He opened the car door and slid out. "Come on, we'll talk later in the pub. If you stay inside the cab much longer, you will die of dehydration. Drink the water."

She jumped down from the seat, turned and gave him an exasperated stare.

"Oh, I think I *know* why he included *me* in his will." She slowly opened the bottle and met his gaze. "He must have been astute enough to foresee a problem with the business side of running the station, and he certainly had concerns about your current accountant. If he'd discussed his worries with my mother, it makes sense he would offer me the job because I doubt business managers with a degree in accountancy are queuing up to work here. You have to admit, the chance of a share in the Winnawarra Station was a very tempting inducement to get me to come to this wilderness." She waved her hand in a frantic gesture to dislodge the flies.

He rubbed the back of his neck. If there had been a problem with the accountant, why hadn't Jock spoken to him *before* he died? He had no idea there was a problem until Jock fired him in his will. "Did your mother discuss this trip with you?"

"No." A shadow of pain moved over her face. "She died some months ago."

He moved closer and laid one arm over her shoulder. "I'm sorry, love."

She wriggled out from his embrace, her face scarlet.

"Thanks, and I'm sorry for your loss too. Well, Mr. — um . . . *Doug*, it looks like we are stuck with each other for at least one year. It's just as well I'm tougher than I look." With an expression of grim determination, she turned and flounced into the shop.

He removed his hat, wiped the sweat from his brow, and self-consciously sniffed under one arm. By the way she glared at him, he had not made a very good impression on her. Bloody hell, she looked fragile, and he hoped she was not kidding about being tough. An English wildcat would stir up the place and have every man shaving and using deodorant. He glanced up into the cloudless sky. "Thanks, Jock, I guess you think this is funny."

CHAPTER TWO

The pub, set amidst palm trees had huge air conditioning units hanging from three of the windows. It differed from the quaint English pubs with their long, polished bars, whitewashed walls, and oak-beamed ceilings she had frequented. Emily gaped at the bare wooden floor and tiled walls in amazement. The place resembled a hospital waiting room with a bar or the sort of large lavatory found in a theatre. The smell of beer and musky male sweat accosted her nose mixed with the nauseating smell of what she recognised as beef stew or perhaps meat pie.

Men in cowboy hats, wearing jeans and boots in what must be the usual dress *du jour* congregated in groups at the bar. Others sat eating pies and drinking light golden beer with a head resembling foam rubber more than the thick milky bubbles on an English pint. The men occupied most of the plastic chairs set around square aluminium tables. The only woman in the pub appeared to be the barmaid who preened at the sight of Doug. She patted her bleached blonde hair then pushed humongous breasts towards him in a blatant invitation.

"*Dougy,* I didn't know you'd planned to be in town this week. Not trying to avoid me are you, pet?"

"*Me,* avoid you, Sandy, nah, never in a million years." Doug strutted to the bar and gave her a salacious wink. "I came over to pick up a new business manager, who is I'm told a hotshot accountant, to look over our books." He indicated to Emily over one shoulder with his thumb. "I'll have two specials and a jug of water thanks, precious." He pulled out his wallet, took out some notes, and slapped them on the counter. "Keep the change."

Sandy gave her a long accusing stare laced with a "keep away, he's mine" warning then turned a wide smile on Doug.

"What, old Mr. Brewster not cutting it anymore?" She raised one brown pencilled eyebrow in question. "Jock must have used him for thirty odd years. Brewster will be miffed you've decided to bring in a girl to do his job."

"It was Jock's idea not mine." Doug shrugged, and Emily noticed the hard muscles of a well-developed back move under his shirt and swallowed hard. "The old bugger set this up before he died." He passed two glasses filled with ice to Emily and turning back to Sandy picked up a jug of water. "Trust me, it wasn't my doing." His head swivelled to look at her. "That's right, isn't it, Em'?"

Surprised but charmed by his familiarity, she cleared her throat and lifted her chin. "Yes, Doug had nothing to do with my position at Winnawarra Station."

"Oh, Gawd you've replaced Brewster with a young English girl?" Sandy snorted in a pig-like laugh. "Just wait 'til that info gets around town."

Emily's heart sank. *That can't be good. I thought English people were welcomed in this country.* Stuck in a strange land and alone with a powerful man she had just met placed her in an untenable position. From his comments to the barmaid, he had not welcomed her intrusion. She flicked a glance around the room and noticed the other men's attention moving over her as if she had suddenly grown two heads. She calculated her options. Doug seemed nice enough, and she prided herself at being a good judge of character. Could she trust him to keep her safe or should she walk to the nearest hotel, take a room, and book a seat on the next flight back to Perth? *Surely, a solicitor would not knowingly place me in danger.*

"Em' ... ah ... Emily?"

Dragged from her musing, she started at his touch and took a step backwards banging into one of the chairs. "Yes, did you want something?"

Doug wrapped his long fingers around her arm and led her to a table.

"I think you'd better sit down. You're not going to pass out on me, are you?"

She dropped into the upright and less than comfortable chair, and offered him a bright smile. There was no way she would allow Sandy to know how much her harsh words had upset her. "I'm fine just wool-gathering."

"Wool-gathering?" He glanced around as if gauging anyone was listening and lowered his voice to a whisper. "You do *know* you're in a pub, right?" He filled the glass of ice with water from the pitcher on the table and pushed it towards her. "Drink. Dehydration does strange things to your mind if you're not careful."

She sipped and regarded him over the rim of the glass. Uncomfortable did not come close to the expression on his face, and his obvious worry comforted her nagging indecision. She placed the glass on the table, and frowned. "I gather you're not too pleased with Jock for including an English woman in his will?"

"It's not *you* being here. It's just that *we*, my brothers and I had no idea what Jock had in mind until the reading of his will. We never discussed what would happen if he died because he hadn't suffered a day's illness in his life and we all thought he would live forever. His death came as one hell of a shock to all of us especially the *way* he died."

The solicitor had not mentioned anything unusual about the old man's death, and she regarded the deep loss in Doug's expression with interest. She had to ask. "If it's not too painful to discuss can you tell me how Jock died?"

"He took a fall down a flight of steps and fractured his skull." Doug shook his head slowly, and his dark eyelashes lowered covering his expression. "Not here, it happened in Perth right after he changed his will."

"So, an accident then?"

"So they say." Doug lifted his gaze, and a flicker of annoyance crossed his expression. "I've never known Jock to take a misstep in his life. He still had his wallet, so the cops said it was an accident and just an old man tripping on the stairs in the dark." He removed his hat and pushed his fingers through his hair making it stick out in all directions. "Funny thing though, his lucky rabbit's foot was missing. It was a ceramic model my grandmother made for him, and he carried it everywhere." He snorted and shook his head ruefully. "He would have had every man and his dog searching for it if he had lost the damn thing, so as it wasn't found on or near his body that in itself is suspicious."

Emily allowed the facts to percolate in her mind and sipped the ice-cold water. Jock sounded like a man on a mission, travelling to Perth to change his will as if he knew his time was up. Dying the same night in suspicious circumstances made the hairs on the back of her neck stand to attention. "I agree. I'm surprised the police didn't investigate more fully." She placed the glass on the table and shrugged. "Especially as we know he had concerns with his accountant."

"There lies the problem. We didn't *know* he wanted to fire Brewster so that information wasn't given to the cops at the time of his death." Doug let out a long weary sigh. "Although, I can't imagine Brewster going to Perth to push Jock down the stairs because sooner or later one of us would discover he'd been cooking the books."

"So, do you think he put me in his will as a failsafe?" She rubbed her temples. Her head throbbed with the implications. *Good Lord what have I got myself into now.* "Do you believe there is a murderer on the loose?"

"At Winnawarra? Nah. To be honest, I don't think he wanted to worry us about the accountant. I was in hospital in Perth, and he came to visit me the day he died and never mentioned him. I guess he thought he could get everything sorted. Anyway, if Brewster has been fiddling the books, I'm sure you'll get to the bottom of it in no time." Doug leant back in his chair and waited for Sandy to place the meals and cutlery on the table. "Thanks, love." He gave a slow, suggestive grin.

"I'll see *you* later." Sandy sashayed away with a sway of her too short skirt and cheap perfume.

Emily gaped at the pie and mound of greasy chips floating in gravy. "Apply straight to the hips."

"You can afford to add a few pounds." He chuckled. "It's a long time before dinner, so eat up, and we'll get going. I've posted a flight plan for departure at three." He smiled. "I made a special trip in the chopper to pick you up, so you didn't have had to wait a day or two in town to catch a ride on Robbie's plane."

She held up a hand to stop further conversation. "I'm happy to discuss modes of transport later but for now can you give me the basics? Your solicitor informed me the size of Winnawarra Station, how many head of cattle you run, and your name. Were there any other deaths at Winnawarra? It might be significant. Jock would know about my studies in forensic science. Do you think he included me as a failsafe because Jock had concerns for his safety?"

His eyebrows rose to the hairline, and he stared at her.

"I've never believed Jock thought someone was out to get him. If he was worried, he'd have told me or at least his solicitor." A nerve twitched in Doug's cheek, and he eyed her with a bemused expression. "I don't know very much about you." He cut his pie then rested his fork on the plate. "Apart from your job of overseeing the books, and your obvious interest in forensic science, I can't see what he had in mind because you have no other skills to contribute to a cattle station."

Emily's stomach dropped. Why couldn't he see the big picture? Hello? Bells and whistles sounded, and she gaped at him. "If your grandfather *was* murdered, either he must have been clairvoyant or he had a very sound reason to include me. Unless you have some other unsolved murders you haven't mentioned."

"Can't say I can think of any offhand, love." Doug stabbed the fries on his plate and his lips quirked into a smile. "Don't stress,

Em'. You'll be as safe as houses at Winnawarra with three men looking after you."

Of course, Jock could have had another reason for including her in his will. She winced. "I hope your grandfather wasn't prone to matchmaking."

"Oh, he tried but never got far. You see, we get heaps of good sorts coming through during the muster." He grinned wolfishly. "Women just looking for a bronzed Aussie cowboy to warm their beds, so trust me, we don't need any help."

She chewed the mouthful of surprisingly good steak pie as she considered the information and came up with a big fat zero. If Jock wasn't a matchmaker and there hadn't been a murder, why had he included her in his will? *This is too difficult for my jet-lagged mind to unravel.* Taking another path, she smiled at him. "Tell me about your brothers and the staff."

"Ah, well I'm the eldest, then there's Robbie, Dr. Robert Macgregor, he is on call for the Royal Flying Doctor Service." He sipped his water and made circles in the condensation forming on the glass with one long finger. "Then there's young Ian. He has a degree in animal husbandry and is the head stockman." He returned her smile, leant back in his chair, and stretched his long legs. "We have around forty staff most times. The amounts of ringers vary. We employ more during the muster, and then there's the cook and the kitchen staff. We cater for tourists as well. Usually, the visitors come for the muster, and get in the way most times, but hey, Jock started the idea yonks ago, and it has become a tradition. It pays well too. Like I said, it gives the lads the chance to meet people, because being isolated has social disadvantages."

I seriously doubt that, Mr. Macgregor. She glanced over at Sandy. The woman was giving her "snake-eyes" over the bar. Oh yes, Doug was certainly a catch, but after coming out of a particularly sticky office romance, she had no plans to get involved with another player. She would admire him from afar. After all, looking did not hurt anyone. *I'm only human, and let's face facts here, Perkins, everything about Doug Macgregor pushes him to the top of my list of hot, delicious men.* She glanced away. Although, a romantic interlude with him would be fun, she doubted he would be interested in her. She cleared her throat. "So where do you fit in with Jock's plans. What is your specialty?"

His gaze darkened for a second before he shrugged.

"I fly the chopper and I manage the place, like I said before."

Impressed she raised her eyebrows. "So do you fly Robbie around too?"

"Nah, he has his own pilot's licence." He huffed out a long sigh. "Before you ask, Robbie obtained his licence because he wanted to join the Royal Flying Doctor's Service but I used to be a pilot in Special Forces."

Her attention went to the scar on his chin, and she looked away not wanting to appear nosy. "And now you're here. Do you miss the men in your command? Those type of friendships last a lifetime."

He tilted his head and regarded her with an unguarded scrutiny as if deciding to give out classified information.

"If the blokes live long enough, they do for sure." He stared over her left shoulder and winced as if reliving a painful memory. "I was two days from completing a tour in Afghanistan and copped an injury. When I arrived back in Australia, nobody told me my parents had died in a car accident. I was out of it for six months or so, and Jock kept it a secret from me until the day he died. With none of us at home, Johnno, one of the hands, had to run Winnawarra alone. All of us were away from home apart from Ian. So, after my recovery in Perth, rather than sign on for another tour, I asked the Air Force to discharge me, and I came home to take over." Dark lashes dropped over his eyes guarding his expression. "I'd rather not discuss my time in Afghanistan, if you don't mind."

The flash of annoyance in his eyes stopped any questions hovering on her lips. "That's your business, Doug."

"I guess you're unfamiliar with life on a cattle station. We use the chopper as well as horses and trail bikes during the muster."

She frowned. "I'm sorry, but I know absolutely zero about cattle husbandry. Although, using a chopper does seem an expensive way to muster cattle."

"Not at all. You said our solicitor explained the size of Winnawarra, and as an accountant, you must appreciate how cost efficient it is to use the chopper. It would add weeks to the job if we only relied on horses and trail bikes." He shrugged. "I gather in the UK a couple of dogs could to do most of the work, but here it takes a little more effort. I could probably fit most of England's farmland on my station." He cut into his pie and glowered at her. "The chopper is used for tourism as well. The visitors pay well for me to take them out over the Kimberly, and show them the sights of this 'wilderness'."

Not wanting to annoy him further, she smiled to lighten the mood. "Oh, I'm sorry." She ran her finger through a drip of water on the table then lifted her chin. "I must appear very rude, but all this" — she waved a hand towards the door — "is foreign to me, and I might as well be on Mars. To be honest, half the time I have no idea what you are saying. I think it may take a while for me to get used to your accent."

"*My* accent?" He grinned and his accent broadened. "I don't *have* an accent, love. I speak the same as everyone else in 'stralia. You're the one who sticks out like a sore thumb the moment you open your mouth." He leant back in his chair, and his blue eyes twinkled with mischief. "Don't worry. A year at Winnawarra will remove the marbles from your gob. Our mob will soon have you talking like a native."

A man sitting at the next table grunted, and his weather-beaten face wrinkled into a smile.

"Too right."

Heat flooded her cheeks, and she straightened moving her attention back to Doug. "Well, that's something to look forward to . . . I guess." She closed one hand around the cold glass in an effort to regain her composure. "What do the tourists want to see in the Kimberley?"

"I gather you know zero about this region? This area is known worldwide for its magnificent scenery and rock formations." Doug waved a hand towards the door in a parody of her earlier gesture. "It may be miles of wilderness out there, but you haven't lived until you've seen the Bungle Bungles in the Purnululu National Park or flown over the rugged gorges and waterways. The sunsets are spectacular and trust me you will never see another ocean like the one here on the Broome, coast. The water is luminous."

She smiled at his enthusiasm. "Yes, I did notice the ocean. It *is* a magnificent blue, but apart from the coastline, all I saw coming here was miles and miles of miles and miles." She placed her cutlery neatly on her plate and decided to move the conversation to another topic. "How about telling me why the people here are so against visitors from the UK? Your grandfather was obviously Scottish and influenced all of your names. Your name is *Dougal,* isn't it?"

"I prefer Doug, and *I'm* not against the English or *you*. In fact, my mother was English, born in London. I guess many Aussies can trace their ancestry back to the UK."

"Yes, many would have come out as convicts at first. Do you think Aussies hold it against us?"

"Nah, this place was built on the shiploads of immigrants, especially in the 1960s most were from the UK. We thrive on multiculturalism." He rubbed his chin and eyed her speculatively. "It would be good to know exactly *why* you're here and it makes me wonder if Jock didn't trust me to run the place." He sighed, and his shoulders slumped. "I guess he had his reasons." He glanced at his watch. "Are you finished, we'll need to head off?"

* * * *

The professional way Doug did the pre-flight check around the helicopter eased Emily's mind a little until he slid into the seat beside her and grinned like a donkey.

"From the look on your face, this is your first time in a chopper, right?" At her nod, he pushed a headset firmly on her head and adjusted the microphone. "Okay, love, hold on tight, and think of England."

The engine roared into life, and through her headset, she could hear Doug communicating with the Air Traffic Control in a clipped, professional manner. The moment the chopper lifted and hovered, her stomach dropped down to her boots, and she gripped the sides of the chair until her fingers ached. Doug appeared lost in the moment or needed all his concentration to fly, either way, his silence did not help her nerves. After what seemed like hours travelling over grasslands dotted with, creeks, waterholes and bottle-shaped trees, he finally turned to look at her.

"You need to keep drinking water, love. You don't look well, and I don't want you to faint." He took a bottle of water from a cooler and handed it to her with a sympathetic smile.

"I'm fine. All what's happened is a bit overwhelming, and I'm a frightened about being stuck in the middle of nowhere." She glanced at him, and her stomach squeezed. "I noticed how the people in the pub looked at me. What if everyone at Winnawarra treats me like the latest 'flu bug'?"

"She'll be right. I trust Jock knew what he was doing by bringing you out here and I'm sure you'll fit in with our mob just fine." He smiled, and she noticed his cheeks had the cutest dimples. "You're female, and that's a bonus for a start. I'm sure everyone will enjoy chatting with you. It's some time since we've had an English person in our midst." He indicated ahead with his chin. "We're almost home. Look straight ahead. Can you make out the group of buildings set some ways from the river? That's the Winnawarra homestead."

Home? Maybe it will be and maybe it won't. I guess I'll soon find out. In the distance, roofs glistened like glass over groups of white buildings shimmering through a heat haze. The station appeared like an exotic mirage in the wilderness. The place was huge, bigger than three football stadiums. "Yes, I see it. I must say the Winnawarra homestead is larger than I expected. In fact, everything in Australia is bigger than I expected." *Including the men.*

The chopper followed a wide river then Doug swung around and deliberately swooped over a massive herd of cattle grazing on the bank. The cows stampeded like a disturbed mound of annoyed ants running in all directions and leaving a cloud of orange dust in their wake. She stared longingly at the sparkling blue water winding away in the distance imagining diving into the tempting depths and cooling down. "I didn't think there was so much water in this part of Australia. The river looks wonderful, but why did your grandfather build the homestead so far from the water? It's too far to walk for a swim."

He gave her an exasperated stare then rolled his eyes skyward. "Crocs."

She swallowed hard. Snakes, spiders and now crocodiles, what else did she have to put up with — man-eating plants? "Oh, I thought they were native to Queensland."

"Nope. They are up here too, and where there is water, there are crocs, unless it is on top of a plateau. You see, crocs can't climb. They haven't reached Brisbane yet, but I hear they have sharks in their rivers. Even the million-dollar Gold Coast homes on the canals have sharks in the water outside."

"Do you have crocodiles *outside* your back door?"

He shrugged dismissively.

"Not really, that river is about two Ks away, and the ones here are fresh water, not as dangerous as the saltwater crocs." He indicated ahead with his chin. "The fences keep them away from the livestock. The cattle shouldn't be that close to the river that's why I buzzed them before. The fence must be down."

She peered out looking for a break in the fence then frowned. "Perhaps they're thirsty?"

"Not likely. They have water troughs, and they're automatically re-filled. We have an efficient irrigation system, pumping water from the river but as soon as it cools down the cattle start moving around, and the grass is always greener on the other side of the fence." He grimaced. "Then they become croc tucker."

Unease tightened her stomach, and she swallowed the growing lump in her throat. "Wonderful."

The herds of cattle scattered around the area were not the only animals surviving on this rugged landscape. They had flown over hundreds of kangaroos bounding across the grasslands plus a few isolated groups of camels and horses. Sipping the bottled water, she glanced at him. "Are the camels and horses yours too?"

"Yeah, if they wander onto our land and don't have a tag. They have been here since the first settlers came to the area and left to run wild. The stockmen round up the horses once a year to keep the numbers down. Some we break-in to work the cattle, the rest we sell. The camels, well, they please themselves. You can't eat them, and they're mean, nasty buggers so are best left alone."

As Winnawarra Station came into view, her heart raced. They headed towards a runway standing out like a red road going nowhere with a wind direction flag at one end on top of a post leaning precariously to one side. They flew over the main house. The huge, long building with wide shady verandas on all sides Doug called "the homestead." Adjacent to the main building windmill powered water tanks sat on high platforms. The reusable energy theme continued throughout the station with lines of solar panels packed on every spare space of roof. She had expected a rundown farm, but Winnawarra was far from what she had imagined. Modern machinery and freshly painted buildings stretched out in all directions. As they descended, she noticed a fenced area at the back of the homestead surrounding a bright green patch. "Do you grow your own vegetables?"

"We have a veggie patch, but it's the cook's domain." Doug grinned at her. "I'm banned from raiding the tomatoes."

Emily inspected her new home taking in a line of massive sheds and a small aircraft inside a hangar. Beside the homestead ran a row of barns piled high with the biggest bales of hay she had ever seen in her life. Stock pens and grain silos rose from the ground, and the entire scene resembled a small town.

She listened to Doug relaying his arrival over the radio and held her breath as he set the helicopter down some distance from the house. The churning blades lifted the dust and created a dense red fog around them. As the engine whined to a stop, she turned to him. "You're a very competent pilot. At first, I thought we wouldn't make it here in one piece."

He gave her a baffled stare and shrugged.

"I'm not sure how to take you, Em'. You're a strange one." He chuckled and held out his hand for the headset. "Let's take it one day at a time, hey. This may be a big place, but it's not like you can take off on your own to get some peace and quiet." He waved a hand towards the open landscape. "It's dangerous out there. So, before you run for the hills come and talk to me. I try to make sure nobody goes stir-crazy and trust me it happens to the best of us." When his full lips quirked into a warm smile, her stomach went into free fall. "Deal?"

How could she resist? She offered her hand, and his long rough fingers brushed her palm in more of a caress than a shake. Her heart missed a beat then thundered in her chest. She swallowed hard. "Deal."

CHAPTER THREE

Emily pressed one hand over her nose and followed Doug through the orange dust cloud. She glanced down in horror at the red dirt coating her new white skirt and stumbled after him tripping over the uneven ground. Barking dogs surrounded her, but they all scampered off at a sharp word from their master. Before she had taken a step, the sun dropped to snuggle against the horizon as if turning out a light, and she gazed at the incredible red and gold streaked sunset. "Oh, that has to be the most incredible view I've ever seen."

"That's nothing. Yeah, it is spectacular, but I'll take you along with me the next time I do a tour of the Kimberley. I think you'll be impressed and may appreciate what Jock has offered you a bit more."

Caught in the last rays of sunlight, he appeared to be bathed in gold and taller with his long shadow streaming out behind him. She glanced at him and smiled. "I *do* appreciate the chance to be part of Winnawarra, and I would love to see the sights. Thanks for the invitation."

"No worries. Come on inside, love, and I'll get you settled." Doug led the way up the front steps of the homestead. "There will be plenty of time in the morning to show you the ropes." He opened the door, and it creaked in a loud whine. "I've got to oil that hinge one of these days." He marched down a passageway and dumped her bags on the floor outside a neat double bedroom. "This is your room. I'm just down the hall." He waved a hand at the bags. "Leave them for now, and I'll introduce you."

She patted at her hair and glanced in horror at her dishevelled reflection in the mirror hanging in the hallway. Dirt smudges covered her face, and her neck had rings of red where the dust had mingled with her sweat. Grabbing his arm before he could move away, she cleared her throat. "Can I clean up a bit first? I look a mess."

"She'll be right. No one stands on ceremony here, love." He grinned and taking her arm practically dragged her down the passageway. "None of us look too good after a long day's work and think what an impression you'll make on them *after* you've had a shower."

Voices engaged in spirited conversation percolated through an open doorway at the far end of the hallway. Thrust before him into the bright kitchen, she gaped at the men sitting around a long table. All eyes turned to her, and the room had fallen deathly silent. A woman's voice preceded the entrance of a rotund middle-aged lady, wearing a red check apron and drying her hands on a floral tea towel.

"Don't go gawking at the poor girl. You're scaring her to death." She waddled across the room and gave her a bright smile. "You must be Emily. I'm Glady, the housekeeper. I'm married to Bob, he's the cook, and has everything underway for your 'welcome to Winnawarra dinner'." She smiled and patted her on the arm. "You might be the only girl living in the homestead, but you're not alone. We have plenty of women working here. You'll soon get to know the kitchen hands, and I'm sure Doug will introduce you to the two Jillaroos in the morning."

"Thank you, Glady." Doug moved to Emily's side and gave the woman a long "mind your business" stare. "I'll introduce her to the guys then she can clean up for dinner."

The four men seated around the table rose with a scrape of chairs. Good heavens, she could not remember a time when one man had stood at her entrance let alone four of them. She searched the faces. Immediately, Doug's two brothers stood out with their similar features and amazing blue eyes.

One of the men smiled at her in a flash of brilliant white.

"I'm Robbie, and this is my brother Ian." He waved a hand at the slightly younger man standing beside him.

Neither of them offered to shake her hand. Perhaps it was not the custom to shake women's hands in this part of Australia. She allowed her gaze to drift over the brothers and placed them all in their late twenties early thirties. "Nice to meet you."

"The big hairy bloke is Brian, our vet, and this mongrel, Johnno, is the assistant manager." Doug laid one large hand on her shoulder. "We live in the homestead but the staff live in the bunkhouses, and you'll meet them in due course." He turned her around and urged her into the hallway. "Now you can take a shower. The press is empty for your gear." He turned and grinned at the men gaping at her. "Do me a favour and go and unload the chopper. Bring in the shopping bags and give them to Glady. Em' will need her new things washed before she can wear them." He waved her towards a bedroom door.

The press? What? She glanced at him over one shoulder. "I'm sure they'll be fine."

"Nah, the jeans will be as stiff as buggery. Don't you worry, Glady will have them back to you first thing in the morning." He grinned at her. "Do you need my help to unpack?"

Exhausted, filthy, and more than a little overwhelmed, she sagged against the bedroom wall and waited for him to drag her bags inside then place them in a line on a chest of drawers. "Thank you. What is a press?"

"It's the cupboard where you hang your clothes." He saw her blank look then smiled. "Ah more Aussie slang. I think it comes from 'linen press' or something."

Emily heaved a sigh of relief. "Okay, thanks. I'll be fine now. What time is dinner?"

"Six." He turned strolled out the door and headed towards the kitchen without a backward glance.

She stared after him admiring the way his jeans fit snugly over muscular buttocks and long, strong thighs. He had a sinfully handsome face but looked just as good walking away. She wet her lips. How did he slide into jeans so tight? Absently she rubbed her fingers on her skirt, to rid the tingle from the need to run them through his thick black hair. Was it the Aussie drawl or just the raw masculinity drawing her to him? She had heard the term "chick magnet" and now she had met one and experienced the pull of attraction she once thought a myth. Oh yes, Doug Macgregor took out that honour in spades and from the way he carried himself, he damn well knew it. *Get a grip, Perkins. He's only a man, and I'm here to work — remember?*

Refreshed from a hot shower, she dressed in shorts and a tee shirt then unpacked her bags. The deep cupboard with mirrored doors stretching the length of one entire wall surprised and delighted her. Inside, one section had shelves, and she laid out her clothes in neat piles. Exhausted, she glanced at the digital clock radio beside the bed and yawned. Perhaps if she rested before dinner, her jet-lag headache would ease, and the huge double bed looked so tempting. She crawled onto the soft grey bedspread and pressed her head on the pillow. *Just five minutes.*

* * * *

Doug wandered past Emily's room at a few minutes to six on his way to dinner. Glady served all their meals in the kitchen although they did use the dining room once a year at Christmas. He scanned the room and met Robbie's gaze. "Seen Em'?"

"Nah, not since you sent her to her room." Robbie rubbed his chin and eyed him critically. "She's a grown woman, maybe she doesn't appreciate being treated like a kid."

"I didn't treat her like a kid."

"Yeah, you did." Ian pulled out a chair and dropped into it then gave him a reproachful stare. "Dragging her in here covered in dirt after travelling all bloody day wasn't a very nice thing to do." Robbie narrowed his gaze. "Are you sure you're all right, mate?"

"Never better." Doug pushed his hands into the front pockets of his jeans uncertain if he should go and check on Emily.

He swallowed hard. Why did his brothers constantly ask him if he was all right? Fine, so he'd suffered post-traumatic stress disorder after his chopper went down under enemy fire killing everyone bar him. Yeah, he felt guilty for surviving with hardly a scratch and taken full responsibility for the deaths of his mates. For a long time during his recovery in hospital, he wished he'd died too. The flashbacks were a problem, but hey, he'd seen the shrinks and had it sorted. Although, nothing erased the crash and broken bodies of his unit from his mind, no matter how many drugs he swallowed or counselling sessions he endured.

The war had paled into insignificance for him the day Jock died. After he'd endured a long time in a psychiatric ward, Jock visited him and informed him his parents had died in a car accident months previously. He had gone ballistic unable to believe the doctors had thought him unstable enough to keep their deaths from him. They had denied him the chance to say goodbye at their funerals. The next day they told him Jock had died. In hindsight, he guessed they couldn't do any more damage by informing him. That second, he decided to take the drugs and pretended all was well. He had to get the hell out of the damn hospital and back to Winnawarra. Problem was, he couldn't always hide the flashback episodes from his brothers.

He noticed his brothers watching him with interest and pushed all thoughts of war and death to the back of his mind. He became very good at concealing his desolation with a laid-back "life is sweet" attitude. He sucked in a steadying breath, refusing to fall to pieces in front of them. *Baby steps. One day at a time.*

"You look like you're going to jump out of your skin." Ian snorted and kicked out the chair next to him. "Sit down and take the weight off."

Doug refused and glowered at his youngest brother. "I'm fine, quit babysitting me." He turned to glance over one shoulder towards Emily's room. "I thought you'd all want to take a look at her, considering Jock thought highly enough of her to give her part of our inheritance."

"He did what?" Brian gave a snort of disgust. "If he planned to share it around you'd have thought he would have included me and Johnno. After all, we've been working here for years."

Robbie smiled and straightened the cutlery beside his plate.

"It's nothing personal. I'm sure he appreciated both of you, but Jock always had an angle and looking at her, my guess is she is part of his matchmaking efforts." He grinned. "You have to admit, she's a good sort, not really built for cattle station life but do any of you really care? I sure as hell don't."

"Yeah, I reckon Jock had a plan to see us settled with more than a tourist or Jillaroo." Ian cracked his knuckles. "So, he arranged for a super intelligent woman to come here in the hope at least one of us would get hitched. She has a business degree and studied forensic science." He frowned. "Although, I can't imagine why he thought we needed a forensic scientist in the Outback."

"I hope I'm not expected to babysit. I have enough work to do looking after the livestock." Brian raised one dark eyebrow.

"You don't have to do a thing, but I'm afraid you and Johnno will have to move in with the ringers because we'll need the space." Ian leant back in his chair. "That will mean taking your meals in the cookhouse as well."

"Fine, we'll start tonight then." Brian pushed to his feet. "Come on, Johnno, I'm not staying where I'm not welcome. I'll get my stuff in the morning." He stormed out the door.

"Too right." Johnno stood and followed him.

"Fine by me." Ian narrowed his gaze then turned and frowned at his brothers. "I bet Jock would turn over in his grave if he knew we'd allowed the staff to have free run of the house."

"Well, things will be back to normal now with Em' here to help out." Doug smiled. "Although giving part of Winnawarra to a stranger came as a bit of a shock."

"I have to admit Emily came as a bit of a shock to me too but Jock always planned ahead." Ian rubbed his hands together and grinned. "Now, before we start treading on each other's toes, we need to inform each other up front if we plan to become involved with her."

"Sounds like a plan." Robbie leant forward in his chair. "In what time frame?"

"I'd say we'd know if we fancied her after a couple of weeks and if the feeling is mutual we should speak up." Ian grinned and lifted his chin towards the door. "Although, I think Doug has made his mind up about her already and by the way she looks at him, so has she."

Horrified at the chance of Emily overhearing their conversation, Doug glanced towards the hallway. "Give a man a break. I've only just met the girl." He went to sit down at the table then changed his mind. "Speaking of which, I'll go and see if she wants Glady to wait dinner." More than a little irritated, he strode from the kitchen.

In the hallway, he caught sight of a man slipping out the back door and stared after him wondering what the hell he was doing in this part of the house. Not even Johnno or Brian ventured near the family's bedrooms, and the bunkhouse was on the other side of the homestead. Could one of the hands be making a nuisance of himself? *Christ!* He paused outside her door and listened. Not a sound came from within, so he knocked a few times. "Em', dinner's ready. You decent?"

When no reply came and worried for her safety, he sucked in a few deep breaths to steady his nerves. *Calm down you idiot, she'll be fine.*

"I'm coming in." He turned the doorknob and peeked inside.

Emily had fallen into a deep sleep curled up on the bed. The poor girl must have been exhausted. He moved into the room and raised his voice. "Em', dinner is ready."

When she didn't stir, he went to the cupboard and retrieved a spare blanket. The temperature dropped considerably overnight and dressed in shorts and a tee shirt, she would be cold before too long. He covered her then lingered to examine the pretty face framed with long blonde hair. He wanted to kiss the tip of her cute upturned nose. She sure was a looker. Reluctantly, he turned towards the door and moved through closing it softly behind him. What Ian had said about matchmaking made a lot of sense, but he wondered why Jock had never mentioned plans for including his old girlfriend's daughter in his will.

He rubbed his chin trying to make sense of it all and walked slowly back to the kitchen. He glanced at his brothers. "Em' is dead to the world, so I guess we'll have the celebratory dinner tomorrow night." He dropped into a chair and turned his attention to Robbie. "She seems a nice enough girl with no ulterior motives for being here. In fact, she seems as ignorant as we are as to why Jock included her in his will." He drummed his fingers on the table. "Before our home is invaded by strangers with an interest in the running of Winnawarra, I think one of us needs to go through Jock's journals. I want to know more about why he wanted Emily here. I find it hard to believe this is an attempt to make sure we marry at least one intelligent woman. He always kept a diary, and there must be a pile of letters somewhere lying around or even emails from Emily's mother. Flying in the dark about his motive for bringing her here is driving me nuts."

Ian's eyes narrowed in concern.

"Count me out. I haven't stepped a foot inside his office since he died. Going through his personal documents will be like invading his privacy." His shoulders slumped. "But you're right. We'll need to sort out his files because you'll have to move into his office to run the place."

Horrified at the prospect of breathing in his grandfather's scent and using his things, Doug shook his head. "No, too many memories. I can work just as well from my own office. I have all the current files and everything I need on my computer." He rubbed the back of his neck. "Robbie, can you read the old letters and check his diary for clues? Someone has to sort out his personal items." He frowned. Anxiety mounted, and his head ached. "I'll look at whatever you think necessary."

"No worries." Robbie gave him a concerned stare. "Look, mate, if you think going through Jock's diaries will trigger the flashbacks, I can handle everything on my own." He cleared his throat. "Are you sleeping okay?"

Doug toyed with the salt shaker twirling it around in his fingers then lifted his gaze to him. "I'll let you know if I'm not coping and you can stick me with a needle. Like I said before, *I'm fine*." He let out a long sigh. "I'm confused about Jock's intentions and think we need to get to the bottom of the situation. I want to know the mysterious plans he had in place for Winnawarra and what he concealed from us . . . because as sure as hell, he was hiding something."

CHAPTER FOUR

A loud clanging shot Emily from a dream of swimming in a blue lagoon. She sat bolt upright and stared into the gloom trying to get her bearings. Someone thumped on the door, and she recognised Doug's voice.

"Rise and shine. How do you like your coffee, love?"

"White, no sugar." She glanced at the bedside table and gawked at the time. "Do you know it's four-thirty in the morning?"

"Yeah, that's the time we get up around here." He chuckled, and the doorknob rattled. "You decent?"

She pulled the blanket up to her neck and realised she still wore her tee shirt and shorts. Her cheeks heated. *Oh no, I slept through my welcome dinner. No wonder I'm so hungry.* She swallowed hard and stared into the gloom in the general direction of the door. "Yes, come in."

Doug stepped inside haloed by the light streaming from the hallway. The scent of freshly showered man, coffee, and toast seeped through her senses in a sizzle of awareness.

"As it's your first day and you missed dinner, I thought you'd like a jump start. We have breakfast about seven, and a strong cup of coffee usually keeps us going until then."

Doug waited in the doorway as if requesting her permission to enter, so she waved him inside. "That sounds great. I don't usually eat this early, but I'm famished."

"Lucky I got the coffee right, and I spread marmalade on the toast. English people like that, right?" He turned on the bedside lamp and placed a steaming mug of coffee and a plate piled high with toast on her lap. "Glady will drop your jeans in shortly." He grinned at her. "I'll wait for you in the kitchen then take you around and show you the ropes. After breakfast, we'll go and check the fences."

Yes, I'd like to see the ropes. Right now, I might just try to use them to hang myself. Pushing her dismay at waking in darkness aside, she smiled at him. After all, he had gone to a lot of trouble to make her feel welcome with breakfast in bed. "Thank you, and yes, this is wonderful. I'm sorry I missed dinner. I must have fallen asleep. When I see Glady, I'll be sure to give her my apologies."

"No worries. People miss dinner all the time around here. I know it's unusual for townies to understand our need to work sunup to sundown but you'll soon get used to it, and you won't have any problems sleeping. The workload has most of us hitting the sack by eight. Some of the younger lads stay up later, but they pay for it the next day." He gave her a brilliant smile then turned to go. "Don't be too long, or the hands will think I've given them the day off."

Emily blinked the sleep from her eyes and watched him move his wide shoulders through the doorway. She inhaled trying to catch the remaining fragments of his delightful masculine scent then shook her head. "Oh, Perkins, you're acting like a schoolgirl with her first crush. You should know better, you fool."

Half an hour later, wearing jeans and a pair of leather, work boots, she strolled into the kitchen. The housekeeper stood at the kitchen sink washing up dishes, and she moved to her side. "Need any help, Glady?"

"I'm good, thanks, love." Glady turned and smiled at her. "Best you set your alarm for four in the morning. Doug likes to be out the door at the first sparrow's fart, so any later than four-thirty and the entire day is knocked out of sync."

Emily glanced towards the front door. "Where *is* Doug?"

"He'll be in the stables." Glady motioned with her chin towards the front door. "It's the building across the way on the left, beside the cattle drenching pen."

"The what?"

"Oh, you *are* a newbie." The old woman chuckled. "Follow your nose. It's the white barn with a gate at the front. Walk straight ahead it's the first building on the left."

Emily pulled her jacket around her against the cooler than expected morning and trudged across the floodlit driveway in the direction of the stable. Voices echoed from a number of different buildings, and people moved around doing a variety of jobs. She squinted into the brightly lit stables, surprised to see so many horses and took a tentative step into the hive of activity. A number of Indigenous men led horses past her and others chatted noisily in a language she could not recognise as they mucked out the stalls. Others rolled wheelbarrows out the door piled high with soiled straw. All the workers eyed her with interest and offered a smile.

"You want something, lady?"

Emily spun around coming face-to-face with a pretty, young woman with flashing brown eyes. She took a step back then one to the side to avoid a pile of horse dung. "I'm looking for Doug."

"Are you now?" The woman gave her a long slow once-over then grinned. "You must be Emily. Doug said we'd pick you out the moment the sun came out." She snorted with laughter. "Too right."

Embarrassed and more than a little annoyed, she lifted her chin. "I have no idea what you're talking about." She straightened and glared at the grinning face before her. "Is Doug here or not?"

"Yeah, yeah, don't get cranky." She waved a hand towards the back of the building. "He's in the tack room."

Emily stood her ground, as a potential owner of this property she needed to state her position. "And you are?"

"Sue. Sue Porter."

"Well, Sue, what do you mean by saying you would recognise me the moment the sun came out? Did Doug imply I'm a vampire and will burst into flames at the first rays?" She balled her fists on her hips.

Sue's white teeth flashed in her suntanned face.

"Oh, he didn't say you were a vampire, far from it — but being English an all, he said the moment the sun hit your face the reflection would blind us." She chuckled seemingly overjoyed by Emily's discomfort. "You being lily-white."

"I see."

"Yeah. I hope you brought a few litres of fifty-plus sunscreen with you. You'll need it." Sue bent to pick up an empty bucket and sashayed away.

Her stomach sunk to her brand new glossy boots and she wanted to turn around, run inside the house, and bury her face in her pillow. She wondered what else Doug had told the hands about her. Perhaps he planned to make her stay as uncomfortable as possible so she would leave and forfeit her stake in Winnawarra. Could such a deliciously handsome man be so devious or was it *normal* to torment newcomers to the Australian Outback? *I am a skilled professional, and I will not allow any of them to trick me out of my inheritance.* She could handle the business side of the running of Winnawarra but would fall short as part of the labour workforce. To make things worse, as a potential part owner, she had allowed one of the hands to disrespect her. There would be no coming back from that fall from grace, not once her show of weakness had become common knowledge.

She stepped around the pools of urine leaking from the wheelbarrows, pushed down her anger, straightened, and marched towards the back of the building. A bright light poured from the doorway, and as she moved closer, she could hear Doug's voice as he issued orders to a small group of men. Then a new voice chimed up.

"You don't expect me to take orders from the new girl, do you? Bloody hell, Blind Freddy could see she's never stepped foot on a cattle station before."

"You're right, but she has impressive qualifications in business management. Don't worry she won't be involved in running anything until I can gauge her ability. You'll take your orders from Johnno or me as usual. She's a *Clayton's* assistant manager, and it was one of Jock's crazy ideas, not mine." Doug's voice lifted above the shuffle of horses and workers' chatter. "Just give her a fair go. She may be useful in the long run."

"I'm not being bossed about by no English girl fresh out of school, either." The man snorted in derision. "I didn't spend years studying Veterinary Science to be demoted to the bunkhouse because we have a woman living at the homestead. We had a good system us blokes, why involve untrained women? They always mess things up."

Dismayed by the men's attitude and not quite sure of their terminology, Emily paused at the door to peer inside. Johnno and Brian plus an older man with grey hair had grim expressions. She caught sight of Ian, standing beside his brother and holding a clipboard. He looked up and smiled at her, then waved her inside.

"Come on in, Emily. We don't stand on ceremony here." Ian prodded Doug in the arm. "Want me to introduce her or do you want to do the honours?"

Doug lifted his dark head, and his blue gaze moved over her as if inspecting her dress code.

"Glad to see you made it, Em'." He glanced at the men standing around him. "This is Em' — Emily Perkins our new assistant manager." He pointed to a grey-haired man in his fifties. "This is Joe, the head ringer." He lifted his chin towards a tall blond man with unusual green eyes. "Pete here is the good lookin' one, so watch out for him. He is a real ladies' man and is in charge of the stables. You'll remember Johnno and Brian from last night?"

"Yes, I do." Emily nodded towards the other men but did not offer her hand. Doug's words had given off mixed signals, and the looks from the other three had been close to evil. *What have I done to upset you?* Earlier, Doug had appeared to accept her in his home, but now, he made her feel like an outsider. Irritable by his sudden change of mood, she bristled with indignation. "Just as well I met you all inside. I'm sure you wouldn't want to go blind by looking at me in the sun." She shot a meaningful stare at Doug. "Would they, Doug?"

To her delight, his cheeks pinked and he cleared his throat.

"Right you are then." He turned to Ian. "Are you okay to handle things while I show Em' the ropes?"

"You mean I get to ride without training wheels today, boss? Sweet." Ian crossed his eyes and grinned. "Now I feel all grown up."

Doug gave him a long, annoyed stare and whistled to a dog lying at the stable door then his full lips quirked at the corners into a phantom of amusement.

"'Bout time." He tipped his head towards the door. "Coming, Em'?"

Emily followed Doug into the early morning sunlight jogging to keep up with his long strides. "This place is very strange. It gets dark or light in seconds. In the UK, it sort of creeps up on a person and in the summer it's light until ten at night."

"I've visited London a few times, but I prefer the wide, open spaces." Doug glanced back at her. "I did appreciate the history, and I liked France too. Now that place has atmosphere. Have you visited the Palace of Versailles? That place is a magnificence of idle indulgence and proves nothing has really changed over the centuries. I don't believe any government whatever party or ruler is truly in touch with its people."

She noticed his brow crinkle into a frown and touched his arm to slow him down. "I thought Versailles was magnificent, but I do understand the history and why there was a revolution. I think if we are going to get along, we should keep politics and religion off the table. What do you say?"

His suntanned face split into a wide grin.

"No worries, love." He headed towards the homestead. "Come on."

Perplexed, Emily stared at him. "I thought you were going to show me around?"

"I will, but you'll need a hat and sun lotion." He took the steps two at a time. "And we need to talk." He led the way down a passageway opposite the one leading to her room and flung open a door. "Take a seat."

When he slid behind a paper-strewn desk and leant forwards clutching his hands together, her stomach clenched with the awful feeling she experienced every time she did something naughty at school and had to front the headmistress. Taking a deep breath, she perched on the edge of the chair opposite him and waited for the dressing down.

He removed his hat and pushed his fingers through glossy black hair then turned an exasperated blue gaze on her.

"Look, love, I know we do things differently here than you're used to. Most of us call a spade a spade and don't beat around the bush." He let out a long sigh. "How can I put this and not make things worse? English are kind of prudish, and I'm not sayin' there's anything wrong with that, but I can see we come over a bit rough, or too familiar with you." He spread his hands wide. "Jeez, in the city, me calling you 'love' could probably be classed as sexual harassment and if I've offended you — I'm sorry."

She opened her mouth to say nothing he could do would offend her. In fact, bathing in the sight of him and his brothers had been better than an entire week at Versailles.

"Just a minute let me finish, and then you can rip strips off me." He lifted a hand to stop her. "First, Sue is a stirrer, and she has a crush on me, well on all three of us, and does her best to ward off rivals. So take everything she says with a grain of salt. I admit I said you would burn up in the sun but it wasn't meant as it sounded." He leant back in his chair watching her reaction critically. "About being a Clayton's assistant manager—"

She clasped her hands and lifted her chin, hoping to appear confident. "I have no idea what that term means, so before you apologise perhaps you should explain?"

"Oh, I see . . . well, *a Clayton's* means a substitute for the real thing. When I said that, I meant you did not intend to take

Johnno's job. Beats me why Jock put you down as assistant manager when you have no experience in running a cattle station." He offered her a smile — a far too sexy smile that sent an embarrassing wave of heat rushing into her cheeks.

Good Lord, now he'll think I'm menopausal. She leant back in the chair trying her best to look like a cool, sophisticated woman. "Now I know why Johnno was giving me the evil eye." She glanced at him from below her lashes. "I'm here now, and I'm sure you'll find *something* for me to do."

"There's always plenty of work to do, love, and I've straightened out Johnno, so no worries there. I hope Jock meant for you to be the *assistant* to the manager, because I need help with a few things on the business side, especially all this paperwork." He waved a hand over the piles of documents on his desk. "It would be good if you could handle the bookings for the muster and chopper tours as well. Oh, and can you answer the phone because Glady is about as useless as tits on a bull when it comes to customer relations. We've set up the web page to make sure calls come in around six, so you'll be available."

She heaved a sigh of relief, those things she could do with one hand tied behind her back. "Yes, I can handle the office duties, but I think Jock wanted me here to look over the books as well." She crossed her legs and noticed his gaze leave her face for a brief moment. "Something tells me he had concerns about your last accountant, or he wanted his business kept in-house. Either scenario, you should consider using me for my expertise." She smiled warmly at him. "I'm a quick learner and will pitch in wherever you need me around the place too. Just show me what needs doing, and if necessary how to do it, and I'm sure we'll get along fine."

"Too right we will." He rubbed his chin as if thinking through his next words. "I'm not sure if it will help, but my mother always used to tell other English folk, the best way to settle into 'stralia was not to compare it with the UK. She said that was the sure road to failure. She always advised people to look on this country as an adventure into parts unknown and give everything a go." He chuckled, and the sound rumbled from deep in his chest. "She hated the term 'whinging Pom,' and did her best not to complain. Although, she kept some of her traditions and always insisted on a Sunday roast with Yorkshire pudding even when it was hot enough to fry an egg on the ground." He glanced into the distance as if remembering. "It's not the same around here since we lost our parents. I know Jock did his best to keep Winnawarra going, but it couldn't have been easy."

Not wanting to intrude on how they died, she offered him a comforting smile. "I'll do my best not to become a *whinger*. Now about giving me a look at the books?"

"There will be plenty of time to get to those later. The accounts are paid quarterly, so the invoices won't arrive until the first week in July." He pushed to his feet scraping the chair across the polished wooden floor. "Get some slip-slap-slop on and your hat. We have plenty of work to do before breakfast."

Utterly confused, she gaped up at him. "Some, what?"

"Oh, you mean the 'slip-slap-slop'? Ah, it means to get some sunblock on — sun lotion. It's a slogan from a government advertising campaign to prevent skin cancer. You'll need to protect your skin all year round because we don't really have a winter as such." He led the way out the door. "There's a bottle of lotion in your bathroom. I'll show you."

She followed him along the hallways increasing her stride to keep up with him. "I don't suppose you have an Australian slang dictionary on hand, do you?"

His laughter echoed through the house. At her bedroom door, he paused grinning at her and his amazing eyes glistening with mischief.

"No, love, but maybe you should write one?" He nodded towards the bathroom door. "Pump bottle with a fifty-plus sign on the side." He frowned then gave her a long considering stare. "Before you go there *is* something else I need to ask you."

"Yes?"

"Ah, did one of the hands cause you grief last night?"

She blinked trying to understand his meaning. "I'm not sure what you mean."

The tips of his ears pinked and he swallowed.

"Did anyone try to get into your room and cause a nuisance?" He shifted his feet like a schoolboy waiting for the headmaster to punish him. "You *did* leave your door unlocked, and I caught one of the hands lurking in the hallway, so I thought I'd ask. The staff shouldn't be loitering near your room." He met her gaze. "We hire drifters, some of them fresh out of prison, and the house is always open so they can gain access to my office. You'll need to lock your door day and night."

There was a creep outside my door when I was asleep? Wonderful. More than a little unnerved by his statement, she covered her distress with a smile. "No one bothered me, and I will lock my door from now on. Thank you for your concern."

"No worries." He grinned broadly. "I'll wait in the kitchen and don't forget your hat." He strolled away slapping his against one thigh.

Prickles worried the back of her neck, and she examined the room, afraid she might find someone hiding under the bed. Heart pounding, she moved slowly towards the bathroom. She listened intently for any sound then pushed at the door. She gulped in a long breath at the sight of the empty room then spun around and ran to lock the bedroom door. With her back flat against the wall, she sucked in a few deep breaths. Had she overreacted? Probably, but Doug would not have mentioned seeing someone in the hallway if he really trusted his men. In fact, it would not have been an issue. She dashed a shaking hand through her hair. At least Doug cared enough to warn her.

Her predicament sunk in like the chiming of a death knell. Alone in the middle of nowhere, she had no idea who she could rely on. To date, her instinct had never let her down, and she trusted Doug to some extent. He may well come over as confident and easy going, but she had noticed the shadow crossing his expression when he spoke of his tour of duty. He had suffered in the past and returned soldiers sometimes never recovered from witnessing the atrocities of war. Doug's brothers seemed normal, but she shuddered at the thought of one of the hands, a vagrant or someone fresh out of prison, sneaking into her room at night and watching her sleep.

I'll lock my door and stick to Doug like glue during the day. She made use of the lotion then grabbed her hat on the way out the door. Strolling into the kitchen, she caught sight of Doug leaning casually against the counter. Her attraction towards him had been immediate, and the thought worried her. God help her, Doug Macgregor might be the sexiest man to have crossed her path but could she risk her heart again. Yet, in this wilderness, she needed a friend, someone she could trust and so far, he was the only candidate. *I hope I can rely on you Doug because right now I don't feel safe.*

* * * *

The first three days passed in a flash and on the fourth night after dinner, she gave the Macgregor brothers a wave, pushed up from the table, and staggered to her room eager to take a long hot shower. She had accompanied Doug to check and repair the stock's water troughs, which she thought would be an easy job. Wrong! Following pipelines until she went close to going insane, dodging snakes, lizards, and mounds of cowpats so thick with flies they looked like strange heaving creatures. She wiped her sweat-soaked brow and stretched her aching muscles. *Why am I here? Is owning ten percent of acres of cow shit, and working dawn 'til dusk worth it?*

The task had taken them a great distance from the homestead, and they arrived home as Glady served dinner. The long discussion afterwards pushed her way past bedtime and keeping her eyes open had proved difficult to the max. She staggered to her room. Exhausted, she hung up her hat and with every overworked muscle screaming, peeled off her dusty clothes. After tossing them into the hamper, she dragged her heavy legs into the bathroom. The hot shower was calling her name, and she turned on the taps to allow the water to wash away the day's grime. Aware of using too much water, she bathed quickly and shampooed her hair. She moved unsteadily, but managed to dry off and yawning, gave her hair a quick once-over with the hairdryer before slipping between the sheets. The air conditioner above her bed hummed sending a cool breeze over her face. She extinguished the light and sighing closed her eyes.

Where am I?

Trapped in a strange dark place, she flattened against the wall. In the middle of the room, a body dangled by the feet with blood pouring from a gash across the neck cloaking the face in a veil of red. The thick, crimson stream dripped from strands of hair in a constant tap, tap, tap on the floor.

Shocked awake, she sat up and peered around the room, heart pounding with fear. *It's just a nightmare.* She reached for the glass of water on the bedside table and sipped to regain her composure. How stupid to be so afraid of a silly dream. She glanced at the clock, relieved to see it was five hours before daybreak. The dream hovered in her subconscious, and she blinked a few times to clear the vision.

Tap, tap, tap.

Tap, tap, tap.

The sound came closer. Terrified, she gripped the sheets and stared at the bedroom door. The hairs on the back of her neck stood to attention and her muscles clenched. She needed a weapon and staying in bed would be a big mistake. *Pull yourself together, Perkins, and do something.* She moved swiftly across the floor and into the bathroom, grabbed a can of deodorant then slipped back into her room. If someone planned to come through the door, she would be ready for him. Listening intently, she heard nothing. Perhaps she had imagined the sound. Staring into the darkness, the dream came back in full Technicolor. Her pulse thumped in her ears, but then the sound cut through the silence again.

Tap, tap, tap

Tap, tap, tap.

Not a dream, she heard footsteps. The sound came closer then stopped outside her room. Heart pounding like a military tattoo, she lifted the deodorant and aimed at the door. She had remembered to lock the door — hadn't she? Frozen with fear, she strained her ears. A slight squeak cut through the silence like a cannon blast. *Oh, my God! Someone is turning the handle.*

Motivated by a survival instinct previously foreign to her, she edged her way to the huge cupboard. She could slip inside and hide. After three steps across the room, she tripped over a pair of boots and crashed to the floor. The deodorant, her only weapon, spun out of reach. Winded, she bit back a cry and lay very still listening intently.

Tap, tap, tap

Tap, tap, tap.

The footfalls moved away and relieved, she dragged in a breath and rolled onto her knees. Pushing to her feet, she moved to the bedside table and turned on the light. Doug's bedroom was two rooms down, and if she screamed, he would come. *I have to know who tried to get into my room.* Snatching up the deodorant, she edged towards the door. The footsteps had moved away, slow and confident.

Without thinking of the consequences, she unlocked the door and flung it open in time to see the outline of a tall man wearing a cowboy hat moving towards the kitchen, his metal-tipped boots tapping on the wooden floor. The sour scent of male sweat lingered in the corridor mixed with a cheap aftershave. She stared at him looking for anything to identify him but all the men at Winnawarra had hats constantly glued to their heads, and the majority of them were tall. Anger overcame her fear, and she stepped into the hallway. "Hey. Why were you outside my door in the middle of the night? Do you make a habit of haunting the corridors?"

Without replying, he stopped walking and rolled his shoulders in a show of masculine pride before continuing on his way, then disappeared through the veranda door and into the darkness. She slipped inside her bedroom, locked the door and leant against the wall. Heart pounding, she allowed the weird incident to percolate through her mind. He may have been one of the hands doing a security check but why did he ignore her? She tossed the can on the bed and shivered then rubbed the goose bumps on her arms. Night had dropped the temperature from hot and humid to cold. She walked across the room to turn off the air conditioner then sat on the edge of the bed, too upset to lie down.

Had she really heard the doorknob rattle or been caught in the throes of a nightmare? Reluctantly, she lay down but left the light burning on the bedside table and the deodorant in easy reach. She would speak to Doug about the incident first thing in the morning. *He will probably think I'm a whinger — too damn bad.*

A soft knock came at the door and her stomach knotted in fear. She grasped the can again then let out a sob at the sound of Doug's familiar voice.

"Em', you okay?"

She ran to the door, flung it open and jumped into his arms. "Oh, thank God it's you."

"What happened? Did you have a nightmare?" Doug held her close to his chest and stroked her back with his rough palms.

Inhaling his intoxicating fragrance, Emily pressed her face against the smooth skin of his bronzed muscular chest and hugged him then stepped back realising he was shirtless. She had clung to him and pressed her breasts against him like some brazen hussy. Her gaze drifted down his body as if drawn by a magnet. Oh boy, he was magnificent. His jeans hung low on his hips, the top button undone and displaying a flat stomach with a line of dark brown curls arrowing down to his zipper. Her cheeks heated as she lifted her chin and forced words over the lump in her throat. "A nightmare, yes I did have one, but I was awake when someone tried to open my door."

"What!" Doug glanced both ways down the passage.

"He went that way." She pointed towards the kitchen. "Out the veranda door."

"Stay inside and lock your door." Doug took off at a run bursting through the veranda door and stamping down the steps.

Emily turned the key in the lock then moved to the window. Moments later, light flooded the front yard, and she could see Doug coming from the barn and heading for the bunkhouse, his dark hair lifting as he ran. Some time passed before he appeared again strolling toward the barn. The lights went out and moonlight cast long shadows from the gum trees. The wind moved the branches, and sinister black gargoyles engulfed the lonely figure returning to the house. When a knock came on her door again, she rushed to greet him. "Did you catch him?"

"Nope." Doug gave her a long considering stare. "Come down to the kitchen, and I'll make us a drink. We'll talk."

A rush of panic gripped her again. "Wait for me." She pulled on her dressing gown and rushed after him.

With the hallway and kitchen flooded with light, Emily relaxed. She sunk into a chair and allowed Doug to make her a steaming mug of hot chocolate with the added bonus of marshmallows. "Thanks." She stared at him across the table feeling rather stupid for causing a fuss. "I'm sorry I woke you."

"No worries, love. I want you to feel safe here." He ran a hand through his thick black hair and smiled. "This old house makes noises, like an old woman with creaky bones. It takes a bit of getting used to. Are you sure you saw someone in the hall? It's windy, and the trees cast strange shadows through the windows."

Annoyed by his casual attitude to her worries, she lifted her chin. "It wasn't the house creaking or shadows. Agreed a nightmare woke me but I heard footsteps, then my doorknob rattled. When the footsteps went by, I looked into the hallway and saw a tall man wearing a cowboy hat. I called out to him, but he ignored me." She raised one eyebrow. "I am sure someone tried to get into my room. What if you have a rapist working for you and if I hadn't locked my door, I could have been his next victim." A sudden thought occurred to her sending a shiver down her spine. "The place isn't haunted, is it?"

"Haunted? No of course not. I believe you, Em', it must have been one of the hands but who is the question. Maybe they just came in to raid the kitchen, although there are plenty of snacks in the bunkhouse fridge." Doug stretched out long muscular legs encased in tight jeans and muffled a yawn. "We employ all sorts here. Many come here for a new start, and some no doubt are running from the law or just out of prison. Casual labourers might last a day or a year, and I have to take their credentials at face value. If they muck up, fight, or cause a problem, they're asked to leave." He closed one large hand around the mug and sighed. "I checked the bunkhouse. Everyone was asleep. Yeah, one of them could be faking but which one is the problem." He leaned forward in his chair. "Trust me, if any of them give you one second's grief they'll be kicked out of here so fast their duds will catch on fire."

She sipped her drink glad he believed her. "Okay, so how can you stop him bothering me again?"

"I'll make sure the house is locked overnight, and you'll continue to work with me, so you'll never be alone. If anyone steps out of line, I'll deal with him personally." He lifted his mug and drank deeply then stood and dropped the cup in the sink. "Now get the hot chocolate into you and try and go back to sleep, we have a hard day tomorrow."

Emily pushed to her feet and taking her mug with her, headed back to her room with Doug at her heels. She turned at her bedroom door. "Thank you."

"I'm only a few feet away, love. I'll hear you if you call out." He ran a hand over her hair in a gentle caress and smiled. "Lock the door."

"I will." She went inside and turned the key, but her mind was no longer on the intruder. She inhaled. Doug's delicious scent clung to her, and she remembered the feel of his hard body pressed protectively around her. The sight of his bare chest and ruffled hair had made her toes curl with delight. "Oh my, now that's what a real man looks like."

CHAPTER FIVE

Emily stuck to Doug like glue over the next couple of days despite the awful feeling someone was watching her. Nothing happened, no stalker haunted her every move, and she started to wonder if her imagination had played tricks on her after all. She strolled into the tack room to grab a couple of drinks and peered inside the refrigerator. The wrapped packets of sandwiches stacked high looked too good to ignore, and she selected egg and lettuce. She heard footsteps, and the *tap, tap, tap* of metal-tipped boots on concrete. The feeling of dread dropped over her. Trapped inside the small area, she would have to face whoever came into the room. Straightening, she pushed the food and drinks onto the bench and spun around. Heart pounding, she snatched up a hoof pick and held it out in front of her like a knife. The footsteps paused outside the door then moved away, and in the distance, she could hear Robbie's voice calling the dogs to heel. *Pull yourself together, Perkins.*

In an effort to discover who found her so interesting they needed to spy on her, she dashed to the door. One of the Jillaroos, Sue, came out of a stall carrying a bridle and gave her a wave. The horses moved restlessly, someone was close by, and Emily shrank back inside the tack room, her gaze fixed on the barn door. When Robbie strolled inside, she turned, grabbed the supplies and dashed out to meet him.

"Hey, slow down." Robbie gave her a lopsided grin. "Let Doug wait for his drink. You're not his slave."

She smiled back at him. "Hey, did you see anyone come out before me?"

"Yeah, Sue. Why is anything wrong?"

Emily shrugged. "I'm not sure, I thought I heard footsteps, and when I looked out the tack room, I only noticed Sue.

Whoever it was had steel-tipped boots. I had the feeling someone was watching me."

"Ah, Emily." Robbie grinned like a monkey. "All the guys are watching you. You're a beautiful woman, and we're lonely guys." He cleared his throat. "Oh shit, now I've embarrassed you. Sorry, love."

Face hot, Emily dashed back to Doug and handed him the drink.

"You okay, love?" He put down the hammer he was using and opened the can.

She refused to explain. It would only make things worse. "Yes, I'm fine."

* * * *

That night, a noise woke Emily from a deep sleep. She turned over in bed and stared at the door. She had locked the door, and for her own peace of mind, Doug had installed a bolt. Confident no one could get inside her room she rolled onto her back. The sound came again, a creaking, like branches scraping on the roof. *Go back to sleep, Perkins.* Moonlight bathed her bed flooding through the open curtains. She enjoyed going to sleep staring out the window, past the roll of the veranda roof to the expanse of endless star-filled sky. The moon seemed closer here and the stars brighter than any place on earth.

A shadow moved outside the window.

She stiffened and stared transfixed at the veranda trying to remain calm. The shadow moved again, and she would swear it looked like the outline of a cowboy hat. She sprang out of bed and ran into the bathroom locking the door behind her. Teeth chattering with fear, she tried to reason with her panic to force sense into what she had actually seen. Dragging in deep breaths, she made an effort to calm down. There were no trees directly outside her room and no logical reason other than she had disturbed a peeping Tom. He would know she had seen him, and she listened intently for footsteps on the veranda but heard nothing. She turned on the light then washed her face and stared at her reflection in the mirror. If she called out to Doug, he would think she had lost her mind or had experienced the after-effects of another bad dream. The window was secure, the insect screens locked, no one could get inside her room. She turned off the bathroom light and counted to twenty then eased open the door a crack.

She had a clear view of the veranda. Nobody lurked outside, and none of the shadows moved. Flinging open the door, she dashed across the room to close the blinds then crawled into bed. There would be no sleep for her tonight, but by the morning, she might have gathered enough courage to inform Doug about the two disturbing incidents. He would probably laugh at her insecurities but speaking to him would calm her nerves. One thing was for sure, she would keep the curtains closed in future.

* * * *

Doug dropped the bag of fence-mending tools into the back of his Ute and flicked a glance over Emily. His mouth went dry as she pulled the sweat-soaked shirt away from her breasts and flapped it in the slight breeze, displaying a wedge of tempting flesh. Covered in grime, her face flushed, and shoulders slumping, she had worked hard all week, but the heat was taking its toll on her. He had tried to explain, during winter the Outback reached temperatures twice as high as an English summer. Surprisingly, she pulled her weight and insisted on working alongside him every day. She never complained but the toll on her body was noticeable, and she moved slower this morning. Her skin had tanned, and she had a cute dusting of freckles over her nose.

To her credit, Emily asked questions and was not afraid to get her hands dirty. In fact, he looked forward to their long conversations into about every subject known to man. He enjoyed a comfortable familiarity with her, which was a new experience.

Most of the women he met wanted a cowboy for the night or a holiday romance but Em' was different. Over the long days, he had gained an insight into her personality but not her life. Yeah, she guarded her past but had an outgoing, friendly disposition he admired. Although he did not need intuition to know some bastard had hurt her and recent too because the moment he moved too close she got the scared rabbit look in her eyes. Having someone lurking in the hallway had not helped her confidence. He hoped the idiot who frightened her had stopped acting like a fool. Locking up every night and insisting the hands give the homestead a wide berth must have worked.

The sweet scent of her perfume and memory of her, small and delicate in his arms haunted his dreams, but he kept his distance. He did not intend to spoil things between them because having her around was as refreshing as the first rain and he appreciated working alongside her. His attention moved to her lips, damp from a swipe of her tongue and he could imagine how good they would taste. Arousal came so fast it made him giddy, and to quell his desire, he glanced down at her rust-streaked hands. He swallowed guiltily at the blisters on her fingers. He should have thought to give her a pair of gloves this morning. They had a damn box of them for the tourists to use, so he had no excuse. Ah well, he would make sure to offer her a pair the moment they returned to the homestead. He removed his hat and stretched. "I'm starving. Are you ready for smoko?"

"Yes, I could eat a horse." Emily rubbed her stomach. "Glady packed chicken sandwiches in the cooler and ginger beer."

Doug wiped his brow. "We're done here and might as well pack up then we can eat before we leave." He accidentally brushed her arm and immediately she took a step back tripping over the wire cutters. He grasped her arm. "Steady."

"Thanks, I'm fine." Emily gave him a smile that didn't reach her eyes.

Bad relationships aside, he would have to be Blind Freddy not to notice the way she looked at him sometimes. Interested but guarded. *She doesn't trust me yet.* Maybe because he'd flirted with the barmaid the day he'd met her and given her the impression he was a player. Yeah, he flirted a lot because he enjoyed the way women openly appreciated him, especially when he'd once believed the scar on his face would kill his chances of ever dating again.

After returning from his tour of duty a mental and physical mess, he'd stayed away from any unattached skirt, but the admiring glances from the tourists saved his life. Flirting with them, doing the rounds of the cattle auctions, and dancing with as many women as possible at the local barn shindigs was good for business as well as his ego. He tried to keep everyone happy.

As he stretched to reach the cooler from the hook on the gum tree, he caught her gazing at him with a heated expression and his mouth spat out a question before his brain had processed the implications. "I know you're single but is there anyone special waiting at home?"

She gave him a long considering stare as if weighing up his intentions then shrugged.

"Not anymore, no." She bent to pick up the wire stretchers then flicked him a gaze. "That was the main reason I took your grandfather's offer. It wasn't only the inducement of land but the chance of a fresh start."

He smiled at her pink cheeks. The admission had obviously been difficult for her. "Trust me, I know how places and stupid things like smells often trigger memories we'd rather forget. I hope you will find the new start you're looking for at Winnawarra. For me, this place is peace personified."

"What about you?" Emily examined her nails as if not wanting to look at him. "Have you anyone special in *your* life? Sandy for instance, is she your steady?"

"Sandy? Jeez, Em', *no*, not her. She isn't my type." He gaped at her in horror at the suggestion. "Nope, there's no one special in my life. I've never experienced the pleasure of falling in love."

"Really?" Emily raised one perfect, pale blonde eyebrow.

He snorted and grinned at her. "I'm never with a girl long enough to fall in love, Em'."

Slowly he turned and dropped the cooler onto the ground under the tree in the only patch of shade for miles around. "Let's eat. We have the south paddock to check, and then we'll head home. Maybe today we'll have time to go over the books. That's if you're up to office work after being in the sun all day?"

"Yes, I'm sure that's what Jock wanted me to do. I only hope I can stay awake long enough." She smiled and pulled open the door to the Ute then dragged out a small bag. "You weren't joking about needing a lot of rest. I could fall asleep standing up." She took a box of wipes from the bag and started to clean her hands then tossed the box to him. "Do we ever get a day off?"

"Sundays, we feed the stock then have a day's rest. In the rainy season — that's in summer — it is difficult to move around the property. Most of the tracks are either flooded or muddy." He caught the box and pulled out a delicately scented wipe before tossing the box under the tree. He diligently washed his hands. *If the blokes could see me now, they would have me straight back in the psych ward.* "Then we'll only have to tend the stock. The rainy season is the time we will all go stir-crazy looking for something to do. Next month is very busy with the muster, and it's all hands on deck."

"That entails rounding up the cattle and branding the calves, right?" Emily grimaced. "I'm not sure I can watch or be involved. It's cruel and barbaric."

He barked out a laugh and her beautiful eyes had rounded in horrified surprise. "Jeez, Em', what have you been reading? We don't *brand* cattle with hot irons anymore. We would have the RSPCA down on us like a ton of bricks. Did you notice the ear tags? They carry the latest technology, and we keep records on each one. The cattle don't feel a thing when we tag them, and before you get into the castrating and cauterizing, we use a method called banding. We use it on selected male calves under three weeks old. These we keep for premium meat production because they yield the biggest price at auction. The rest we use to fill overseas orders, and they go on the road train." He smiled. "The muster is heaps of work. It entails the counting and sorting of our stock. This is where Ian's expertise comes in. I'm a good judge of cattle, but Ian selects the bulls he wants to run on. He's made a pretty penny selling his prize Black Angus bulls for breeding, but you'll notice most of our cattle are Brahman."

"I wouldn't know one breed of cow from the other, I'm afraid, but if you show me, I'll learn." Emily stared out into the distance. "Do the visitors come mainly for the muster or just the scenic tours?"

"Both and they're a good money spinner. Next month we'll be hosting a bunch of tourists and hiring a mob of ringers for the muster." He sighed. "There's always work to do on a station, but the lads will feed the stock in the morning. In case you've lost track of time, tomorrow is our day off, and tonight I'll open the bar."

"The bar?" She looked at him from below her lashes. "We have a bar?"

He grinned and sat down leaning his back against the tree. "Yeah, it's in the hangar. During the muster, we hold a couple of dances there too, but every Saturday night, I open the bar and put on some music. It gives us something to look forward to each week."

"That sounds like fun, but I guess you don't do the type of dancing I'm used to?" Emily opened the cooler and peered inside. "You'd all be into country and western music I guess?"

He took the packet of sandwiches she offered him and grinned. "Is there any other kind?"

She giggled and sat down beside him in a cloud of honeysuckle perfume.

"*You* are such a cowboy."

When she gave him a friendly punch on the arm, every male hormone in his body went on full alert. He wanted to drag her into his arms and kiss her sassy mouth. Instead, he gave her his best sexy smile and watched her pupils dilate in a sexual response. He could reach out and take her full mouth, and she would not resist, but then he would ruin their friendship. He pushed down his primal urges and chuckled. "I'm true blue, love, true blue."

Emily grinned at him. How couldn't she? Her heart raced every time he came close, and he made her feel safe. She wanted to discuss her insecurities with him because recent incidents had only escalated her unease. Apart from the Macgregor brothers, the men working on the homestead terrified her. Taking a deep breath, she glanced at Doug. *It's now or never, Perkins.* "I need to tell you something."

"You're married?" Doug tipped back his hat and stared at her down his long, straight nose.

She gawked at him. "No! I'm worried about my safety here, and I need to discuss it with you as you're the boss."

"Okay. What's happened now?"

Gathering her wits, she tried to put her concerns forward in a precise manner without elaborating her fears. "Well, nothing really." She sucked in a breath and let it whistle out between her teeth. "I have the feeling someone is watching me, and I heard the same sounding footsteps as I did the other night but this time outside the tack room. Last night I'm pretty sure someone was loitering outside my window." She waited for a reaction, but Doug stared at her blankly. "I heard a noise on the veranda, and a shadow passed over my bed."

"You mean we have a peeping Tom?" He rubbed his chin. "Shit! Did you see him or the person outside the tack room you think was watching you?"

"No, but I'm sure it was the same man who tried to get into my room because he has metal tips on his boots that make a clicking sound when he walks."

"It could be anyone. Heaps of the men have metal tips on their boots." Doug wrinkled his brow. "Whoever he is, he has no business being outside your window. I'll talk to the lads again and tear strips off them. Don't worry, I'll make it *very* clear to keep away from the house and to show you some respect and stop gawking at you." His eyes flashed with anger. "Can you give me anything, any description of this bloke?"

"Not much, unfortunately. He wears a cowboy hat and is about your size, tall with broad shoulders. He could be any one of ten or more of the men here. He kept to the shadows and the moment he moved away, I pulled the curtains. I'll be keeping them shut all the time now." Lifting her chin, she narrowed her gaze on him. "I've been keeping my door locked as you suggested but I think he is watching me and it makes me feel uncomfortable."

When he snorted, she glared at him. "Look, I know you think I'm a 'townie' and I'm not fit to be on Winnawarra, but one of your men is a peeping Tom. You're the boss, so consider yourself informed."

Doug's expression softened.

"No, love, you have me all wrong." He rubbed his chin. "Most of the lads we have working here have been here for years and never put a foot wrong, but this type of behaviour is way off base. I'm not sure who he is or what his game is, but I'll find out. Best you stay close to me. I'll get you a satellite phone. Keep it with you when you're on your own." He shrugged. "He might just fancy you and is waiting for a chance to talk to you, but that's no excuse to invade your privacy. I'll keep a close eye on you, and if you don't mind, I'll ask my brothers to do the same."

Relieved she smiled. "Thank you."

"No worries." Doug cleared his throat. "We all want you to think of Winnawarra as your home." He dropped his gaze. "I really want you to be happy here, Em'."

She glanced at Doug from below her lashes, she hadn't missed the expression of longing in his eyes, but he'd never made a move on her. Did she secretly want him to? His raw male sexuality pulled her towards him like a magnet, but her last disastrous relationship still hung around like a bad smell. Oh yes,

George Bradshaw had done a number on her all right. She should have seen the "I'm married" signs way before she fell helplessly in love with the cheating bastard. Then she had to take the brunt of the "other woman" on her good reputation in a messy divorce and an even messier breakup. As if she would want him after he'd dragged her to hell and back. Especially after discovering he cheated on and divorced three previous wives.

Her attraction to Doug was real, but his "love the one you're with" attitude frightened the hell out of her, even if his long black lashes and the expanse of smooth skin stretched over tanned, muscular flesh made her nerve endings tingle. Did she want him wrapped around her? Oh, yes with a passion, but what if he discarded her like last night's pizza the moment another woman took his fancy? She glanced at him, and the look of need in his eyes made her stomach quiver. *Maybe not.*

* * * *

After dinner, Emily joined Doug and his brothers in one of the many offices. Some year's previously, Jock had converted what Doug referred to as a "sleep out" at one end of the house into four offices and a communications room, the latter holding an older type two-way radio, now used around the farm, and a satellite system for everything else. Phone calls, bookings, and enquiries for the coming muster came in from six to seven each night, and she dutifully took bookings. Surprisingly her knowledge of French and German came in very handy, as many of the tourists were backpackers from Europe.

She glanced around at the brothers' serious expressions, all with identical creases between their eyebrows. Robbie offered her a smile then tapped a leather-bound book against his thigh and waved her into a chair.

"Take a seat." He closed the door behind her. "Doug told us about one of the men pestering you, and we'll keep an eye on you, but this isn't why we asked for this meeting. We need to discuss a few family matters with you."

She smiled at him and sat down glad to be included. "Yes, of course. Is there anything I can do to help?"

"Maybe." Doug sat behind the desk and leant back in the squeaky office chair. "To be honest, love, we're not sure if we're dealing with the truth or an old man's fancies."

As Jock had been the shining light of the Macgregor family, Doug's statement caught her off guard. "Perhaps you'd better explain."

Robbie cleared his throat looking uncomfortable.

"I'm a doctor, and as far as I know, Jock was of sound mind. Although anything could have happened after our parents died. You see, none of us were living or had lived at Winnawarra for over a year before our parents' accident." He sat down opposite her and smiled thinly. "We were all wondering why he included you in his will, so I started reading his correspondence. Nothing unusual came up in his letters apart from the usual conversational kind of things, but I found an entry in his day–to–day journal that gives a hint of why you are here."

Intrigued, she clasped her hands. "Really? That would clear up a lot of speculation. What does he say about me?"

"Nothing specific." Robbie slapped the book on the desk. "Jock was a trusting soul. He found keeping books and paying accounts a pain in the arse, so he left everything in the hands of the accountant." He sighed and rubbed his chin. "He mentions he had concerns about Mr. Brewster and lists accounts for feed he never received, and payments made to companies he didn't know. He thought he might be going nuts." He cleared his throat. "This was around the time our parents died, so I imagine with the stress of the accident he either forgot to mention anything to us or decided he could handle the situation alone."

"So, we're guessing he made you a beneficiary in his will because *if* he thought he was suffering from dementia, he didn't want anyone to know and if he wasn't you would be the failsafe."

Doug cleared his throat. "A man like Jock, so strong and in control wouldn't have been able to cope with anyone thinking he'd lost his marbles."

Emily gripped the arms of her chair. "So how do I fit in? The solicitor mentioned Jock wanted me to oversee the bookkeeping side of things, is that correct?"

"You obviously have the skills to manage the business side of Winnawarra, and we can keep the cattle and tourism side running smoothly. I have to admit, I relied heavily on old Brewster, but he's an accountant, not a business manager." Doug bent one leg to rest his boot on his opposite knee." He heaved a deep breath and let it go in a sigh. "We would like you to take over the business side of Winnawarra. You could start by looking over the books to get an idea of how we run the station. Everything we order comes here by road train, feed, salt licks and the like. We keep a copy of the delivery invoice, but we have accounts with the companies involved, and our accountant handled all the payments. Before Jock's death, Mr. Brewster handled the various accounts, distributed the profit share, and kept the cash flow running. Up to now, we were happy because all we really had to do was run the place and do the payroll. Jock put an end to that by stipulating in his will we fire the accountant. If Jock had doubts about Brewster's honesty and there was any funny business going on, I'm sure you will get to the bottom of it. Can you go over the accounts and put our minds at rest?"

She nodded in agreement. "Not a problem but I can't work outside all day as well. I will need to work out a management plan, which will include the payroll as well. Everything needs to be in the same place, so all the owners can check the financial status of the business at any time. I will set up everything and give you a financial report each month. I would rather not have carte blanche control over the accounts. I'd rather have one of you approve and co-sign before any payments are made." She frowned. "I will need to download some accounting software as I gather everything here is out of date."

"Whatever you need." Doug smiled at her. "Problem is we think Jock's worries about Brewster weren't recent." He rubbed the back of his neck and stared at his hands as if to hide his feelings. "You have to admit including you in his will was a pretty drastic step. He could have just fired Brewster and hired another accountant, but then he did mention your forensic science skills would come in handy. Why on God's earth would he think we needed a forensic scientist? Nothing makes sense, and we believe the answers are in his diaries. Something was going on, and it all started around the time our parents died."

"I know he wasn't happy about the inquest." Robbie let out a long, patient sigh. "He stormed out of the hearing calling the coroner a blind fool. After the inquest, everything changed. According to Glady, he didn't trust any of the men working here and started locking the house overnight. I think he must have become paranoid and couldn't come to terms with the fact our parents died in a freak accident and wanted to blame someone."

"That may be the reason he included me." Emily frowned. "I would be a fresh set of eyes examining the situation."

Her mind was running riot. Had Brewster sent someone to Winnawarra to scare her into leaving so she would not discover his crimes? The idea made terrifying sense and perhaps, he had been behind the accident after all. If Jock's son had been aware of his father's worries, he could have started investigating Brewster. The idea made perfect sense. By taking out the son and Jock, it left three grandsons oblivious to the problem — until she showed up. Icy fingers ran down her back. She needed more information and had to force words past the lump of fear in her throat. "We know Jock had issues with the accountant. Did Mr. Brewster benefit in any way from your parents' deaths?"

"Brewster? Nah, the only people who benefitted are the three of us, we inherited our father's portion of Winnawarra." Doug scratched his stubble making a rasping sound then stared into space for a few moments. "I can't connect anything my parents did with Brewster. Jock ran Winnawarra and was in charge. My dad worked beside him but wasn't involved in too many decisions. With Jock, it was better to go along with his way of doing things and keep the peace."

Emily met his gaze. "Yes, but if Brewster is fiddling the books, with a place this size we could be talking six figures over the years. How can you be sure he wasn't involved in Jock's and your parents' deaths?"

"Christ, Em', you're getting as bad as Jock." Doug's Adam's apple moved up and down. "After he died we found out he refused to believe the coroner's findings into their accident. Apparently, he was at the cop station once a week complaining. They thought he had lost his marbles. The old bugger never said one word to us about wanting the case re-opened."

"Maybe he was onto something, and that's why he needed a fresh set of eyes to look at things? None of you have been involved in the business side of things or know if your father noticed any discrepancies and questioned Brewster. If the accountant had been fiddling the books for years, it would mean prison time, and that is a motive for murder."

"And since someone has been trying to scare you back to London since you arrived, you probably believe Brewster has planted someone here to prevent you from uncovering his money-skimming racket." Doug met her gaze with an amused quirk of his lips. "Trust me, love, old Brewster isn't that smart."

"Best you concentrate on the business side of things." Ian flicked a "get on with it" glance at Doug. "The solicitor mentioned Jock informed him he'd left a letter explaining why you were included in his will. It was in Jock's safety deposit box, and he is sending it along. His instructions were not to give you the letter until you had decided to stay. We will have to wait for it to arrive to find out but for now, our immediate problem is keeping the business running and paying the bills. If Brewster was fiddling the books, I'd like to know, and trust me, charges will be laid." He sucked in a deep breath and let it whistle out between his teeth. "As to the idiot bothering you, when we find out who he is, he won't be working here any longer. In the meantime, we'll have your back, and you'll be safe as houses."

I hope so. Emily wet her lips. Untangling problems and reorganising companies just happened to be her area of expertise. "If you are talking about going back five years or more, it will take some time." She cleared her throat and turned to Robbie. "Does Jock mention any specific dates so we can narrow down the search a bit?"

"Yeah, he does. We thought if we gave you his diaries as well, you could look through them for us." Robbie rubbed a thumb over the cover of the leather volume in his hand. "We're a bit raw at the moment, and there's a lot of personal stuff in them. I'm sure you'll understand our reluctance to go through his thoughts?"

How could she refuse the three despondent faces before her? She drew a deep breath. "Yes, of course. I understand completely. Thank you for trusting me, it means a lot."

She would do as they asked but reading another person's private diaries was like an invasion of Jock's privacy. Yet, she really wanted to determine if the old man had discovered something fishy going on with his books and what evidence he had if any about his son's death. She wondered if he'd decided to confront the accountant with the issue. Surely, he would have gone to the police or at least spoken to them about his concerns. She glanced at Doug from below her lashes noticing his distress. Perhaps he'd suffered more than the cut to his face during his tour of duty and Jock didn't want to put more pressure on him, but the others? She turned to Robbie. "I know Doug was overseas for some years but why haven't you and Ian been more hands-on since your parents died?"

Robbie pushed one hip onto the corner of the desk, and his expression changed from concerned to one of interest.

"Well, I came back months ago, but Ian arrived late January, Doug sometime later. I had finished my residency in Darwin Hospital, but Ian had to finish his degree in Melbourne. Before that, we all lived here, but our parents and Jock ran the place. After our parents died, I decided to move back to help Jock, but he never mentioned anything to me about Brewster."

Ah, that made sense. Jock wouldn't burden his grandsons with his worries so soon after their parents' deaths. She offered them a reassuring smile. "You can leave this to me. I will have Winnawarra running like a top. I do appreciate how hard it is for you to go through Jock's personal diaries. Don't worry, if anything unusual shows up, I'll let you know."

Doug's handsome face broke into a relieved smile.

"Thanks, Em', although, I'll miss you. I've got used to your nagging." He chuckled and rubbed his knuckles along the scar on his chin.

She would miss him too, and had started to treasure every moment with him. "Then I'll work the morning with you and organise the office after lunch. It's too intensive to give it twelve hours a day, so you will have to put up with me after all."

"That sounds like a plan." Doug flashed a wide grin and pushed to his feet. "Are we done here?"

Robbie handed her the diary with obvious reluctance.

"The other diaries are in the office next door. You will find them in the bookcase. Some of them go back forty odd years. The ones you need are in the brown leather covers nearest the door. The ledgers with the accounts are old school up to three years ago. The new ones are on Jock's computer and backed up on an external drive, but the operating system is old." He pushed a laptop with two books balanced on top into her hands then made a sound as if he wanted to clear a lump in his throat. "We don't need to know the personal stuff, just anything that affects the running of Winnawarra."

She gave him her best attempt at an Aussie accent. "No worries, love."

Ian burst out laughing, and his blue eyes sparkled with mischief.

"I told you she would fit in just fine." He gave her a friendly punch on the arm. "Do you want to come out with me in the morning and get away from Doug for a while?"

"No, she doesn't." Doug moved to her side and gave his brother a "back off" stare. "We're riding up to the falls. It's about time I discovered how she sits a horse. I might even allow her to ride Bolt." He smiled at her. "He is a very special stallion and not for the weak of heart."

She grinned at him. "Oh, I've ridden a stallion before, I am—"

His blue gaze moved over her in an intimate embrace.

"I bet you have, Em', but let's not discuss your old boyfriends in front of my brothers." He grinned at her like a donkey.

She gave them all a dramatic roll of her eyes. "Men!" She turned and marched out the door clutching the books and laptop to her chest. *I'll never get used to Aussie humour.*

CHAPTER SIX

After deciding to forgo a night watching Australian Rugby League Football for a cup of hot chocolate and three of Jock's diaries, she climbed onto her bed and reverently opened the first page. She found a very detailed account of day–to–day life on Winnawarra, from the price of hay to the cut on a stockman's hand. She skimmed through the first three diaries checking for any reference to the accountant, Mr. Brewster, and only found the slightest reference to attending a meeting with him for signing taxation returns. The fourth diary was completely different; it contained a disagreement with his son, Jamie.

February 14

Jamie returned home from his Valentine's Day dinner with Jenny in a right mood. He mentioned running into old Bill Wilson from the assay office. Apparently, last month I ordered a company to take core samples from the edge of Rainbow Gulley and requested him to forward the assay to Brewster. Bill must have been mistaken because I've never ordered any damn core samples and I had a right old barney with him. He accused me of going behind his back and disrespecting the land. It took me some time to convince him I hadn't made plans to sell out to the mines.

After calming him down, which was no mean feat. I persuaded him to take the chopper into Broome first thing so we can talk to Bill Wilson and find out the truth of the matter. I need to have a few words with Brewster too. I have no recollection of ordering drench, not when we have six month's supply in the shed, and yet it seems he paid an invoice for a year's supply last month. I ordered a bank statement and discovered Brewster made payments to companies I've never heard of for items I don't use. I'll discuss the Brewster problem with Jamie the moment I have the other problem sorted and get his opinion.

February 16

I'm losing my mind. Must be because Bill insists Brewster dropped in the request for the core samples personally on my behalf, yet I have no recollection of ordering any tests or authorising the company to send the results to my accountant. As if I would allow anyone prior knowledge of what lies beneath Winnawarra? It makes no sense. I made a promise when I purchased Winnawarra not to allow mining. The local Indigenous tribe informed me about the Dreamtime and gave me respect for the land. I've passed down the need to cherish and appreciate Winnawarra to my son and grandsons. I can't believe Jamie thinks I have a secret agenda and have allowed an offer of money to change my ethics.

When I spoke to Brewster, he denied everything and said he thought Bill was in the first stages of dementia. I tend to believe him and think I am heading in the same direction. After all the years Brewster's worked for me, why would he go behind my back or try to skim money from our accounts? Jamie is still convinced Bill is telling the truth and Brewster is covering for me. I cannot for the life of me, understand what is going on. I wanted Jamie to front up at the assay office with me again and ask Bill which company I had supposedly arranged to do the testing. He refused and decided to wait for an invoice to arrive to prove Bill's statement one way or the other. If one turns up, he will contact the company directly for a copy of the request and test results.

Emily pulled out a notepad and jotted down the date then reached for the corresponding accounts journal and flicked through looking for an account for the tests — and found nothing. She leant back on the pillow and chewed on the end of her pen. Perhaps this was the start of something unusual happening at Winnawarra, or old Bill had made a mistake. Curiosity had her slipping off the bed and going into Jock's office. She scanned the shelves and noticed all the family's journals stacked neatly on the bookshelves. It would seem Doug's parents also kept a day–to–day account of Winnawarra. She ran the tip of one finger over a stack of volumes with the name James Macgregor embossed in silver on the spine and hesitated. She had a very deep respect for people's privacy and dead or not, looking without asking somehow did not seem right. She turned and almost ran into Doug passing in the hallway. "Oh, good. You are just the person I wanted to see."

"I'm getting some half-time munchies — want something to eat?" Doug led the way to the kitchen.

Why not? She had a ferocious appetite since starting work at Winnawarra and followed him inside. "Yes, thanks."

"What do you fancy? Chocolate? Chips?" He flung open the door to the walk-in pantry and turned on the light.

Her stomach made a low growling sound at the thought of a bar of chocolate. She had no idea this delicious treat was supplied. "Oh, chocolate please."

"You're a girl after my own heart." He grinned and tossed her a huge bar. "You know, you can help yourself anytime. You're family now." He collected an armful of snacks and backed out turning off the light with one elbow. "What did you need to see me about?"

Basking in his presence, she almost forgot to ask permission to look at his father's diaries. "I've found something unusual concerning Mr. Brewster in Jock's ledger. He mentions his worries over a company taking core samples without his consent. He seems to think Brewster was involved in some deception and had reason to believe he was cooking the books. I am sure if he discussed his concerns, your father might have made a note on the subject. Would it be possible for me to look at your father's journal? If I could cross-reference the incident, it might give me a better handle on what Jock suspected."

The grin on his handsome face vanished, and he heaved a sigh.

"Yeah, go for it. You have my permission to read everything in Jock's office. My grandfather never mentioned any worries to me, neither did my dad, so it may just be an old man's fancy. I guess you will need to read everyone's journals if you want to get the full picture. My mum wrote one as well, and they used them as a backup to keep track of things. None of my family had confidence in computers." He gave her a long look then one side of his mouth quirked into a smile. "I trust you, Em', and I believe Jock did the right thing bringing you here."

Embarrassed, her cheeks heated but she returned his smile. "I won't let you down, and if there is anything amiss, I'll find it. I'm like a dog with a bone."

"Don't work too late. I'll be hammering on your door again before daylight." He sauntered past her. "I want an early start."

She hesitated before turning for the office. Surely taking core samples would scar the landscape. "Just one more thing, he mentioned a place called, Rainbow Gulley, is that far away?"

"Not really, it's about two hour's ride on horseback. I haven't been there for years, but we could take a ride out there next week. Do you think it's relevant?"

"Yes, I do." She chewed on her bottom lip. "Jock believed a company took core samples from that area. We should at least take a look and if there's no proof we can at least dismiss Jock's worries about companies taking illegal core samples." She sighed. Australians were so laid back it seemed everything happened in slow motion. "Why can't we go tomorrow?"

"Tomorrow? Nah, sorry that's impossible. I had planned to take you on a ride out to the waterfall first to make sure you can handle a horse. It's a tough ride to Rainbow Gulley and once we hit the plateau its single file on a narrow track and the horses get skittish." He smiled. "Don't look so concerned, if a company were after the mining rights, they would have contacted one of us by now. I wouldn't mind betting Jock had words with Brewster and let his imagination run away with him. People can go a bit crazy in the Outback."

Jock's words resonated in her mind. He had been so sure something was wrong. She wanted to stamp her feet and demand he take her to Rainbow Gulley at first light. "What if we fly over in the chopper?"

"Sorry, no can do. There's no place to land, and we wouldn't be able to get in close enough to check for drilling holes." He let out a long sigh. "We'll have to go on horseback because not even a trail bike will make it up the mountain and I'm not taking you anywhere until I'm sure you can handle one of our horses." He frowned. "We'll go during the muster."

"I've already told you I can ride a damn horse. I have ridden since I was a kid." She gripped the chocolate bar so tight it crumbled in her hand. "How much proof do you need?"

He raised one eyebrow, and his eyes sparkled as if he enjoyed her anger.

"As you get to know me, Em', you'll understand, I do things a little differently than most people. Being in the military and leading men, I tend to make sure a person is right for the job before I risk their lives." His Adam's apple bobbed on a swallow. "We'll go out for a short ride tomorrow, if I can persuade Robbie to check the fences in the south pasture for us. I'll tell him you deserve a break. I guess it's not a lie. I have been working you pretty hard." He turned his head towards the noise in the lounge room. "Gotta go the game's started."

With the broken chocolate bar gripped to her chest, she stomped back to the office. *He is going to drive me insane.* The muster was a fortnight away. One four-hour round trip and they could validate or dismiss Jock's claims, but no, Doug would rather leave his grandfather's theories up in the air for another two damn weeks? She needed more proof and pushing the chocolate bar into the back pocket of her jeans, re-examined the bookshelves. Each journal had the year embossed on the spine with the name of a family member. Collecting the dates she required, she returned to her room.

Settled in bed, with the chocolate close by, she opened each volume with respect. Reading Jamie Macgregor's journal brought the man to life. He came over as an efficient yet compassionate man, devoted to his family and Winnawarra. Although from Jenny Macgregor's impressions of the same period, he kept his worries to himself, which surprised her because of the open relationship between their sons. All the Macgregor boys discussed everything, from cow drenching to personal hygiene. All had voiced opinions about her inclusion in Jock's will with blunt honesty.

She flipped open the page and read a similar account to what Jock had described then moved through the diary to June, looking for any further reference to the incident and came across a brief entry from Jamie.

16 July

I collected the mail from Broome today and didn't find an invoice from a drilling company. Dad insists he had nothing to do with ordering tests, and now I believe him because no company drags a crew and equipment out here for nothing. Bill Wilson must be missing a cog or two but just to be sure, I'm riding up to Rainbow Gulley with Jenny in the morning to poke around and see if anything has been disturbed.

17 July

We never made it to Rainbow Gulley, but I'll be sure to take a sweep over the place in the chopper next time I'm out that way and see if anyone is camping thereabouts. We went as far as Old Man Rock when a sudden rock fall spooked the horses. Jenny insisted someone was watching us and refused to ride into the entrance of the gulley. As none of the Indigenous tribesmen offer any threat and have always offered advice and help when necessary, her reluctance surprised me. It would be very unlikely for tourists to be this far west unless they had followed a road train.

I heard a crack, and it could have been lightning or a shot from a rifle, but with the echo from the surrounding plateau, it was difficult to tell. The weather forecast had predicted a storm and clouds were rolling in, so either was possible. I didn't want to place Jenny at risk if some maniac had wandered onto our land and decided to do some target shooting, so we turned tail and headed for home.

Tomorrow I'm taking Jenny away to do some shopping in Darwin. I plan to take her on a picnic at our usual place. I've made an appointment with the assay office in Darwin. If anyone carried out testing on Winnawarra, the assay office will have the details, and I'll discover the truth one way or the other. Trouble is, if old Bill was fair dinkum then Brewster is lying but for what reason remains to be seen. It's not as if he can gain by anyone mining our land and I wonder if he has an ulterior motive. I'll suggest going with another accountant, but Dad is set in his ways.

The entry was the last for Jamie on the subject. The next heart-breaking entries from Jock told how Jamie and his wife died in a car crash in a remote area outside of Darwin. He made no mention of Jamie's trip to the assay office. Surely, if Jamie had discovered any information, he would have telephoned his father and Jock would have mentioned the conversation.

Moving on she read the entries in Jock's diaries written on the day prior to his visit to Perth. The contents made her blood run cold. He'd made it very clear he believed someone had caused the accident resulting in Jamie and Jenny's deaths. He had fears for his own life and mentioned an inquest returning the verdict of "accidental death" then went on to say how the police refused to investigate his observations. Even though, after examining the car, he was convinced someone had cut the brake line.

Had Jock been correct?

Unease covered her like a shroud, and her mind reeled. Perhaps Jock's death hadn't been an accident after all. It made sense someone would have wanted him out of the way if he was getting close to the truth and making complaints to the cops or speaking to others about his suspicions. *Why didn't he tell his grandsons?* She drummed her fingers on the cover then remembered a brief notation in Jock's diary about Doug's injury. He'd been angry about the lack of information, but when he arrived in Darwin, he discovered Doug's helicopter had come under heavy fire, and he'd been the only survivor. He'd managed to fly the damaged chopper into friendly territory before crashing, and his injuries had not been life-threatening. Doug had arrived in Darwin a few hours before his parents' accident. *He was critical then found to be mentally unstable enough to be hospitalised in a military psychiatric hospital. No wonder Jock kept Jamie's death and his suspicions a secret.*

Doug had mentioned doubts about his grandfather's accident, so perhaps her summation was not far from the truth. She had to discover the details surrounding Jock's death but if she did find anything suspicious what could she do about it? *I'm not a bloody cop.* The next moment, the conversation with Jock's solicitor dropped into her mind, and she gasped. As if Jock had turned on a light to show her the way, everything became clear. *Oh, my God! Jock included me in his will because he didn't trust the cops. He must have believed he was next on the list.*

She wanted to leap from the bed and tell Doug, but the sitting room had a number of stockmen watching the game, and she doubted the Macgregor boys would want everyone at Winnawarra knowing their business. Emily chewed on the end of her pen and went through the evidence. Assuming the accountant was corrupt, Brewster's motive stuck out like a lighthouse on a stormy night. Jock was an old man, and he'd tried to make him appear incompetent in the first instance may be to cover his tracks. He knew Jock well enough to push the right buttons, and from what she gleaned about him, Jock had a short fuse.

Throwing a fake mining company in the mix would have sent Jock crazy and taken his attention away from Brewster's scam, but then Jamie got involved. If Brewster arranged the car accident and murdered Jock, he would be in the clear as he would be aware the rest of the Macgregor family were blissfully ignorant of Jock's worries. As an old acquaintance, Brewster would know Jock would never lose face by informing his grandsons his trusted accountant had tricked him.

However, Brewster was an old man and must have had an accomplice. She would keep checking the diaries for further information and discuss her theory with the brothers. Surely, together they would know what to do. She pushed her hands through her hair and shivered with apprehension. Mr. Brewster probably believed he could go on taking money out of Winnawarra without detection and would not have bargained on Jock bringing her into the picture. *So, he sent someone here to scare me off.*

Emily closed the journals with a long sigh. She had to think rationally and place each piece of information in order. Leaning back on the pillow, she stared at the ceiling for a long time. First, she would consider the facts. Jock had brought her to Winnawarra to oversee the books, so he suspected Mr. Brewster had played him for an old fool. From Jamie's entry, Mr. Brewster had been involved in the request for core samples probably as a smokescreen to cover his dishonesty.

If Mr. Brewster *had* made some sort of deal with a mining company, there would be a paper trail, and Jock would have needed to sign off on any drilling request. Perhaps, he was one of those men who trusted his accountant implicitly and failed to read every document he signed. How easy it would be for an unscrupulous person to slip an assay request or even, God forbid, a mining rights lease transfer into a pile of tax documents? Jock could not dispute the documents if he was dead and Brewster would walk away with millions.

This alone would be reason to murder Jock. In fact, if Mr. Brewster witnessed and lodged the document, the mining company could rape the land at will leaving the Macgregor boys helpless to do a thing. They might be wealthy but fighting a billion-dollar company in court without one shred of evidence would be futile.

She repeatedly went over Jock's journal entries in her mind. As he changed his will to include her the day he died, he might have discovered a threat closer to home and documented his concerns to her in a letter. Jock had insisted someone had murdered his son and believed he and his grandsons were in danger. She had to admit, Jock's "accident" the day he changed his will was more than a little coincidental.

After admiring photographs of Jock standing proudly beside a prize bull, she could plainly see he had not been a small man. Images of him falling to his death flashed into her mind, and she hugged her stomach. She glanced at the door, and her heart thumped wildly. *If someone close by killed him, I could be next.* After she sucked in a few steadying breaths, she tried to force her mind back to rational thought. *Pull yourself together, Perkins.*

She made a list of priorities then stared into space. Informing the family about the mining rights concerns would be the first step. She would ask Doug to do a search via the assay office to discover if anyone had lodged a claim. If nothing showed up, she could dismiss the mining rights angle because the Macgregor brothers would respect Jock's wishes and as long as they owned Winnawarra and the rights, no mining would take place. If a transfer of rights showed up, the boys would have to go to court and fight the legality of the document. She tapped the end of the pen on her bottom lip trying to make sense of everything. The next step would be to discuss her theory with the brothers and reluctantly added, "Who would benefit if they all died?" to her list.

Could someone be willing to kill the entire family to gain Winnawarra? She sighed. The idea seemed a bit far-fetched, but Jock had included her in his will, and she had the necessary knowledge to protect his grandsons and his property. She slipped from the bed, collected up the diaries, and headed back to the office. After returning them to the shelves, she leant on the desk and stared out the window into blackness. Jock might have left her a hint, *something* concrete about Mr. Brewster for her to investigate. Right now, she had nothing but insinuations, and they would do nothing to help his grandsons or Winnawarra. Had he relied on her skills to uncover Mr. Brewster's involvement in duplicity? *I can do nothing positive until the letter arrives.*

She heard men's voices in the hallway and waited for the hands to leave. When Johnno turned and smiled at her, she returned the gesture. He immediately turned mid-stride and came back into the hallway.

"It's a beautiful night, and I'm restless after watching the game. How about coming for a ride and maybe a swim. Just the two of us?"

He was a good-looking man, tall with broad shoulders and his shorts hugged tanned, muscular thighs but she had her eye on Doug. She gave him a warm smile. "That sounds like fun, but I'm very busy right now."

"Then come to the dance with me." Johnno's dark brown gaze moved over her.

"I have a date." Emily shrugged. "Sorry."

"No worries. Save me a dance." He turned and strolled out the door his feet flapping in a pair of rubber thongs.

She watched him meet the other men on the veranda then made her way to join the Macgregor brothers in the kitchen. They all turned to look at her with the exact same expression of interest. She lifted her chin and straightened. "I think I know why your grandfather brought me here. He wanted me to use my skills to examine the deaths of your parents and possibly him too."

"What?" Robbie frowned and his piercing blue gaze fixed on her. "I think you'd better explain. My parents died in a car accident, and Jock fell down the stairs at a hotel in Perth, after a night on the town."

"From the entries in his diary, he believed someone murdered your parents." She took in the horrified expressions on the three brothers and quickly explained her concerns. "He doesn't offer any real evidence apart from insisting the brake hose was cut on your parents' car, but I'm sure he included me for two reasons, first because he had reason to believe Mr. Brewster was involved in some way. I'll audit the books for the last five years and see if I can uncover anything suspicious. Second, because I can look at the forensic report from the accident and might find something the coroner missed."

She sighed. "I would suggest one of you contact the assay office or wherever mining rights are lodged to get to the bottom of this, but that's where your parents were heading before they died. This may be a coincidence or something more sinister. You need to be very careful, and I suggest you don't mention the visit to anyone outside this room. In fact, we shouldn't speak about any of this to anyone before we work out who we can trust." She moved her attention over the three faces. "I'm worried you may all be in danger and the threat might be closer than you think. Jock believed whoever is involved is implicated in your parents' murder and if he was correct, then we must consider they would be capable of killing him too."

"I find this all a bit far-fetched, Em'. Why didn't Jock warn us if he thought we were in danger?" Doug hooked his thumbs into the front pockets of his jeans. "How could anyone get their hands on Winnawarra?" He shot a glance at Robbie as if asking for confirmation. "First, we the three of us, own the mining rights. Jock made sure of that when he purchased the land. Jock's will gives us ninety percent hold on the property and one hundred percent of the assets. You get ten percent of Winnawarra but if you die the land reverts to the family. If we all die then Winnawarra goes to any surviving relative, failing that it goes to the local Indigenous tribe lock, stock, and barrel. As far as we know, we are the only living relatives. Jock had a distant cousin on his mother's side, but he died last year. The local tribe would never hurt a fly, and they're happy with our commitment to the land, so count them out." He sighed and rested his attention on Emily. "I can't believe Jock had concerns about someone with a blood claim on Winnawarra planning to kill us all. So, I'd say he was more worried about the accountant stealing our money."

The tightness in her chest eased, and she nodded. "If your grandfather trusted his accountant before he had his suspicions, Mr. Brewster could have added a core sample request to a pile of documents for his signature." She lifted her chin. "Making Jock believe someone was planning to mine Winnawarra would certainly take his mind off his suspicions about Brewster."

"It sure would. Jock would go ballistic. I think Brewster slipping in documents for him to sign and maybe fiddling the books make more sense than murder. I wonder what tipped Jock off. We've been using Brewster for years." Robbie shrugged. "Unless the old bugger has been gambling again, but for someone like him to be involved in murder and intrigue to pay his debts seems a bit much." He crossed his arms and eyed her suspiciously.

She flicked a glance at Doug. "I believe Jock was convinced Mr. Brewster was defrauding your company."

"Right, but I think it's too late for you to discover any new leads in our parents' accident. We have their personal effects, but I have no idea if the police keep evidence after the case is closed. Do you?" Doug raised one dark eyebrow.

"I think they keep everything just in case the investigation is re-opened." She chewed on her bottom lip. In truth, she had no idea but made a stab in the dark. "This being the case, I gather Jock believed my forensic expertise might be able to determine the cause of death."

"That was covered at the inquest." Robbie moved to the coffee pot, poured a cup and offered it to her. "I must admit, the idea Jock had concerns about a company taking core samples seem more likely. He was an old man and went to pieces when my dad died. Perhaps he blamed himself for sending him to Darwin on a goose chase and needed to pass the buck after the accident to ease his conscience."

"From what I've read he blamed everyone else *but* himself." Emily moved to Robbie's side and took the mug inhaling the rich aroma. "Is there really anything of value to mine here? I mean anything worth killing for?"

"Jeez, Em', everyone knows Winnawarra sits on a bed of iron ore. Did you notice the red soil? It's that colour because of the ferrous oxide." Ian grinned. "There is a possibility to find gold and diamonds too, but we really don't want to know. Jock made us promise years ago never to allow anyone to take core samples. He always said the land was precious and should be left untouched." He rubbed the back of his neck thoughtfully. "What lies underneath Winnawarra is probably worth billions, but we'll never allow anyone to destroy the land by mining, not ever. We make enough money with the cattle and tourists."

She leant against the door frame thinking back over the journal entries and sipped her coffee. "Jock was very concerned about someone gaining the mining rights, and I think Brewster used it against him to cover his tracks."

"Like I said before, we *own* the mining rights." Doug pushed a hand through his dark hair in a show of agitation. "What else did you discover?"

Emily listed Jock's suspicions to bring them up to speed. "Somewhere between his last entry and the time he altered his will, he must have discovered something else. We will need to find out exactly what happened during the week prior to his death. I want to know where he went, and whom he met in Perth. If it's people you know, you'll have to call them and ask what they remember about his visit and if he mentioned having any concerns." She looked from one man to the next. "We'll need a list of everyone he met then we can cross-reference them with anyone you know who may have been in Darwin or Perth about the same time Jock and your parents died. I gather passengers' names are logged on all flights in and out of Broome so maybe one of you can sweet talk someone at the airport for the list." She placed her cup on the table then rubbed her temples to dispel a throbbing headache. "We'll need a list of everyone back and forth from Winnawarra on those dates as well. I don't want to discount anyone, not even people you trust."

"I have those names, no worries." Doug wrinkled his brow. "I'll go through our logs and make a list but getting the info from the airlines is a different matter. Passenger lists are not on public record. It's a privacy issue, and we'll have Buckley's chance of seeing them." He rubbed his chin. "What was the date of his last journal entry?"

She gave him the date and sighed. "It's a shame he didn't take his journal with him when he went to Perth because the gap between the last entry and the day he died might be crucial."

"He visited me in hospital and never even mentioned he'd planned to visit his solicitor, let alone his suspicions." Doug shrugged. "But I guess he thought I wasn't in my right mind to deal with it."

"I'll make some calls in the morning. I might be able to find out if anyone requested a mineral assay." Robbie eyed her over the rim of his cup. "Anything else we need to consider?"

"Right now, I believe there are two things we need to address first and they are, who ordered the core samples and Mr. Brewster's honesty." She pushed a lock of hair away from her face. "If you can't find anything from the assay office about core samples, then Doug and I will ride out to Rainbow Gully as soon as possible to see if anything has been disturbed. I will start an audit and see what I can discover about Mr. Brewster's ethics."

"I can't see him doing all this on his own." Ian rubbed his chin. "Did Jock mention anyone else?"

Emily shook her head. "Not so far, but I agree about an accomplice. You must know Brewster's acquaintances. It wouldn't hurt to do some digging to find out if anything unusual has happened in his life in case it's relevant. All this intrigue might be an old man's fancy for all we know."

Robbie eyed her intently.

"And if it isn't, Jock covered his bases by including you to help us with his suspicions about our parents' accident. Although, I can't fathom why he thought someone planned to murder him as well unless someone had threatened him. This seems the case because he obviously believed he was a target. If there is a threat to our family, we need to be on our guard. The muster is in two weeks, and we could be walking into a trap."

Emily stiffened as dread hung over her like a shawl. "What does the muster have to do with this problem?"

"Strangers. We have twenty visitors arriving, and any one of them could be a threat." Robbie rubbed the back of his neck and sighed. "We'll have to deal with this investigation in secret." He snorted, and his gaze rested on his brothers. "It is just as well Emily found out about this *after* she arrived."

She narrowed her gaze. "What's that supposed to mean?"

"Can you imagine Doug meeting you at the airport and explaining all this shit to you? 'Welcome to Winnawarra, Miss Perkins. We're on somebody's hit list, and you need to discover the murderer quick smart before he picks us off one by one'."

CHAPTER SEVEN

Emily followed Doug through the stables and into the tack room. He moved with an easy stride towards a row of saddles then turned and cocked one eyebrow at her.

"Can you saddle a horse, Em'?"

She offered him her best "oh, doh" expression. "I think I can manage." She waved a hand towards the saddles. "Which tack and which horse?"

Doug gave her a lopsided grin, hoisted a saddle over one arm and handed it to her then reached for a bridle.

"'Bolt'. The bay stallion with one white foot in the loose box by the door." He gave her the bridle and saddle blanket then jerked his thumb over one shoulder in the direction of his brother. "I'll need to speak to Ian before we leave. I'll be right behind you." He wandered away with a trio of farm dogs at his heels.

Staggering under the weight of the stockman's saddle, she gave him a curt nod and headed towards the stable door. The *tap, tap, tap* of boots on the flagstones behind her made the hairs on the back of her neck stand to attention. When a figure moved into her peripheral vision then slid into the shadows, her stomach clenched in fear. She stared into the dark corners, trying to discover who found her so interesting but nothing moved. The man was a phantom. Her skin pebbled as if an ice-cold wind had brushed over her. Damn he made her uneasy — no, more than uneasy — he frightened the hell out of her. *I can't show him I'm afraid or I'll play right into his hands. He probably gets off scaring women.*

Glad that Doug was close by, she took a few deep breaths to calm her nerves. Horses could feel emotions, and she refused to enter a stallion's stall showing signs of fear. Keeping one eye out for anyone creeping around, she strolled along the rows of horses, peering at each one. The only light in the stable came from the front door, and the dim conditions made all the horses appear bay. Moving towards the last stall, she caught sight of a proud head, ears pricked, and large soft brown eyes watching her with interest. She moved closer and rubbed the horse's long nose. "Hello boy."

He snorted a greeting, and when she unlocked the gate, he stepped back allowing her to enter. This in itself was a good sign, she'd known many stallions to challenge anyone entering their space, and she moved with caution keeping one hand on the horse's neck. Speaking in calm tones, she pushed the bit into his mouth and fitted the bridle. Thank God, Bolt appeared to be easygoing. She took a deep breath in relief then glanced towards the tack room expecting Doug to walk out at any moment and inspect her abilities. She didn't want to appear like a novice in front of him or the other men. The horse stood still allowing her to fit the blanket and saddle. She bent to reach for the girth strap and froze at the *tap, tap, tap* of boots on the concrete floor. Head pressed against Bolt's ribs, she pushed down the rising fear and waited. This time, she would get a good look at who was stalking her, but the stallion moved blocking her view. She ducked down to peer under the horse's wide girth but only caught sight of a pair of jeans and scruffy boots moving away. *Damn!*

The next moment, a ripple of tension moved through Bolt's muscles. The big stallion snorted his disapproval, stamped his feet, and his hindquarters moved dangerously towards her. In this position, if he kicked, she would suffer serious injury. Worried her fear might have caused the stallion's reaction she ran a comforting stroke down his back and murmured to him. The *tap, tap, tap* of boots passed the stall again, and all hell broke loose. Bolt shook his head and danced sideways, his huge rump pinning her against the wall, her scalp prickled. *What is the idiot up to?* She crooned at the stallion and hitched the girth. If she could mount him, she could gain control and calm him down. Bolt screeched in terror, his head flew up, and she could see the whites of his eyes. Ducking away from his chomping grin, her stomach dropped at the sight of a two-metre-long snake at the entrance to the stall.

Struck dumb with fear, she gaped at the reptile and reached for the horse's bridle in an attempt to calm him. Bolt let out a piercing scream, flattened his ears then reared pawing at the gate with his front legs. At the crack of wood splintering, she wrapped the reins around one arm and pulled. The horse's rump swung around and smashed her into the wall. Cold brick hit her back, and air rushed from her lungs in a *whoosh* of pain. Agony slammed into her head and fighting to keep conscious, she pushed helplessly at the immovable hair covered crushing machine. *I must keep on my feet.*

Men barking orders and running feet came through her muddled senses. She heard Doug's voice speaking softly and then his strong body moved in front of her, shielding her from the writhing terrified beast.

"Whoa boy, good fella, calm down." He turned the horse and pushed him to the back of the loose box. "Ian, get your arse over here, there's a dead snake in the straw."

"Got it." Ian lifted the huge brown snake on a pitchfork and carried it away.

Bolt appeared to calm the moment the snake disappeared and made grunting sounds as if explaining to Doug the reason he had crushed her half to death. Her head ached, and she tried to make sense of what Doug was saying over the ringing in her ears. "What?"

Doug ran a gentle hand over her shoulder and peered at her with deep concern etched in his expression.

"I asked if you're okay, love."

She tried desperately to stop her teeth chattering, and stared at him through a strange distorted tunnel. *I'm going into shock.* She gripped her ribs running her fingers over the sore spot and winced. As she took stock of her injuries, crushing chest pain prevented her drawing a deep breath. Her head throbbed, and she wanted to vomit. If this happened to be some kind of a prank, she did not think it was at all funny. She ground her back teeth and straightened. "I'm not too sure, but I *do* know who threw that snake in here. It was the same person who was outside my room the other night. I heard him walk by, stop then move on a second before Bolt went ballistic." She touched the egg forming on the back of her head and glared at him. "If this is some kind of stupid initiation for the new girl, you should all be ashamed of yourselves. I could have been trampled to death, and you could have lost a valuable stallion."

"Have you lost your mind?" Doug rubbed the back of his neck. "Do you really think I sent you in here to set you up for a bloody joke?"

Ian, his face grim, moved into the stall and gave her a once-over then moved his concern to the horse. "We don't pull stunts like that, and I doubt any of the men would do something so stupid. Everyone here knows Bolt has a fear of snakes." He ran a hand down the stallion's legs then turned to Doug. "You'd better get Emily back to the house and check that bump on her head. I'll ask Brian to give Bolt a once-over, he's got a nasty cut on his fetlock."

"Walk him until he settles down and put him in the empty stall on the end." Doug narrowed his gaze at her. "Can you get back to the house on your own?"

She gaped at him. Obviously, her welfare came in second place to a horse on this station. She straightened and willed her bottom lip to stop trembling then lifted her chin. "Yes, and I'm sure Glady will give me some ice for my head. Go about your work. I wouldn't want to inconvenience you."

With one hand on the wall for support, she stumbled towards the open door. Her mind raced at the implications of the situation. She glanced around, making sure none of the men were watching her before making her way across the dusty expanse. Having a creep outside her bedroom and trying to peep at her as she slept was one thing but now, he'd gone too far. Bolt could have killed her. *Maybe that's his plan.* She gazed into the sunshine, and the ground moved in waves. The distance to the homestead spread out before her like a vast expanse, more like miles instead of feet. She blinked not comprehending why the distance had grown or how the house appeared to be down a long dark tunnel. Determined not to ask for help, she dragged leaden feet step by painful step along the pathway gasping breath into crushed lungs. Her vision moved in and out of focus, and the steps of the homestead appeared to bend at the edges. The next moment the shimmering red soil rushed up towards her and she floated into peaceful darkness.

Doug ran towards the crumpled figure and dropped to his knees. "Em', for Christ's sake why didn't you tell me you were hurt?"

She didn't move and face ashen lay with her arms spread out in the dirt. He pushed back her hair and swallowed hard at the sight of the huge bruise on her forehead. "Shit!" He scooped her up and dashed towards the homestead taking the steps at a run. "Glady, come here, Em's been hurt."

The housekeeper poked her greying head around the kitchen door. "What happened?"

"Bolt crushed her. Bring your set of keys, her door will be locked."

The moment Glady opened the door he moved swiftly into Emily's bedroom and laid her gently on the bed. He rubbed her ice-cold fingers. "Come on, open your eyes."

His service in a war zone had its benefits. For the first time since his horrific chopper crash, he didn't panic and sent up a silent prayer of thanks for his medic field training. He ran his fingers over Emily's head wincing at the bump on the back then unbuttoned her shirt to examine her ribs.

"That bump looks nasty." Glady moved to the bedside.

"Can you get some ice? She has a nasty bump on the back of her head as well. She hit her forehead on the ground, but I think she's okay." He lifted her shirt trying to avoid looking at her lacy pink bra and gingerly touched her ribs. He ran his palm over her soft bruised skin and flinched at her moan of pain. "I don't think her ribs are broken. Get me two ice packs wrapped in a cloth. She will have one hell of a headache when she wakes. I'll get her comfortable then radio Robbie. I want him here to check her ASAP."

"Go and call him now." Glady waved him towards the door. "He only had one call next door this morning. After, he planned to head into Broome for supplies. You'll miss him for sure if you don't hurry." She frowned down at Emily. "She isn't going anywhere. I'll get the ice and sit with her until you get back."

"Okay." Doug patted Emily's cheek in an attempt to wake her. She was sheet-white and leaving her unconscious worried him. She needed a doctor, and with luck, Robbie was only one-half hour away. He got to his feet, strode towards the office, and made the call. After explaining Emily's injuries to the best of his ability, he listened intently to Robbie's instructions.

"Keep her head elevated, apply the ice packs for twenty minutes then remove. I should be home by then. Any discharge from the ears or bleeding from the eyes or nose?"

Dread crept over him, and he swallowed the panic rising in his chest. "Nope, all good but she is out cold. She walked out of the stables and collapsed."

"Check her pupils. I'm worried if she's still unconscious. You said she staggered, has bruising on her forehead and a bump on the back of the head. She could have a fractured skull so get back to her. My ETA is about twenty minutes." He sighed. *"The ice is imperative, and checking her vital signs every ten minutes."*

He cleared his throat trying desperately to remain in control. Damn, he hadn't had a flashback in ages, and things like this triggered them nine times out of ten. "Roger that, Doug out."

After pushing to his feet, he marched down the hallway in grim determination. He would keep it together if it killed him.

After collecting a small flashlight from the kitchen drawer, he headed towards Emily's bedroom. Relief washed over him the moment he set foot inside and looked at her. It seemed Glady had already supplied the ice pack and left Emily sat propped up on the pillows holding the cold compress to the back of her head, and her eyes flashed angrily at him. *That has to be a good sign.*

"Shut the door and make sure no one is listening." Emily's voice came out in a raspy whisper.

He glanced into the hallway, looked both ways then closed the door and stood at the foot of her bed feeling a little like a kid in trouble. "What's wrong?"

"What's wrong?" Emily glared at him. "You tell me. How did a dead snake get into Bolt's stall? The arsehole who is stalking me put it there, and I know why he is trying to frighten me into leaving. He is the link — Brewster's accomplice and he knows I'm here to do an audit."

"Did you see who it was this time?"

"No, the bloody horse was blocking my view, but I heard his boots." Emily held her ribs and moaned. "You must have seen who was in the barn when Bolt went crazy. Check them out, see who has steel tips to his boots."

"When I came out with Ian, Sue was standing at the entrance chatting to Brian." The idea Brian might be Em's stalker seemed crazy. He'd known the man for years. He rubbed his chin uncertain how to proceed. "I'll check both of them out and ask them if they noticed anyone else hanging around the barn."

"Go now." Em' grabbed his arm. "I need to know who is doing this to me."

"They're not going anywhere, and right now, you need me. I'm not leaving your side until Robbie arrives to check you out." He offered her a small smile. "Robbie said I should test your pupillary response. Lift up your chin." He flicked the flashlight over her eyes and to his relief her pupils contracted. "They look fine."

"Has Brian or any of the other men done anything like this before?" She narrowed her gaze. "Could the snake be a prank?"

What could he say? The men did play pranks on each other sometimes like pouring ice down each other's backs but not anything dangerous. "I've known Brian for some time. He started working here about four years ago, and he doesn't seem the type to disrespect women. We have heaps of women visiting during the muster. It's a time when the family tries to get together, so I have seen how he acts around tourists. I know he thinks he's some kind of stud but I've never seen him do anything to deliberately hurt anyone." He shuffled his feet trying to think of something to say to calm her. "Look, Em', the snake had been dead for a while by the look of it, so it could have been concealed in the straw and missed when one of the boys mucked out the stables. You walked in and disturbed the bedding and uncovered it is all."

"So these kinds of things happen every day?" She snorted then held her head as if the movement bothered her. "Can you remember *one* other time this has happened?"

"Yeah, and I've seen snakes in the straw, heaps of times." Doug shrugged trying to appear nonchalant. *Brian might be a loudmouth, but I'm sure he wouldn't deliberately hurt her.* No, he would put her worries down to being upset about seeing a man outside her bedroom and the bump on the head. "You have to admit, it *is* possible it was missed."

"Bloody hell! It was two metres long and as thick as my arm." She wrapped both hands around her middle, and her blue eyes narrowed to slits. "Someone would have been blind not to see it, and it would have weighed a lot too. Nope, I think this was a deliberate attempt on my life. I'm not going crazy. I heard someone walk past the stall just before Bolt went ballistic." She gave him a look of pure desperation. "I don't feel safe here." She covered her mouth with a shaky hand, her eyes large and round with terror.

He pushed down the need to pull her into his arms and took her hand. "I'll see if Brian has metal tips to his boots and ask Ian who was working in or around the stables."

"Yes, make a list in case he kills me next time."

He huffed out a long sigh. "We usually have the same group of men working in the stables every morning. It's part of Brian's job to check the horses before he moves onto his other chores. You didn't actually see him throw the snake in Bolt's stall, did you?"

"No, I didn't *actually* see Brian, but whoever is doing this has won hasn't he because I'm leaving?"

He rubbed his chin. "You can't leave, Em'."

Before she answered him, a knock sounded on the door, and he went to open it. Robbie stood in the hallway doctor's bag in hand and a worried look on his face. Doug beckoned him inside. "She seems okay but is raving a bit."

"I am *not* raving." Emily moved then moaned and clutched her ribs. "This idiot won't listen to me."

"What?" Robbie raised both eyebrows to his hairline. "I think you'd better explain."

Doug gave Robbie an abridged version of the incident and Emily's concerns. "It's because of the bump on the head, right?"

A shadow of worry crossed Robbie's face.

"Concussion does strange things, but you did mention seeing a man near her room on different occasions, so don't be too hasty disregarding what she is saying." Robbie frowned. "She could be right, and the person stalking her is Brewster's accomplice."

"There, *he* believes me." She glared at him. "*You* think I'm a raving lunatic."

Ouch! "I didn't say I *didn't* believe you, Em'. I said it was out of character for any of the men particularly Brian to act that way." He touched her cheek. "I'm sorry, love. It's my military training. I don't jump to conclusions, but I did see someone in the hallway the night you arrived, so I don't think you imagined seeing a man outside your room."

"And just before, in the stables." Emily lifted her chin then winced. "Do you believe I heard the same tapping of boots? People walk differently, and I heard the same stride pattern outside the stall."

"Then I believe you, Em'. What I can't understand is why someone would do such an irresponsible thing, and that's why I don't think it's Brian." Doug glanced at Robbie for support. "He wouldn't risk Bolt by doing such a stupid thing, he's a vet, remember?"

"Yet it was obviously okay to risk killing me?" Emily snorted in derision. "Trying to scare me into leaving Winnawarra is one thing, but now they've progressed to attempted murder. I want to leave."

"I hope you reconsider. I like having you here." Doug's heart twisted at the thought of the long days ahead without her.

He wanted so much more than friendship, but now she didn't trust him to keep her safe. How could he sweep her into his arms and convince her to stay with Robbie breathing down his neck? He stared into her eyes trying to convey his feelings and not look like a pathetic idiot. He could never do the sexy eye thing most men perfected. "Emily, you being here means a lot to me. I've never met a woman like you before, and I think we're good together." He let out a long sigh. "Please stay. I *promise* to keep you safe. I'll never leave your side until we sort out this mess, okay?" He bent down and brushed a kiss on her cheek and embarrassed by his brother's amazed expression lowered his voice. "You must know, I have feelings for you."

His pulse thumped in his ears as he waited for her response but her angry expression melted away. Her big blue eyes drifted over his face, and her mouth curled up at the corners.

"No one has ever promised to keep me safe before, and I like you too." Emily's cheeks pinked. "Very much."

"Have you finished making cow's eyes at her because I'm feeling like a third wheel here? Give me some space so I can take a look at her." Robbie gave him a long, puzzled stare then sat on the edge of the bed and examined her. "That's a nasty bump on the head. Rest up and leave the stalker to us." He smiled at her and patted her shoulder. "I'll talk to Ian, and then we'll all have another word with the men about keeping their distance from you."

"Is there any of the men you can trust?" Emily frowned. "I mean apart from Ian?"

"The cook, Glady's husband, has been here since we were born. You can trust him. I honestly can't see Brian or Johnno stalking women." Robbie rubbed the back of his neck. "They've been here for years, attended musters, and never acted inappropriately against women or anyone else that I am aware."

"What about Pete? He looks at me a lot, and Joe dislikes me intensely."

"Pete thinks he's God's gift to women but he usually has a more direct approach and Joe, well honestly I don't know." Robbie turned to Doug and raised both eyebrows. "Best we check out everyone within cooee of the stables this morning and see who has steel tips to their boots."

Doug nodded in agreement. "We'll assign work away from the homestead to anyone we think is suspicious then if the bugger shows up here and causes strife we'll have him to rights."

"Can you explain 'within cooee of the stables'?" Emily's brow wrinkled into a frown.

"Ahh, when we call out to each other, we shout 'cooooeeeee' and the sound carries, so if anyone is in cooee of the stables it means within shouting distance." Doug grinned. "Now you get some rest, and we'll deal with the stalker."

"I'm not staying here alone in the house to be used as bait. I'm booking a flight back to Perth first chance I get." Emily's eyes filled with tears and she stared down at her hands.

"You can put going anywhere right out of your mind." Robbie patted her hand and spoke in a soothing tone. "I can't stop you leaving, Emily, but I will not allow you to fly until I'm sure you're okay."

Emily stared at the two brothers with incredulity. Fine, she would rest but would keep her door locked day and night. "Okay, I'll rest, but I'm going to keep Doug to his promise to keep me safe."

"Good. Take it easy and I'll check on you again in an hour." Robbie rubbed his stomach. "I'm famished. I'll grab something to eat and see you later." He collected his things and strolled out the room.

"Don't worry." Doug bent down and to her surprise placed a lingering, warm kiss on her lips then pulled away. "I'll send anyone suspicious out to mend fences for the rest of the week, and I'll stay close by. If the stalker makes one false move, he will have me to deal with, and trust me, it won't be pretty. You have my word." He tapped the satellite phone on her bedside table. "I'm only a phone call away, and Glady is in the house. Next time you go outside attach it to your belt like the rest of us, it's no use to you sitting here on the table." He turned to go.

She grabbed his arm, needing to have him close and he sat beside her with a silly grin on his face. He had melted her heart by baring his feelings and promising to protect her. Speaking so frankly in front of his brother must have been difficult. His tender confession of his attraction towards her had warmed her heart. She thought a relationship with Doug Macgregor had been a foolish dream but the moment he sat on the edge of the bed her heart raced in anticipation. The scent of fresh man and aftershave enveloped her. *I could become addicted to his delicious smell.*

She gazed into his deep blue eyes and all doubts fled. *I am so going to regret this.* "Okay, I'll stay and do as you say because I trust *you* — and your brothers of course but most of all because I really wanted to make my home here. Winnawarra is so beautiful, too lovely to leave and I understand how devoted you are to the land." She offered him a small smile. "The problem is I think the snake incident scared me more than you realise. Yes, I know I may be overreacting, but when I'm with you, it's great, but the moment I'm alone with the ringers, I have this awful feeling someone is watching me."

"You don't have too much trust in men, do you, Em'?" Doug reached for her hand and rubbed one rough thumb over the back in slow circles. His gentle touch sent tingles of awareness dancing over her flesh. "I'm guessing some bastard hurt you and this business has brought it all back." A sad expression touched his eyes, and he shrugged as if dismissing his feelings. "You're not alone in being a bit off-kilter. We all deal with problems in different ways. I've been through my own personal hell too. Robbie and my shrink tell me I hide my worries under false bravado, whatever that means." He snorted and smiled at her. "I've suffered from PTSD since my chopper went down in Afghanistan under heavy fire. It's under control to a degree, but it emasculates me because stupid things trigger flashbacks." He sighed, and a spark of uncertainty crossed his expression. "I really like you, Em', and hope my illness won't be a problem."

Astounded by his admission, she covered his hand and returned his smile. "I like you too, and I think you're a hero. I understand PTSD and what it can do to a soldier."

"I'm no hero." Doug looked away. "I should have died along with my men. I wonder why I was spared."

Emily cupped his face and pressed kisses to the corners of his downturned mouth. "I think you were saved for me. I need someone to believe in, Doug. You're correct though, my trust in men is practically non-existent."

"What happened? Did someone hurt you?" He frowned then shook his head. "I'm sorry, I shouldn't have asked. It's none of my business."

She squeezed his hand. "If we are going to be friends, then we should have no secrets, and as you've bared your soul to me, I'll tell you about my sordid past." After taking a deep breath, she met his interested gaze. "I left England after being involved as the 'other woman' in a very nasty divorce case." She glanced away disgusted at the memory. "I had no idea the man I'd dated for a year was married. He had three kids and a pregnant wife."

"That wasn't your fault, Em'." Doug cupped her cheek, his palm a soothing balm to her anxiety. "He was a dog, pure and simple. Me, I'm just a basket case, and because of my tour of duty, I haven't had a girlfriend in over four years."

She bit back the overpowering need to lean into his warm hand and smiled. "As we're both basket cases maybe we can take it slowly and see how things go?"

"I can do slow." He chuckled. "Well, I can try. I was thinking, maybe, if I told the men we were an item, the stalker might pull his head and leave you alone." Doug shrugged. "But I'll understand if this makes you uncomf—"

"That makes me feel *very* safe." She leant forwards and brushed a kiss over his deliciously full lips.

Tingles of awareness sparked between them, and she pulled back staring into hooded eyes. Doug's pupils had dilated with passion, and he slipped one large hand to the back of her neck. The masculine scent of him infused her senses. At his touch, her mind went blank, and she stared at him in awe. She melted into his kiss, and her lips opened at the gentle teasing of his tongue. He took control exploring her mouth, and for a man who hadn't had a girlfriend in four years, he certainly hadn't forgotten how to ignite every erogenous zone. He tasted like sin, and his lips sizzled over her flesh. She slipped her hands around his neck then sunk her fingers into his thick black hair pulling him closer. Her nipples hard and erect pressed against his muscular chest and she gasped. Tingles of pleasure curled around her, and she moaned into his mouth. She wanted him.

Lost in the moment, she forgot her injuries and let him devour her. Oh, he was so good at kissing, she wanted the embrace to go on forever and groaned her displeasure when he pulled away.

"Jesus, you're hurt, and I'm taking advantage." Doug smiled and cupped her chin in his warm hand then rubbed the pad of his thumb over her bottom lip.

She stared into his slightly unfocused eyes and smiled then licked her lips tasting him. "You can take advantage any time you like."

CHAPTER EIGHT

A knock came on the door, and Robbie walked back inside. "I forgot to tell you the letter from our solicitor arrived. I've left it in Doug's office. He can give it you later when you're feeling better. Let her rest, Doug." He turned and strolled out the door.

"I'd better get back to work. Ian is going to be working in the barn today and be in and out of his office all day, so you'll be fine." Doug got to his feet then shot her a concerned gaze. "Will you be okay here with Glady?"

"I'll be fine." She stared at him, and her face grew hot remembering their kiss.

As if he'd read her mind, he gave her a lopsided smile.

"I'm happy to continue where we left off when you are feeling better."

"That would be nice. Damn this headache, I'm anxious to find out what's in that letter. What if we have a serial killer close by and Jock has named him?" She rubbed her temple trying to alleviate the endless throbbing.

"I'm sure he would have gone to the cops. You need to rest. The letter can wait another day." He met her gaze his expression serious. "There have been a number of serial killers in the Outback over the years, and if there is one at Winnawarra we'll find him."

She wet her lips, tasting him and her stomach gave a strange twist. As she peered up at him from below her lashes, she caught his intent focus on her mouth. "That's good. In case you are in any doubt, the kiss was wonderful, but my head is aching, can I have a rain check on the next one?"

"My heart is shattered, but I'm an understanding lonesome cowboy." He grinned in a flash of white, even teeth and placed one hand over his heart. "Rest. I'll speak to Glady and come back with a tray. You need to eat something." He strolled from the room.

His retreating footsteps made a soft squeaky shuffle so unlike her stalker's distinctive tread.

She grinned then winced at the rush of pain in her temple. She hoped the brothers would discover which of the men was stalking her and perhaps help her find out the truth behind the deaths. She leant back into the pillows and adjusted the ice packs. A warm fuzzy feeling enclosed her, and she sighed. Doug would be close by keeping her safe, and for now, she could rest.

* * * *

After a reasonable night's sleep, Emily ate breakfast in bed then dozed. The morning sped by, and by ten her gaze drifted to a bowl of fresh fruit Doug had placed beside her bed. He had turned down the temperature on the air conditioner for her comfort, and she'd kicked off the sheets five minutes after he left. Her head no longer ached and she soon became bored lying in bed auditing the books. She wondered why the old man had given his accountant so much power. Rather than have a separate account for him to pay the outgoing invoices every cent went into one account. Mr. Brewster had been able to withdraw his "expenses" and any other sum at will without permission. The accountant had handled everything including, taxes, wages, and quarterly profit shares. From the number of withdrawals into his personal account, any fool could see the accountant had been skimming money from Winnawarra. The turnover for the property was considerable, and Mr. Brewster was very astute at concealing his deceit.

Convinced Jock must have hidden more details in his journals, she decided to grab a couple more diaries and some of the ledgers from Jock's office. She wanted to explain Jock's concerns with facts.

Reluctantly, she slid out of bed then glanced out the window pausing to admire the variety of birdlife drinking from a water trough. Apart from the birds and the odd bellow from one of the bulls, Winnawarra was as quiet as a church graveyard at this time of day. There would be no one around to bother her or tell her to get back to bed. She could sneak past Glady in the kitchen without her knowing, grab a couple of books, and be back in her room in seconds. With hesitant steps, she moved to the door and pressed her ear to the wood panelling. No sound came from the kitchen, and Glady usually had the radio blaring all day. The old woman must have slipped out to help her husband in the cookhouse.

She unlocked the door and peeked outside. Seeing the passageway empty, she closed the door then moved to the kitchen and poked her head around the corner. She sighed with relief at the empty room and hurried through the kitchen then took the passageway to Jock's office. Once inside, she scanned the shelves to select diaries and accounting ledgers with corresponding dates. She could cross-reference any details with the files on the laptop. Selecting a number of books, she turned towards the door and heard the front door hinge whine then click shut.

Tap, tap, tap.

Tap, tap, tap.

Oh, my God. It's him again. Doug had sent anyone suspicious out to mend fences during his absence. Ian would be close by, but Ian didn't have metal tips on his boots, and Robbie was making house calls. The confident stride and the sound of metal tips striking the floorboards were frighteningly familiar. Her heart pounded, and sweat trickled down her face. Whoever had come inside had to be the same man who tried to get into her room, and the incident with the snake left no doubt in her mind he was dangerous. With the house empty and not one soul close by in the yard to hear her calling for help, her pulse raced. She glanced around for an escape route and centred on the window behind Jock's desk.

The steps came again.

She would never make it across the room before he reached the office door and the fly screens would block her way. Panic froze her limbs, and she stared at the door unable to breathe as if a fist had closed around her windpipe. Willing her feet to move, she sneaked across the room and flattened her back against the wall behind the open door.

Tap, tap, tap.

Tap, tap, tap.

Terrified he would hear her heavy breathing she covered her mouth, and peered into the hallway through the tiny crack between door and frame. *Where is he?*

Tap, tap, tap

Tap, tap, tap

She listened intently and let out a relieved gasp. He had taken the other hallway and moved towards the kitchen. Once there, if he were looking for her, he would take the passageway on the far side and reach her bedroom in seconds. What would he do when he found the room empty? She forced her mind to think rationally. He would know she hadn't left with Doug. Ice-cold fear chilled her sweat-soaked flesh raising goose bumps on her arms. The conversation with Doug slammed into her memory. He admitted serial killers roamed the Outback. She had to get outside and find Ian. He planned to enter a couple of the bulls in the next show and would go online at lunchtime to complete the entry forms. She glanced at the clock and relaxed a little. *He will be heading here soon.*

Perhaps she'd allowed her overactive imagination to run wild, and one of the hands had come inside looking for him — but why not take the direct route to Ian's office *unless* he was doing a sweep of the house to make sure she was alone.

Oh, God! The stranger would have to walk straight past her to check if Ian was in his office. She stared down at her trembling hands. *Pull yourself together, Perkins.* Pressed against the wall, she tried to listen over the heartbeat thundering in her ears. She stared through the gap between hinge and frame and fixed her attention on the kitchen doorway.

Tap, tap, tap

Tap, tap, tap.

Terror clenched her stomach. The moment he turned into the hallway, he would see her through the crack in the door. She needed to find a better place to hide. Her attention slid to Jock's old desk, the front went to the floor, and the back had two sets of drawers with a gap between. She dashed across the room, the creaking from the floorboards under her bare feet sounding like gunshots, and dove into the space under the desk.

Pain shot into her ribs, and she pressed her fist to her mouth to muffle a sob. Holding her breath, she listened to the footsteps move to the office doors then pause at each one as he looked inside. Teeth chattering with fear, she swiped at the sweat dripping from the tip of her nose. If he attacked her, how could she defend herself? One sudden move and the pain of her bruised ribs would make her helpless.

She let her breath out slowly and in horror remembered the pile of books she'd left on the desk. Since her arrival, Jock's desk had been as neat as a pin. By the confident way the stalker moved around the house, he was familiar with Winnawarra. He would notice something out of place and might investigate. When his footsteps disappeared into Doug's carpeted office, she dragged in a deep breath, crawled out and grabbed the books, then heart thundering louder than a military tattoo, returned to her hiding place.

Tap, tap, tap.
Tap, tap, tap.

He stopped outside the door and was so close she could smell the cheap aftershave he used to cover his sweat. She slammed her jaw shut to prevent the scream threatening to erupt, and dripping with perspiration, she trembled with dread. She heard him sigh then his footsteps continued down the hallway and headed towards the veranda door. The door creaked, and she sucked in deep breaths to steady her nerves. Barefoot, she could run back to her room and lock the door without anyone hearing her. If she ran to the end of the passageway and went through the kitchen, she would avoid him seeing her through the French windows to the veranda.

With her arms wrapped around her ribs, she dashed along the hallway and into the kitchen. She skirted the long scrubbed wooden table and limped out the far door heading towards her room then stopped mid-stride. Her heart leapt into her mouth at the sight of a tall, broad man with his back to her leaning one shoulder casually against the wall outside her door. Trapped in a web of terror, Emily shrank back. Her heart thundered as if it would leap from her chest. Unable to move or utter a word she panted, dragging air into her damaged lungs. The strong scent of male sweat poured over her like a stinking blanket. If she made a sound, he would hear her. *I have to get away.*

CHAPTER NINE

She edged backwards, skirted the table then headed towards the back door and slipped outside. The barn appeared a hundred kilometres away, but she could make out Ian moving around inside. With adrenaline pumping through her veins, she increased her speed towards him and screamed out at the top of her voice, "Ian, Ian."

"What the bloody hell?" Ian thundered towards her and wrapped his arms around her. "Big breaths, that's better." He rubbed her back then held her gently away from his chest and looked at her. "What's wrong?"

"The stalker, he's inside the house." She hugged her painful ribs and gasped then glanced over one shoulder towards the house. "Outside my room. I was in Jock's office, and he searched the house. I know he was looking for me. When I returned to my room, I saw him in the hallway waiting for me."

"Who is it?" Ian stared over her shoulder at the house. "I'll deal with him right now." He took her hand and attempted to lead her towards the homestead. "He's not getting away with terrorising you."

Emily hung back. "I didn't stick around to see who it was, Ian. I only saw his back, brown cowboy hat, black tee shirt, blue jeans, and brown boots. He looks like Robbie from the back, not as tall as you or Doug but big. Dark hair too." She grimaced. "He might be dangerous."

"Hey, Joe." Ian waited for the grey-haired man to lumber out of the stables. "Go round the back and use the kitchen entrance. Someone is snooping around inside the house. We'll use the front door."

"No worries." Joe headed in the direction of the rear of the homestead.

"Do you want to wait here?" Ian gave her a long assessing stare. "You don't look too good."

She glared at him. "If you don't get a move on, he'll be long gone before you get inside."

"Let's go." Ian led the way up the front steps.

She stuck close to Ian as the men moved through the house and searched every room.

They found no one.

* * * *

The moment Doug walked into the homestead instinct told him something had happened. He headed towards Emily's bedroom and knocked on the door. "Em', it's me, Doug, I'm back."

"Can you leave me alone for a bit please?"

What the . . . ? He removed his hat and dashed a hand through his hair staring at the door. "Are you ill? Do you want me to radio Robbie to come home early?"

The door opened a crack, and Emily stared at him, ashen-faced and wide-eyed.

"I'm fine. I'll get dressed. I'll need to read that letter."

"Did something happen?" He noticed fear shadowing her eyes and his heart ached for her. "Please, Em', no secrets, remember?"

"I can't discuss this now. We'll talk later, okay?" She closed the door, and he heard the key turn in the lock.

He rubbed the back of his neck and stared at the white wooden panelling for a long moment before reaching for his phone and calling Ian. He headed towards his office and dropped into his chair. "Hey, can you come to the house? Something's wrong with Em'. Did anything happen while I was in the back paddock?"

"Oh yeah, something happened all right." Ian cleared his throat. *"She claimed someone was in the house. I searched the place with Joe, and we didn't find anyone lurking about. She didn't see his face again, either. I'm wondering if she has a mental condition and hallucinates or something."*

Doug frowned. He had worked with her for some time, and she certainly did not have a mental condition. "Nah, I don't believe she is mentally ill. If she thinks she saw someone, I believe her. Anything else happen?"

"I stayed inside until Glady had finished in the cookhouse and Emily only came out of her room once, to ask me for the list of people travelling from Broome to Perth around the time Jock died, so I gave her what you had so far. I informed her you hadn't finished the search for the time our parents died."

Doug ran a hand down his face. "Yeah, well it's difficult getting information from airlines. As it is, I had to pull in favours and I've probably broken the law. I do have the logbooks for our chopper, but they only list the passengers leaving and returning to Winnawarra, but if she is fingering old Mr. Brewster, I can tell her he was the first person I asked them to check. He goes to the pub every night for dinner, and Dolly insisted he hasn't missed one evening in four bloody years."

"Well, then that covers both deaths, doesn't it?" Ian let out a long sigh. *"One other thing. I know you sent Johnno to mend fences, but he dropped in about an hour ago. He said he'd left his watch in the bathroom in his old room."*

"Did you say Johnno was *inside* the house?"

"Yeah, but not for long. He checked the room and found his watch then left. He wasn't here for more than five minutes."

A chill curled around his neck like a noose. "Who else was in the house?"

"Apart from Emily and me, no one, as far as I know. Glady was in the cookhouse. Why?"

Oh, Jesus. "What was Johnno doing here anyway? I sent him ten miles away." He pushed to his feet and headed towards Emily's bedroom to find her standing in the hallway eyeing him with speculation. "Hurry up. I think I need backup" He closed his phone and clipped it back on his belt.

He walked towards her hat in hand. "Is something wrong?'

"You might say that." Emily would not meet his gaze. "You promised me, no one would bother me and the moment you leave, a man slips into the house and scares the hell out of me."

Abashed he swallowed hard. "Yeah, Ian told me. I'm sorry, Em', I had no idea. I told the staff to keep away from the homestead."

"That wasn't good enough, was it?"

Emily straightened and levelled her gaze on Doug's concerned face. She wanted to trust him, *needed* to trust him and not because the sight of tall, dark, and cowboy made her heart miss a beat, she liked him as a person too. Tragically, after the stalker incident, she had spent some time sifting through papers and letters and found another reason *not* to trust him. She didn't consider Ian a threat. He had been forthcoming with documents and had given her the password to read Jock's emails. The latter had been most illuminating about the extent of Doug's injury and the need to move him to Perth because of his mental condition. *Why didn't he tell me he was in Darwin when his parents died?*

She needed to get some distance between them. "May I use your grandfather's office to read his letter? As it is for my eyes only, I'd like some privacy to read it if you don't mind?"

"No worries. I'll get it for you." Doug fingered the brim of his hat and smiled warmly.

"Thanks."

He returned moments later and handed her an envelope. "I'll ask Glady to make up a tray as well." He turned and moved away, his large frame filling the hallway.

Emily strolled to Jock's office, but before she could shut the door, she heard Glady humming and waited for the old woman to set the tray, laden with coffee and biscuits, on the desk. "Thanks, I'll be fine now." She closed the door behind her and turned the key.

Emily dropped into Jock's chair and poured the coffee then tore open the envelope and unfolded a sheet of white paper.

Dear Emily,

You must be wondering why I brought you here. I have reason to believe my son and daughter were murdered. I have two motives. The first, to cover up embezzlement by my accountant, Mr. Brewster and the second, I believe he plans to sell the mining rights to Winnawarra against my consent. He is money hungry, and I no longer trust him. I had planned to call in another accountant to help me uncover his scheme but then Jamie died, and no one would listen to me. I think Brewster had a hand in Jamie's murder. He is too old to do the deed himself, so look for a partner or maybe two with free access to Winnawarra. You will need to be very careful of Brewster. He has far-reaching influence in many places.

I have made a lot of noise challenging the coroner's findings about Jamie's death. Your mother told me you excelled at both business and forensics, a strange mix, but one I need very much to help me solve this mystery.

If I am dead within a few weeks of writing this letter, I believe it is because I am getting too close to the truth. Prove Brewster is behind all this and keep Winnawarra and my grandsons safe."

Emily dropped four lumps of sugar into her cup and stared at the wall. She would have to discuss the letter with the brothers, and would ask if they had time for a meeting in the morning. She swallowed hard. First, she had to clear up a few points with Doug, and the questions she needed to ask would come close to accusing him of murder.

CHAPTER TEN

After leaving Emily in Jock's office, Doug needed to speak to someone about how to handle her change of attitude toward him. He strode out the front door of the homestead and headed across the floodlit driveway towards the barn to find Ian. He wanted to speak to him some distance from the house where they would not be overheard. Okay, so Emily blamed him for the stalker, but he felt it went deeper than that and he wasn't sure how to fix the problem. The idea she didn't trust him after their heart-to-heart talk made his stomach cramp. One thing with Emily, her emotions showed on her face, especially her eyes. The man who had betrayed her love had wounded her deeply.

He sighed wondering how he should approach the subject with Ian. His brother didn't suffer fools easily and had a realistic approach to life far above his twenty-one years. With Robbie gone most days, with the Royal Flying Doctor Service, Ian had held the fort and kept Winnawarra running. In fact, Ian could run the place with one hand tied behind his back. Why Jock had made him the manager instead of Ian confused him. Ian could run rings around him when it came to running a cattle station and breeding stock.

When Ian stepped through the barn door and into the sunshine, he raised a gloved hand in greeting.

"Hiding from Emily?" He grinned and tipped back the brim of his hat to wipe the sweat from his brow.

"Nah, we need to talk and away from flapping ears." Doug strolled towards the cattle pen. He leant on the wooden railing placing one foot on the bottom rung and turned to his brother. Casting a quick glance around to make sure no one could overhear the conversation he took a deep breath. "I'm concerned about

Em'. I thought we were getting along fine, but since I left this morning, everything has changed."

Ian raised both black eyebrows and rubbed his chin.

"I'm not surprised after what happened to her today."

Doug pulled a toothpick out of his back pocket and jammed it between his teeth. The small slithers of wood had become his failsafe. He needed a smoke or drugs — anything to stop the panic welling up and making him crazy. Drawing a long breath through his nose, he flicked a glance at Ian. "Last night, I had a heart to heart with Em', and to cut to the chase, due to an incident in the UK, she doesn't trust men, period." He moved the toothpick across his lips to the other side of his mouth. "I promised her I'd keep the men away from her after someone tried to get into her room the other night and now she is certain the same person is responsible for throwing the snake into Bolt's stall." Anger bubbled, and he snorted. "I sent everyone apart from you and Joe ten miles in every direction to work, and the moment I left, someone sneaked back and went inside the house."

"I didn't see anyone, mate. I'm starting to believe she is a bit unstable." Ian tipped back his hat. "Have you spoken to her?"

"That's the problem, she hasn't said a word, but she is pissed to the max and now has just about locked herself in Jock's office." He dropped his forehead on the weathered railing and sighed. "I thought Em' was over-exaggerating at first, but now I'm not so sure."

"Do you really believe any of the hands could be stupid enough to chuck a snake in Bolt's stall?" Ian removed his hat and smoothed his sweat-soaked unruly hair.

"I dunno what to think." He shook his head slowly trying to go over his conversation with Emily. "Whatever happened outside her room the other night frightened her. If one of the hands *did* try to get into her bedroom, why risk doing such a stupid thing with all of us sleeping close by? If she'd screamed and woken the house, he would get an arse whooping. I'm wondering if she had a bad dream. Nightmares can be real enough, and I've had my fair share of them lately." He glanced at Ian's concerned face. "You know, I came home on leave for the last two musters, and no one ever laid a complaint against one of the men. Let's face it we have heaps of women falling at our feet, and they all leave here happy. If Emily is telling the truth this sudden change of behaviour is unusual, to say the least."

"*If* it is true." Ian blew out a breath and hunched his broad shoulders. "Emily is an unknown quantity and men are men. Any one of them could have come on strong and worried her. I'm not surprised Emily believes we've let her down." He pushed his hat firmly on his head. "If you'd told me about this earlier, I would have remained in the house until you returned. It was quiet, and I thought she was resting. I had no reason to believe anything was wrong." He slapped him on the back. "We'll just have to keep a closer eye on her."

"I had intended to tell both of you tonight. I didn't get time this morning with Robbie taking off before dawn. I told Em' to keep her door locked and asked Glady to take her some lunch and keep an eye on her. She had no need to leave her room, and I wasn't gone *that* long. She is acting as if it's my fault some arsehole went into the house." Doug spat out the toothpick and turned to stare at the homestead resting his elbows on the fence. He indicated towards Emily watching them from the veranda. "I guess she has read Jock's letter. I guess we'd better hear the verdict."

As he walked, he moved his attention to Emily, but she refused to meet his gaze and stared at the floor. What the hell was going on? He led the way up the steps and removed his hat. "Is there anything wrong?"

"May we speak inside?"

"Yes, of course." As he waved her towards the door, dread fell over him like a shroud. "Would you prefer to wait until Robbie gets home, so you don't have to repeat everything twice?"

"No, that's not necessary." Emily moved into the kitchen. "Glady has laid out a snack for us and will give us some privacy while we discuss matters."

Doug frowned and flicked a glance at Ian who looked equally bemused. "No worries." He followed her to the kitchen and went to the sink to wash his hands.

Ian moved to his side and dropped his voice to a conspiratorial whisper.

"She is not happy."

He snorted. "Noticed that, did you?" He moved to the refrigerator took out two beers and handed him one.

He smiled at Emily and leant on the table. "What is worrying you, Em'?"

"I've spent a lot of time reading your family's diaries and today some of your father's emails. Ian gave me the list you compiled of the people who flew in and out of Winnawarra with their destinations on the date Jock died." She gripped her fingers together on the table and lowered her attention to her hands in obvious discomfort.

"I know you were in Perth at the time Jock died." Emily raised one eyebrow in question. "I also believe you were in Darwin when your parents died."

"Yeah, he was in the medical facility at RAAF Base Darwin." Ian laid a hand on Doug's arm. "What are you getting at?" He snorted, and his grip tightened. "You're not trying to infer my brother had something to do with their deaths, are you?"

"I'm not inferring anything" Emily lifted her head to stare at Doug and caught the hurt expression in his eyes. He stared at her and his lips compressed into a thin line. She placed her hands in her lap to hide her shaking fingers from him and lifted her chin determined to clear the air. "As you are aware, I have been mapping people's movements and need to clarify a few things." She lifted her gaze back to Doug's face. "If I am correct Brewster or his accomplice murdered your parents and Jock to conceal fraud then it makes sense, the person responsible would be in both places at the time of their deaths." She dragged in a breath. "The thing is maybe you know who else was in the same place at the same time. Did anyone else from Winnawarra visit you for instance?"

"What the hell did Jock say in his letter? He's not blaming me, is he?" Doug settled a puzzled gaze on her. "I can't believe this shit." He scrubbed trembling hands over his face and sucked in a deep breath.

"How could I possibly be aware of anyone else in those locations? I arrived critically injured in Darwin the day my parents died. I'm not exactly clear on the precise timeline. I was in surgery having a bullet removed. The head injuries were a bonus, and in case you believe I am capable of murder you should be aware I couldn't stand let alone drive fifty kilometres to kill my parents. The moment I *could* travel the doctors flew me to a psychiatric ward in Perth." He stared at her with so much pain she wanted to cry for him. "I didn't *know* my parents had been killed, not until Jock came to see me the day he died. The family kept it from me because they thought I couldn't take any more guilt." He pushed back the chair and stood. "Yeah, I'm a murderer. I killed my unit. I'm guilty of that, but Jock and my parents, dear God, no." He dropped the bottle of beer into the garbage bin, and it spewed foaming pungent liquid then without a backward glance, he stomped out the door.

"I'd never think such a thing," Emily stared after him needing to go to him and apologise. When she heard Ian swearing under his breath, she swallowed the lump in her throat and turned to him. "I'm so sorry, Ian. I didn't mean to upset him."

"Sorry?" Ian got to his feet reaching for his phone. He glared at her and shook his head. "Do you know what you've done?" He pulled out his phone pressed it against one ear and relayed an urgent message to Robbie then flopped down in a chair and stared at her. "Robbie is on his way. Your questions have probably triggered a PTSD episode."

Emily rubbed her temples. Her relationship with Doug had been going so well. He would never forgive her. Guilt made her face hot, and she stared at the table. "Yes, but he told me he had it under control."

"Obviously not."

She stared at his angry face. "I'll go and speak to him."

"I suggest you leave him to settle down first." Ian sighed. "He'll be okay, and we still need your help. Just keep looking for any clues."

Emily sipped her coffee. "Okay. I'll finish searching through your family's personal documents, but we'll need more information. "What's the chance you can get a look at the forensic reports?"

"We'd require a letter from the solicitor stating our reasons to view the documents and Doug would have the authority to make those arrangements with him. Right now, I doubt he'll cooperate."

Emily pushed to her feet. "Then I'll go and see if he'll talk to me. I don't think he needs to be alone right now."

"Good luck. You'll need it."

Outside she scanned the shadows surrounding the massive yard and listened for voices. She could hear the *squeak, squeak,* of the windmill pump above the barn, the bellow of one of the prize bulls but not the raging of an angry man. She moved down the steps and headed towards the stables. If the men had nothing to do or wanted a snack, they hung around the tack room. The refrigerator held bottles of water, soft drinks, sandwiches, and slices of cake. "Grab food" Doug called the mountains of supplies. She could hear his words in her mind. "*When men work hard they need a supply of snacks.*" The ringers would drop into the tack room for what he referred to as "smoko." She gathered the term came from the break workers had for a smoke in days gone by.

She moved inside the dim stables on high alert for any snakes and strolled down the centre aisle towards the tack room. Hearing a soft rumble of voices, she hesitated at the sound of a man's raised voice.

"Take the damn pills, boss. You're acting crazy."

"For God's sake, I'm not having a bloody flashback, I'm just angry." Doug strode out of the tack room, stopped mid-stride, and gaped at her. "What do you want, Em'?" His narrowed blue gaze bored into her but not one shred of anger filled his voice.

She swallowed her fear of rejection, moved in close and slipped both arms around him. Under her palms, every muscle in his broad back stiffened and his chin lifted with a grunt of disapproval. Her instinct told her he would never hurt her because his touch had always been gentle, reverent. In her heart, she understood his feelings of guilt. He had taken the blame for an enemy attack because he had *lived*.

She inhaled the comforting musky smell of him, she snuggled against his chest and lowered her voice to a whisper. "Calm down. You're frightening me."

She caught his sudden intake of breath, and he rested his large hands on her waist.

"I'm *sorry*, Em', I thought you doubted me." He sighed and drew her closer. "That hurt a lot." His Adam's apple moved up and down. "I want to know what Jock said in his letter. Did he blame me for not being here? He was angry when I joined the Air Force." A tremble went through him, and his fingers tightened a little. "If I hadn't left home, my parents would still be alive."

"You have to stop blaming yourself for everything that happens. Jock loved you and was so scared when you were injured. He never wrote a bad word about you. From reading your father's diary, I know your parents planned a shopping trip and a picnic in Darwin so it wouldn't have made a difference if you *had* been here, unless you usually made a habit of going on romantic picnics with your parents?"

When he snorted in reply, she moved both hands up and down his back, lifted her chin, and stared into his confused expression. "I thought as much. Look, I asked you about being in Darwin and Perth in case anyone else apart from Jock and Robbie visited you in hospital, that's all." His thumbs caressed her waist, and she wet suddenly dry lips at the thrill of his intimacy.

"So why give me the cold shoulder when I came to your room before?" He raised one black eyebrow in question. "I thought you'd changed your mind about us."

"I had every reason to be angry with you because the moment you left the stalker was back and you'd promised to send the men miles away." She dragged in a deep breath. She had to convince him without being overdramatic. "After what happened today, I'm convinced he is trying to hurt me." She shuddered at the memory and caught a flash of concern in his expression. "I know you think I'm overreacting."

"I don't." Doug rested his chin on her head. "Ian explained everything, and we're going all out to discover who is doing this to you."

Relieved she sighed into his chest. "I bet they'll all deny even being near the house."

"Not all of them. Johnno was in the homestead. Ian told me he'd spoken to him on the way out." He smoothed a strand of her hair behind one ear in a familiar gesture. "You'd recognise if it was him, right?"

She lifted her chin considering the possibility. "Yes, I think so, but from the back in the same clothes, it could be at least ten of the staff plus you, Ian and Robbie. Ian was wearing a blue tee shirt today, so it wasn't him, you and Robbie weren't here, so I guess if Johnno was around, yes, I'd put him on the list."

"He's a big bloke, almost as big as me, so why didn't you scream for help?" He held her close and stared into her eyes his face etched with concern. "I'm sure Ian was close by, and Glady or the staff in the cookhouse would have heard you."

"I hid under Jock's desk until I thought he had left but I saw him outside my room leaning against the door frame as if he was waiting for me." She pressed a hand to her chest. "Yeah, it could have been Johnno, but he had his back to me, and I wasn't hanging around to find out. I made a run for it and found Ian."

"Has Johnno even spoken to you since you arrived?"

"Once." She nodded. "The other evening after the football game, he asked me to go for a ride up to the falls."

Doug snorted. "Did you agree to go on a moonlight swim with him?"

Emily gaped at him. "Of course not, I'm not stupid. He asked me to go to the dance with him as well, and I told him I had a date. He wanted me to save a dance for him, but I didn't agree."

"Okay. Has he bothered you again since?" He cupped her face and stared at her.

"No. He seemed to take the refusal okay, courteous in fact." Emily chewed on her bottom lip. "I don't think Johnno is the one stalking me. I'm sorry, but I can't identify who is doing this to me. I know it sounds like my imagination is running riot but I'm telling the truth."

Doug dropped his warm hand from her chin, but his eyes never left her face.

"Look, love, I believe you, and I promise to find out who is responsible for frightening you. I think you should move into the bedroom next to mine and keep your door locked. I sleep light, so I'll wake if you bang on the wall or call out. During the day, we'll stick close together then he won't get another chance to bother you."

Relief fell over her like honey on hot toast, warm and so sweet her eyes misted. "Thank you, but won't you be going on the muster soon?"

"Yeah, most of us go on the muster, even Glady. We only leave a few hands behind to tend the stock." He chuckled and turned out the door, and they headed towards the house. "We usually need her to help the cook and to make sure the women are well cared for. I'm hoping you will come along too. Camping under the moonlight is very romantic, and you'll be safe with me, not to mention the twenty or so other people around the campfires." He slipped one large hand around her waist and pulled her into the shade of a tree. "Say you'll come."

A shiver of awareness tingled through her, and she smiled. "I wouldn't miss it."

"Great." He drew her into his arms and his warm breath brushed across her ear raising goose bumps down her arm. "I love your scent. It makes me want to hold you and inhale."

She turned to reply but found his lips, soft and so tender. After she slipped her hands around his neck she drew him closer and welcomed his teasing tongue. She moaned into his mouth. Winnawarra slipped away, and Doug surrounded her, feeding her with sensual delights. The way he held her, his gentle caresses, made her weightless, and she floated on the taste of him. She wanted more, but he controlled the kiss, and with a sigh lifted his head and stared into her eyes.

"You would tempt a saint, Em'." He pressed kisses to the sides of her mouth. "If I keep this up I'll forget my manners and carry you inside to my bed."

She blinked then touched her tingling lips. He made her giddy with lust. "Would that be so bad?"

"Oh, darlin', don't you think I want that too?" He cupped her cheek and passion showed in his eyes. "Em', you have concussion and sore ribs. I'm frightened I might hurt you, and I want our first time together to be perfect."

Emotion rolled over her, and she stared at him speechless. *He wants me.* She swallowed hard trying to keep back the tears of joy threatening to overflow. "So do I."

The throbbing hum of an engine filled the air. Doug tipped back his head and stared into the darkness.

"Ah, here comes Robbie's plane. After what happened, he'll be planning to pump me full of drugs. I'll have to convince him I'm fine." He rubbed her back. "I'd love to stay here and cuddle you all night, but I really need a shower. I stink."

"You smell great to me, but okay go take a shower. Call out if you need someone to scrub your back." She gave him a teasing grin and stepped back with reluctance. "I'll help Glady with dinner."

"Thanks, Em'." He led her up the front steps of the homestead and groaned. "Now all I can think about is sharing a shower with you." He gave her a rakish grin then pushed open the screen door and strolled inside.

She stared after him, then shook her head and made her way to the kitchen. The tempting aroma of roast meat filled the room, and suddenly famished her stomach growled. She strolled to the counter and collected plates to set the table. Heavens above, Doug had invited her to the muster. *And his bed.* Sleeping under the stars would be very romantic. *I can't wait.*

CHAPTER ELEVEN

After seeing Emily to her room, Doug took his shower alone. Refreshed, he strolled from the bathroom with a white towel tied around his waist surprised to see his brothers waiting for him. Robbie sprawled in a chair by the window, and Ian sat on the end of his bed, hat in hand and eyeing him with suspicion.

"What?" Placing both hands on his hips, he grinned. "You know you can hide from the stalker in your own rooms, there *are* good sturdy locks on the doors."

"I want to talk some more about the episode you had today." Robbie rested one booted foot on his knee and leant back in the chair. "Getting mad won't help you know."

He snorted his indignation. "You mean walking out rather than arguing. Well, brother dearest, the doctors told me to avoid confrontation, which I did." He opened drawers and pulled out underwear, blue jeans, and a black tee shirt. "Are you staying to watch the show?" He turned his back and dropped the towel. "No? Ah, well no photographs please." He stepped into his underwear and reached for his jeans.

"It's no good trying to cover up by trying to be funny." Robbie dropped his boot to the floor and banged a fist on the arm of the chair. "You need to face reality and stop living in a dream world."

Doug turned slowly. Bloody hell they were serious. He cleared his throat and composed his features. "Ask Ian, he'll tell you what happened." He pulled his tee shirt over his head. "I'm not sure what Jock had in his mind before he died, but whatever it was he said nothing to me. He came to the hospital to visit me twice. The first time he'd come straight from the airport and said nothing." He pushed his fingers through his damp hair and rested his backside against the chest of drawers. "The second time, he told me about Mum and Dad's accident, and I lost it." He turned and glared at Robbie. "Especially after *you* came to see me in Darwin hospital and told me they hadn't visited me because they had the flu." He rubbed his chin. "You thought I'd lost my mind and couldn't handle the truth. I'm right, yeah?"

"You were scheduled for emergency surgery and raving like a madman." Robbie pushed to his feet and moved closer. "Telling you our parents had died wouldn't have been the responsible thing to do. You had enough on your mind." He placed one hand on his shoulder and squeezed. "I tried to see you, but the Air Force had you under guard and whisked you away to Perth before I had a chance to speak to you again." He sighed, and his mouth turned down. "You *do* know they wouldn't allow anyone to visit for ages. Jock flew to Perth the moment he received permission."

"What happened after Jock told you? You've never told us." Ian straightened, and his dark blue eyes held a deep sorrow.

Doug grimaced at the memory. "The usual. The doc shot me up with drugs until I stopped raving. I had a long talk to the doctors, and they gave me a couple of options. Stay in the looney bin until they decided I was fit for duty or retire from service." He drew a deep breath and let it out slowly. "The next morning, I made arrangements to be de-mobbed. That afternoon they allowed Jock to visit because I had my shit together and I needed to explain my decision with him. Jock told me he'd changed his will and divided his estate equally between the three of us. Like I told you before, he never mentioned including Emily."

He scrubbed both hands over his face. *For God's sake, why do they have to drag this up now?* He didn't want to rehash his time in the psych ward and would prefer to bathe in the comfort he had with Emily. She would keep him sane. The way she'd cuddled him even though he'd frightened her humbled him. He needed someone like her in his life. Her calming influence was better than any drug.

"Did he say anything else?" Robbie eyed him with his professional air. "Did he mention anything at all about his suspicions concerning Mum and Dad's accident or the outcome of the inquest?"

"No! I've already told you a thousand times. We talked about Winnawarra and me coming home. How he was happy we'd decided to return to Winnawarra to help him run the place." He glared at him, wanting to stop the interrogation. He had his fill of questioning for one day. "And for the record, no one else visited me."

"Okay, so what happens now?" Ian pushed to his feet.

"Now we eat and get some rest. First thing in the morning, I want you both with me when I tackle Johnno." Doug frowned. "We need to make it clear he is no longer welcome in the house."

"Why?" Robbie looked at him as if he'd gone mad.

"I'm not sure, but he could be Em's stalker."

* * * *

After breakfast the following morning, Doug looked at Emily and pushed to his feet. "We have something urgent to attend to." He headed for the door and motioned to his brothers. "Coming?"

"Do you have time to discuss Jock's letter before Robbie takes off again?" Emily stared at him. "It's important."

"I have time. I don't have anything urgent today." Robbie smiled at her. "Give us five."

Doug cleared his throat. "We'll talk in Jock's office it's more private."

Without waiting for the reply, he led his brothers outside and noting Johnno's rig parked near the barn, headed for the bunkhouse. He turned to Robbie and gave him an update on the stalker problem and Johnno being the only man in cooee. He shrugged at Robbie's bemused expression. "Yeah, I can see you came to the same conclusion as Ian but trust me, she's not delusional. I'm convinced she is telling the truth and we have to look into it no matter what you believe."

"I didn't say I didn't *believe* her?" Ian pushed his hat firmly on his head and matched his stride. "I can't see Johnno doing something so stupid, although, I did see him near the house at the time."

Robbie laid a firm hand on Doug's arm. "Who is going to speak to him, we can't all go at him like a pack of angry dogs."

Doug snorted in disgust. "What if it is him stalking Em'? He is not going to admit to anything. We don't know if he does this to women, do we? A tourist might brush it off and not bother complaining, who the hell knows?" He rolled his shoulders. "I'll do the talking."

"I'll go and get him. We'll speak to him out by the bullpen." Ian strode towards the bunkhouse.

A few moments later, Johnno came through the door with a silly grin on his face. Ian followed close behind with his lips pressed into a thin line. Doug led the way to the bullpen and turned to him. "I need to ask you a few questions."

"Sure thing, boss." Johnno tipped back the brim of his hat, and his mouth twitched into a smile. "Fire away."

Doug balled his fists on his hips and pushed down the need to slap the smile off Johnno's face. "Why were you hanging around the house yesterday? I told you to go to the west paddock and check the fences."

"I'm the assistant manager, right? I was taking care of things while you were away." Johnno gave a snort of disgust. "You don't really trust the Jillaroos to do their work without supervision, do you?"

"You had no reason to be here. The Jillaroos were moving the bulls to the pens on the north side." Ian narrowed his gaze. "I did see you at the homestead, and I don't believe for a moment you were looking for your watch. I spoke to Glady, and she's already cleaned your old room. She didn't find a watch in your bathroom. You're lying, and we want to know why."

"Okay, you've got me." Johnno held up both hands, but the smirk never left his face. "Maybe I had a date with Emily, and we had to wait until everyone left to get cosy." He lifted his gaze and Doug noticed a flash of triumph in his expression. "She promised to dance with me on Saturday night."

"No, she didn't." Doug shrugged. "Sorry to upset your plans but that's not going to happen. She's my girl."

"Bullshit! You're trying to cut my grass." Johnno's eyes narrowed to dangerous slits. "She said she'd dance with me the other night after the footy game."

Doug bit back a sigh of relief. "So, you haven't spoken with her since then?"

"Nope." Johnno removed his hat and ran a hand through his hair. "Okay, I admit I went inside to speak to her, but I only got as far as the veranda when Ian showed up. I lied about the watch, I didn't want to disobey your" — he made quote marks with his fingers — "orders." He snorted in disgust. "I've noticed the way Emily looks at me, she fancies me. What red-blooded Aussie bloke wouldn't make a move on an English rose? I wanted to ask her to come to the dance as my date. Now you reckon she's *your* girl. She sure doesn't act like she's involved with anyone."

"Even if she wasn't my girl, she couldn't get involved with you." Doug rolled his shoulders, stood in an at-ease position and stared Johnno down. "In your terms of employment, it states relationships between staff and owners are not permitted and may be grounds for dismissal. In case you've forgotten, Emily has shares in Winnawarra."

"You have to be bloody joking?" Johnno glared at him, and his hands balled into fists. "Are you jealous, boss?"

"Of *you*, no." Doug fixed him with a nonchalant stare. "The non-fraternisation clause is to protect employees from unwanted advances." Doug fixed his gaze on him. "It goes both ways, so stay away from Em', or I'll fire you. That means the dance, the muster and everything in between. Since we have a new owner living on the station, the homestead is out of bounds for everyone but family members. There has to be a place she can feel safe, so if I see you or any of the other hands near the homestead without a specific invitation from me personally, I will fire the lot of you. Understand?"

"This is crazy." Johnno removed his hat and slapped it against his thigh sending out a cloud of dust. "This rule never stopped you, did it? I've seen you snogging with the women on the musters and sneaking off into the sunset with them all the bloody time." He waved a hand at Ian. "Him too, the randy little bugger couldn't keep his hands off them."

"The tourists aren't employees, so the clause doesn't apply." Robbie cleared his throat. "We all enjoy the company of tourists and making them happy is part of the job. Allowing you to become romantically involved with Emily is a different matter. We've never had an unmarried female owner at Winnawarra, so up until now, the clause didn't apply. You've never see any of us making out with the Jillaroos, have you?" He pushed both hands into the back pockets of his jeans and sighed. "Look, Johnno, that's the rules accept them or leave. Make up your mind because right now we've more pressing things to attend to."

"Staying or leaving?" Doug took in Johnno's belligerent stare. Yeah, he could see the anger welling just below the surface.

"I'm staying but under protest." Johnno hooked his thumbs into his belt. "You sure aren't like Jock. He'd have looked the other way."

"I don't think so. He's the one who drew up the contract." Doug sighed dismissively. He had spent too much time on him already. "Get back to work." He waited for Johnno to walk away then headed for the homestead.

"Why didn't you mention the snake incident?" Ian fell into step beside him.

He offered him a grim smile and shook his head. "It couldn't have been him. Why try to kill a woman you intend to ask out on a date? We'll keep a close eye on him, and if he steps out of line again, he's out of here."

"He wasn't the only one here yesterday morning either." Ian flicked his brothers a worried glance. "When I went into the bunkhouse, Brian came out the bathroom fresh from the shower."

"Did you see him earlier?" Robbie frowned. "He wears metal tips to his boots too."

"I was busy all morning, and he could have rolled up at any time without me noticing." Ian pushed back his hat. "It could have been Brian stalking Emily, and he's made it clear he doesn't like her."

"Better keep an eye on him as well." Doug scratched his cheek and sighed. "I'm not looking forward to the muster, anything might happen."

"Right now, we should worry about what Jock found so secret, he had to bring Emily here to sort it out."

Doug straightened. "I guess we're going to find out soon enough." He headed for the homestead.

* * * *

In Jock's office, the brothers sat staring at Emily in stunned fascination as she finished reading the letter to them. She lifted her head and took a deep breath. "I think Jock makes his position on your father's accident very clear."

"It's mind-blowing." Ian's face had paled. "Do you think it's true?'

"I do remember him storming out of the inquest." Robbie shook his head. "I put it down to emotional distress."

"If he felt that way, I'm not surprised he wanted the case reopened." Doug reached for his coffee cup then took a wedge of fruitcake and placed it on a plate. "Jock was not a person to settle for anyone's opinion that contradicted his own. Have you found any evidence?"

Emily leant back in the chair and sucked in a deep breath. "I need to check a few suspicious entries in the accounts but so far, I think there is a fair chance embezzlement is a motive and Mr.

Brewster is a suspect. Right now, until I can verify the accounts Brewster owns and the amounts transferred, I don't have enough evidence to go to the police. I have nothing to prove either way if he was involved in a scam to transfer Jock's mining rights. That part of the problem died with Jock because the rights transferred to all of you on his death. There has to be something else Jock wanted me to find, so I'll keep looking."

"What about unusual lump sum payments, especially to people who work at Winnawarra." Robbie pushed a slice of cake onto a plate, sniffed the fruit-filled confection, and moaned with delight. "Sorry but this looks so delicious. Oh, where was I? Ah, yes, if Mr. Brewster had an accomplice he wouldn't commit murder for nothing. He'd be getting a cut." He popped a small piece of the cake into his mouth and groaned appreciatively. "People who believe they can't be discovered make mistakes and if we're lucky he'll leave a nice paper trail for us to follow.

"We need to find out if Brewster or any of our staff were in Perth the day Jock died." Robbie pushed more cake into his mouth and washed it down with a sip of coffee. He glanced at Doug. "I gather you obtained airline passenger lists for that week?"

"Yes, I pulled a few strings and managed to get a copy." Doug shrugged.

Emily frowned. "Problem is we can't take the evidence to the police without getting you into trouble." She handed the list to Robbie then cleared her throat. "I've checked the list and a couple of the men, Pete and Johnno went to Darwin the week Jock died. They both arrived home the day Jock's body was discovered, but Johnno came via Perth. As the airports are on either end of Australia, it wasn't a normal flight path, but I did discover three other Winnawarra ringers visited Perth the same week as well. You'll remember Doug was there too but in hospital."

"We need a starting point." Doug drew a deep breath and tapped the letter with one long finger. "Jock had worries about his accountant, so I think you need to look a little closer at Mr. Brewster, Emily. The amount he was skimming might be more than you think especially if he deposited the money in a phoney company's account."

Emily sighed. "Why kill the man laying the golden egg?"

"Perhaps Jock discovered the missing money trail after he became suspicious about Brewster's involvement in ordering the core samples. If Brewster had an accomplice working here, he could have overheard Jock discussing his worries with our dad." Doug refilled his coffee cup from the pot on the tray. "With Jock and our parents dead, we would come home none the wiser, and his secret would be safe." He grimaced. "Look for a substantial payment to a phoney company, because I doubt Brewster would be stupid enough to move money to an accomplice from his personal account."

Emily finished her coffee and placed the cup on the tray. "I'll get on to it straight away."

"I'm finding it difficult tying in the guy causing you strife with Brewster. Robbie sighed and rubbed his temples. "Peeping Toms are cowards and not usually violent. Unless he is trying to frighten you into leaving, it doesn't make sense. A serial killer would murder you without a second thought and usually by his own hand not by frightening a horse with a snake." He glanced at her. "Have you noticed anyone checking you out?"

Emily drummed her fingers on the desk. "Just about all of the hands stare at me."

"Murderers are usually the last person one would suspect." Doug shrugged. "If Mr. Brewster comes up clean and we can't find an accomplice then I'm afraid it is someone we have probably known and trusted for years."

"Then we need to discover three things about him." Emily held up three fingers. "We have to place him in Perth at the time of death." Folding down one finger, she frowned. "He must gain in some way from Jock's death." She folded down the next finger. "He is here and free to roam the place without suspicion." Her fist curled into a ball. "All we have to do to reopen the case is to offer the coroner fresh evidence. This would mean naming a suspect, proving his proximity to the crimes, and a motive for the public prosecutor to reopen both cases." She frowned. "It looks like we'd better watch our backs. If this person killed Jock and your parents, we may be next on his list."

"What do you plan to do, Em'?" Doug stared at her. "I have no idea where to start."

Emily poured more coffee for the three brothers. "I can't do everything myself. Reading the diaries is one thing but this is one hell of a job for one person, and I need to delegate some of the work."

"Okay, let's hear the list of things you want us to do with a little explanation along the way if you don't mind." Robbie waved a hand at his brothers. "This is the first time we've been involved in a potential murder investigation."

Emily leant back in the office chair making it creak loudly. She tapped a pen on her bottom lip. "We'll need your Mr. Biggs to ask the coroner's office for the accident reports. I will need to see any evidence collected from the scene, especially photographs. Can you handle that, Doug?"

"I'll call him later." Doug narrowed his gaze, and a frown creased his handsome brow. "I would imagine our solicitor already has the relevant information plus the photographs. Robbie instructed him to look into Jock's death again, and I gather from the letter, Jock had a reason to query the findings of our parents' inquest. I'll ask him." He leant back in the chair and a nerve ticked in his cheek. "I can't believe Brewster would murder members of our family no matter what Jock implied. Jock was grief-stricken and wanted to blame someone. This idea about Brewster paying an accomplice to kill them and trying to trick Jock out of the mining rights is a bit far-fetched." He let out a long impatient sigh. "I'll do what you ask to respect his wishes but I think it's a waste of time and in any case, we won't have time to investigate anything until after the muster."

Emily folded her hands in her lap and smiled. "If you could possibly get the ball rolling now I can start when we return." She lifted her chin. "Have you had much to do with the local police? The reason being, many cops will be forthcoming with information. For instance, I need to know if Jock made any complaints about police procedure regarding the accident or his worries about Mr. Brewster. If he *did*, I need to know if the police followed up or shelved the complaint." She wrinkled her nose then blinked. "By the way, do you do background checks on the men you hire?"

"No, we check their work references." Doug rubbed his chin making a rasping sound. "Many men come here to hide or start fresh. I don't have a problem with them as long as they keep their noses clean."

"What about visiting the assay office in Broome? Jock mentioned he'd made enquiries about core samples apparently taken from Rainbow Gulley." Emily stared at her notes then lifted her chin and smiled at Doug. "Has anyone followed up on that lead yet or contacted the local office?"

"Not yet." Doug shrugged. "I could give them a call."

"What's the chance of flying to Broome to visit the assay office and have a word with the local cops?" Emily rubbed her hands together and smiled. "You have every right to ask about core samples taken on your property but do you think the cops would cooperate with me and show me the evidence from the accident scenes?"

"Maybe." Doug stretched out his long legs and smiled. "I think if a beautiful woman rolled up to see Detective George Standish he'll probably do backflips down the main street." He chuckled and winked at her. "We don't get too many tens rolling into Broome. Okay, I'll take you to Broome in the morning to speak to the cops. We can't go today, we have wasted too much time already and we all have duties to perform. I'll have to do my chores first, but we can leave at seven-thirty. If you need to do some shopping for the dance I'll make time, but I'll need to be back here by two, I'm expecting a bunch of ringers to arrive for the muster."

Emily's face grew hot, and she broke eye contact with Doug. *Wow! He thinks I'm a ten.* She scribbled absently across the notepad on the desk and completely lost track of the conversation.

"Em' is coming on the muster with us." Doug grinned broadly.

"Are you sure you want to tag along?" Robbie cocked one eyebrow. "It's damn hard work, long hours, and sleeping rough."

"And tourists pay a fortune to be included. I wouldn't miss it." Emily chuckled. "It's a great way to learn the workings of a cattle station." She smiled at Doug. "I can't wait. It will be fun."

"You'll be as safe as houses." Doug leaned across the table and squeezed her hand.

"I gather even with the firearms restrictions, you'll be carrying rifles?"

"Yeah, it's necessary. Mainly on the off-chance an animal is injured, and we have to put it out of its misery. We're all licensed to carry a rifle and a shotgun." Doug gave her a long look. "Why?"

She met Doug's intent gaze. "Just in case Jock is correct and we might be out in the wilderness with a murderer."

"Jeez, Em', no one has been shot, so *if* there is a killer, then he or she is a little more cunning." Doug's handsome face broke out into a wide grin. "Not to mention the forty or so witnesses on the trail with us." He met her gaze. "You trust me to look after you, don't you, Em'?" He moved around the table and sat beside her.

"Of course." Her gaze drifted over the solid strength of him and the sad puppy dog look in his remarkable blue eyes.

"We'll leave you to it." Robbie pushed back his chair and gave Ian a meaningful stare. "Catch you later."

Emily grinned as the two brothers marched out the door. "Was it something I said?"

"Nah. They know when they're not wanted." Doug chuckled.

"Did you speak to Johnno?"

"Yeah, but I don't think he is your stalker. He told us he fancies you and came to the house to ask you out. I reminded him about the non-fraternisation clause in his contract then I happened to mention you were going to the dance with me. He wasn't too pleased, but that's just too bad." He took her hand, and his expression softened. "If he steps out of line, I'll fly him to Broome myself and put him on a plane out of the state." He smiled down at her and squeezed her hand. "I know you think I let you down and I'm sorry. I'm used to men obeying orders, and up to now none have completely ignored me."

She slipped her hand inside his palm, and a surge of pleasure shot up her arm. Mesmerised by his closeness, she gazed into his eyes. "I don't blame you. I'm just happy you believe me." *And he thinks I'm a ten.*

"Oh, I believed you, love, and I'm not leaving you alone until we discover who is stalking you."

She sighed with relief. "It seems I'm always thanking you, Doug."

He flashed a sexy grin.

"No worries." He laced their fingers. His warm gaze drifted over her face, and as if he could read her mind, he smiled. "Yeah, and I *do* think you're a perfect ten."

CHAPTER TWELVE

The following day in Broome, Doug introduced Emily to Detective George Standish then leant against the wall and watched her work her magic with interest. Although Detective Standish was not any man or woman's fool, he agreed to cooperate to some degree but refused to show them any documents. Doug caught Emily's flash of annoyance and smiled at the detective. "You see, Jock left us a letter about his concerns regarding our parents' deaths. If you could clear up a few points, it would put our minds at rest."

Detective Standish let out a long "at the end of his patience" sigh and gave him the gimlet eye.

"I can give you a copy of the coroner's findings and the accident report for both deaths." He tapped away on his computer, and a whine came from the printer on the far bench. "What else would you like to know? Did Jock come in here making complaints about the investigation? Yes, about once a week. To be honest, I had started to doubt his sanity."

Emily leant forward in her seat and adjusted her green linen skirt.

"Do you remember the last time he came in to make a complaint and did he ever mention his accountant, Mr. Brewster?"

"Old Mr. Brewster? No, he never mentioned him. He went on and on about someone cutting the brake line on his son's car. He wanted the coroner to take another look at the cause of death but couldn't offer any new evidence." He scratched his head and stared at the blank wall. "What else did he say? Let me think. Ah yes, he said he had to catch a plane to Perth. That was the last time I saw him."

"I see." Emily pursed her lips. "Did the Perth police contact you about Jock's accident?"

"Yes, they asked me to arrange for a family member to identify him, and I contacted Robbie." Detective Standish eyed her suspiciously. "They never mentioned having any suspicions about Jock's death."

"Did they send you any reports or photographs from the scene?" Emily cleared her throat. "They would be most helpful."

"Not to me personally but I'll see if there is anything in Jock's file." Detective Standish tapped away at his keyboard then glanced at Doug. "We usually keep this type of evidence away from relatives . . . I'm not sure if I can release this to a family member."

"But *I'm* not a family member, Detective Standish." Emily smiled serenely. "I have studied forensic pathology. I can assure you, I will keep any sensitive documents well away from the family. I am not a ghoul, but I do want to make my own conclusions."

"Very well, in that case, I'll be happy to cooperate." Detective Standish raised both eyebrows and swept his attention over her. "You know, we could really do with someone like you here in Broome. Have you ever thought about opening a private detective agency? I can tell you, we could use a hand with the cold cases. You have no idea how many people go missing in the Outback." He smiled warmly. "If you ever decide to stay, I'm sure this department would be more than happy to take you on as a consultant."

A prickling sensation lifted Doug's hackles, and he blinked at the man, trying to compute his words. *Many people go missing.* "Exactly, how *many* people went missing from this area in say the last three years?"

"From Broome, you mean?" Detective Standish sucked in a deep breath and let it out in a whistle. "Too many. He waved towards two posters pinned to an overcrowded board. Those two women, both tourists are the most recent. You may have met them. I know they went along on the muster at Winnawarra last year. They arrived on the coach from Winnawarra safely enough, and I know they booked into rooms at the motel. One, the young French woman hired a car and never returned, the other the English girl, she was only eighteen, disappeared on a trail ride. We had choppers out, men on horseback, and trail bikes looking for her for two weeks. The horse came back, so we thought she'd been thrown." He shook his head slowly. "I don't know how many times we tell visitors not to go off on their own and to make sure they log in their trips but they don't listen."

Doug moved towards the noticeboard, and his stomach dropped to the floor. He *recognised* both the women. The small pretty, dark-haired one was Sally Miller, he'd spent time with her, had a few dances and kissed her, but she was far too young to interest him. Johnno was all over the other one, Rosa Matisse, but the two women hadn't been friends. "I do recognise them, Sally was in my group, and Rosa was with Johnno. We had a drink with them in Broome just before I left on my last tour. Nice girls. I hope you find out what happened to them."

"Have you found a body?" Emily moved around on her seat. "Or no trace of them whatsoever?"

"Not a thing. You have to remember, some people come to the Outback to drop out of society, and not everyone is involved in a crime. It is a big place to hide if you want to disappear." Detective Standish took a manila folder from a desk drawer and pushed to his feet. He moved to the printer, gathered the documents and placed them inside the folder before handing it to Emily. "Here you go. If there's anything else you need let me know, and keep in mind my consultancy offer."

"Thank you. I'm sure I will." Emily took the documents and pushed the folder under one arm. "Just one more thing. Did you question everyone on Winnawarra Station about the missing women? Did you have any suspects?"

"From Winnawarra? Nah, the women disappeared from Broome. If they'd vanished on the muster or during a trip to Winnawarra, I would have made the effort to interview everyone."

Detective Standish shrugged dismissively. "I did speak to Jock. He confirmed the women's involvement in the muster and gave me their itinerary but by the time their families reported them missing most of the casual ringers, and all the other tourists had left the country." He rubbed the back of his neck absently. "To be honest, we found nothing, no leads at all. It was as if the women never existed once they left the tour." He sighed as if his patience was at an end. "Like I said before, people go missing all the time. Some are victims of crime, others get lost in the bush, but we usually find them if they stay with their vehicles, then there are the idiots who go swimming and end up as croc tucker. They don't follow the rules." He waved to a poster on the wall. "That list is posted everywhere and in six different languages but most don't bother to take notice. It's like the airline safety speech before a flight, most people believe it will never happen to them, and then when something happens, they become a statistic. Cars have a habit of breaking down, catching fire or their tyres get shredded, and the chances of finding someone who leaves their car and wanders off the road is little to none."

"It sounds like heaven for serial killers." Emily snorted in disgust. "You really do need a specialised team working alongside your department. If I decide to stay and meet your country's requirements for living here, I might take you up on your offer. It would be interesting to discover how many of the people who vanish are victims of crime rather than misadventure."

"I think it's a brilliant idea and we have the funds to back such a venture." Doug pushed his hands into his back pockets and shrugged. "Plus, we have expertise in different fields to offer. The idea has merit and sure beats going stir-crazy during the rainy season."

"A joint venture, now that sounds like a plan." Emily grinned at Detective Standish.

Detective Standish smiled and waved away a persistent fly perching on the end of his nose.

"Right you are then. Let me know when you get organised and in the meantime, I'll speak to my superiors." He turned his attention to Doug and frowned. "I'm reluctant to see those files going to Winnawarra. They are not suitable for close family members to view. I would be much happier if you left the files in the hands of Miss Perkins."

Doug offered his hand and met the detective's concerned gaze. "Don't worry, I won't read the reports. I have enough crazy in my head already." He smiled. "Thanks for your cooperation." He turned and ushered Emily from the building.

Outside, he removed his hat and ran a hand through his hair. The fact two women from the Winnawarra muster had vanished without a trace made his blood run cold. He hadn't wanted to push Detective Standish, but he needed to know more information about the other disappearances.

"You thinking what I'm thinking?" Emily touched his arm. "If I were running this show, I'd be checking all the other missing women against the list of visitors to Winnawarra."

"I'm wondering why Detective Standish is sitting on his hands and not doing his job." He took Emily's hand and squeezed her long fingers in an effort to lift her sombre mood. "We need to talk, and I'm sure you need a cold drink and something to eat before we tackle the assay office."

He led the way to the pub, settled her in a quiet corner and ordered club sandwiches and colas. His mind reeled at the implications of the Winnawarra muster being somehow involved in the disappearance of two or more women. *Why has no one mentioned this to me?* He stared at her, and she watched him with expectancy as if he could sort out the damn mess. Looking for any excuse to gather his wits, he indicated towards the toilet. "Excuse me a minute."

He strode into the men's toilet and pulled out his satellite phone. By the time Robbie answered, his anxiety had lessened. "I've just walked out the cop shop after a conversation with Detective Standish that made my head spin. Do you know anything about two women going missing after a muster here last year?"

"*Not much.*" Robbie let out a long sigh. "*I do recall reading something about them in the newspaper, but there's always someone going missing. Unless it's a kid, I don't think they make the newspapers until someone finds a body. Most times, the cops file them away as a missing person, I guess. Those two came into the news because their parents made a noise. The cops searched for a couple of weeks, but nothing showed up as far as I recall.*"

"I remember them, well their faces are familiar. I could have danced with one of them. Sally was her name. Nice girl but a bit clingy. She came to Australia looking for a husband I'd reckon." Doug wiped the sweat from his brow. He stared at the white tiled bathroom and chipped sink complete with a rust stain from the leaky tap. "The shit must have hit the fan after I returned to duty. The only weird thing I remember reading about was a tourist who escaped from a man who murdered her companion, but that was some years ago. Did they ever catch him?"

"*Yeah, but they never found a body.*" Robbie cleared his throat. "*If the girlfriend hadn't escaped, he'd probably still be out there picking off tourists with no one the wiser.*"

"Bloody hell, there could be any amount of crazies out there just waiting for their next kill." Doug stared sightlessly at the dust-smeared frosted window. "I know people wander off and get lost, but I don't think people realise how many criminals haunt the Outback."

"*Yeah, unfortunately, there's always some sick bastard hanging around no matter where you live on this planet.*" Robbie blew out his breath. "*It happens everywhere, mate. That's why Jock insisted visitors took the tour busses to and from Winnawarra. Travelling in three busses behind the road train is a much safer option than driving.*" He chuckled. "*It's not as if we don't drum the safety spiel into them before we go on a muster. In all the years we've had tourists here, we've never lost one — thank God."*

Doug grimaced. "Maybe we have and didn't know it. Look, I have to make tracks Emily is waiting. I'll fill you and Ian in on everything we've discovered at dinner." He listened to Robbie's sign off and closed his phone, although speaking to him had not eased his concern.

Emily sipped her cola and stared at the men's bathroom door. Something had freaked out Doug, and he'd retreated to think. Perhaps the fact both of the missing women had been on the Winnawarra muster had upset him. When he returned, he appeared normal. She smiled at him. "The moment we get home, I'm going to call Detective Standish and ask if he is prepared to give me a list of missing persons. I'll see if Google can find me a newspaper archive available online. Newspapers are a font of information."

"What are you thinking?" Doug lifted his gaze.

"I'd like to see how many missing women attended a muster at Winnawarra. The killer, if there is one, might be one of the tour organisers, or one of the people the tourists come into contact with at the ten or so stopovers on the way to Winnawarra. He could also be my stalker." She leant back in her chair and sighed. "Or not. The women may have wandered into the bush and got lost for all I know."

"What do you think of the idea of starting a private detective agency?" Doug drummed his fingertips on the table. "Do you have any idea how lucrative such a venture would be? It's certainly worth some thought — *if* you decide to stay."

Emily ran a block of ice over her heated cheeks and frowned. "Christ, let's get Jock's problems sorted before we take on anything else. My head is spinning with the implications already." She rolled her eyes towards the ceiling. "I thought this trip would be relaxing, but I'm working ten times harder than at home."

"You haven't started working yet." Doug chuckled. "Wait until I get you on horseback."

Emily smiled at him. "I thought you'd be up in the chopper chasing cows?"

"Robbie and I will be taking the choppers out from tomorrow. You can come with me if you like?" Doug sat beside her and pulled his plate towards him. "We'll drive the cattle down from the back paddocks. The ringers start moving them towards the homestead then the visitors join in for the last week or so. Or it would take six months to find the buggers." He lifted his sandwich and looked at it longingly. "I have to admit I'm a little disturbed about those women going missing after a Winnawarra muster. What if it happens again this year?"

"We have zero evidence they came to harm. Standish said the tour guide checked everyone on and off the coach from Winnawarra, so we can't tie the women's disappearances to the station. We'll concentrate on Jock's worries for now and if we discover anything about the missing women along the way we deal with the information at the time." Emily swallowed a mouthful of food. "Right now, it would help if we could eliminate a mining company conspiracy because I haven't found a paper trail to tie in Mr. Brewster so far. We only have hearsay." She sighed. "Although, Jock seems to think he was behind ordering the core samples." She rubbed her temples in slow, soothing circles. "I'm sorry, Doug, but I'm starting to wonder if Jock was delusional."

"Well, I guess that's why he brought you here." Doug reached for his drink and his lips quirked up into a wicked smile. "Unless his ultimate plan was to introduce his sad and lonely grandson to an English rose."

Emily melted under his hot gaze, and her heart raced. She wanted to say something cute, but his grin had pushed all reasonable thought from her head. "I don't think any of you have a problem meeting women."

"Nice of you to say but I think you're biased." Doug winked at her. "I'm your boyfriend, remember." He chuckled and flicked a glance at his watch. "As much as I'm enjoying this conversation, I think I'll wait here and let you do some shopping. Don't be long. Remember we have to go to the assay office, and I wouldn't mind dropping in to see old Mr. Brewster. Take no more than half an hour, or I'll have to lodge another flight plan."

* * * *

An hour later, Doug gaped at the pimple-faced clerk behind the assay office desk in disbelief. "What do you mean by 'Jock ordered the tests'?" He slammed a hand on the polished wooden surface, and the man stepped back wide-eyed. "No way, he would never do such a thing. Show me the order form."

"I can't do that, Mr. Macgregor, because I don't have it here." The clerk's eyes flashed to Emily as if to gain her support. His Adam's apple bobbed up and down countless times. "I took this job last week, so it's no use getting up me. I have to go on what is in the files." He drew a deep breath. "Says here, mineral tests were completed, and the results picked up at the Darwin office."

"Give me a copy of the results."

"I don't have them, I'm sorry." The clerk's voice came out in a squeak. "You must understand things of such a delicate nature are private between the company and the landowner." He straightened his shirt and cleared his throat in an almost comic gesture. "I suggest you contact the company involved."

Doug's mind reeled, and he turned to Emily for information. "I think you mentioned something about my father never making it to the Darwin assay office, is that right?"

"Yes, Jock made mention of his intent to go but nothing after that. I assume he would have mentioned something so important." Emily frowned and her blue eyes narrowed. "If the results were confidential then someone had to sign for them. You'll have to contact the Darwin office to see if they keep a record of important document disposal."

"They should do. It's a government office, isn't it?" Doug leant on the desk and glared at the clerk making the small man chew on his bottom lip.

"Yes, it is a government office." The clerk gathered himself as if he'd just remembered the police station was across the road. "I suggest you make enquiries at the Darwin office. I'm afraid I can't help you."

"Just a minute." Emily pushed a strand of hair behind one ear, and her lips curled into a coaxing smile. "Does the order by any chance state that copies of the results were released to Mr. Brewster, the Macgregor's accountant?"

The small man paled and tapped on the keyboard in front of his computer.

"A request was sent to halt the testing, and any results would be collected by J Macgregor." His brow creased into a frown. "This request is an amendment added one week after the initial order. The original instructions have been deleted."

"I guess when Jock found out about the tests he had the instructions changed." Emily squeezed Doug's arm and smiled. "There's nothing we can do here. I think we should speak to Mr. Brewster."

Doug covered her hand, glad to have her calming presence close. "Yeah — ah, I'm sorry to come on so strong, mate." He offered the clerk his hand. "It's been a difficult time with half my family dying. We have heaps of things to do. I'm sure you understand. No hard feelings?"

"No." The clerk shook his hand. "I understand completely, Mr. Macgregor." He smiled. "I'll print you a copy of the order I have here. You'll need the number to follow up with the Darwin office." He went to his computer and bent to collect a sheet of paper from a printer below the desk. "Here you are. I hope you get things sorted."

Doug led the way across the road and into Mr. Brewster's office. The man didn't have a secretary and lifted an astonished gaze at him.

"Yes?" He peered at him over his square spectacles.

"I just need to ask you a question." Doug ushered Emily inside then smiled encouragingly. "When did you last see my grandfather?"

"About a week before he died. Why?" Mr. Brewster removed his glasses and narrowed his gaze.

"Did he mention anything about ordering core samples from Rainbow Gulley?" Doug eyed him closely and noticed beads of sweat forming on his brow. "Or asking them to be sent to you?"

"No." Mr. Brewster pulled a check handkerchief from his pants pocket and wiped his brow. "If Jock ordered any testing, he didn't do it through me, and I don't recall an invoice for anything of that nature." He gave him a dark stare and anger flashed across his expression. "You have all the Winnawarra files so why are you bothering me? I no longer work for you, and I'm far too busy to chat."

Doug straightened and noticed a muscle tick over one of Brewster's eyes. The man was hiding something he would bet his last dollar on it. He forced his mouth into a smile. "Fine. Thanks for your time."

He led Emily out of the building, and they made their way back to the airport. His head ached from the implications of what their visit had revealed. Had Jock lost his mind after his parents died? He took Emily's hand and gave it an affectionate squeeze. "Mr. Brewster sure acted guilty, but I doubt we'll find proof to implicate him in this mess because it looks like Jock accidentally deleted the evidence by having him removed as the collection agent for the sample results. That's if the tests were undertaken at all. Jock could have stopped them in time by rescinding the order." He waved a hand absently in the air. "Or the accusations were a figment of his imagination."

"Could be, so far we only have Jock's written account of his suspicions and no actual proof."

"It seems that way. We know Jock suspected someone was after the mining rights and if he was correct and the same person tried to prevent my father collecting the results, it looks very suspicious."

"Unless" — Emily stopped walking and stared at him — "it was a ruse to get your father away from Winnawarra. Jock mentioned when your father went to Darwin, he always took your mother shopping, and they never missed the chance to go to a special place for a picnic."

Doug's stomach went into free fall. "Yeah it was common knowledge, Mum used to talk about it all the time. My dad proposed to her there." He swallowed hard. "The rock pool is at the bottom of a steep hill. So, if Jock was correct and someone tampered with the brakes, it would account for the accident."

"Oh, shit." Emily squeezed his hand. "But someone collected the results from Darwin. If not your dad then who?"

"It's someone we know, someone who knew my dad well." He flicked a glance at her. "We'll need a list of everyone who went to Darwin the same time as my parents. Something stinks, and I'm starting to see Jock's angle." He rubbed his chin. "We'll need to get hold of the airline passenger lists, and that's near impossible."

"But that won't cover the people on busses or those driving, will it?"

"I doubt very much anyone would take a bus from here to Darwin let alone drive. It's close to two thousand kilometres away. Nah, whoever collected those results flew up there, or they would risk someone noticing them missing. It takes over twenty hours to drive or longer by bus. I'll check the logs and see who left Winnawarra around the same time." He wiped the sweat from his brow with his arm and sighed. "They would need identification, a driver's licence or passport to collect the documents. I gather by saying J Macgregor would collect them, Jock meant my father, so how the hell would some stranger get my father's ID let alone pass as him?" He sighed. "Nothing makes sense."

"It had to be someone with a phony ID." Emily frowned. "Australian driver's licenses look pretty hard to fake."

Doug stopped walking and stared down at her. "We know my father didn't collect the results." He rubbed the back of his neck and walked around in circles thinking. "If someone stole my dad's licence he'd have to resemble him to pull it off, so that takes Brewster off our list of suspects."

"But not his accomplice." Emily wet her lips. "Tall, dark and cowboy is the norm at Winnawarra, including the stalker and you and your brothers."

Doug swallowed the lump in his throat. To obtain his father's licence, the killer would have to have been on the scene of the accident before the car caught fire. He remembered his father's licence. It was nearly ten years old and coming up for renewal. His father had always said he wished he still looked as young as the photograph. His stomach clenched with the implications. He and his brothers all had their father's looks, in fact, Jock had stamped his dark hair and blue eyes on all of them. A cold sweat coated his skin. "We've made a list of every man working for us who fits the description right down to owning metal-tipped boots." He lifted his chin and stared at her. "Yeah, Ian, Robbie and I fit the description as well, but have you considered, if anyone at the Darwin Assay office has ever met J Macgregor? I can tell you it's not a place we frequented, so the chances of someone using a fake ID is more than possible, which throws the tall, dark and cowboy theory out the window."

CHAPTER THIRTEEN

Later that evening, Doug, white-faced and sweating, pulled Emily into the office he shared with Robbie and closed the door. "What's wrong? You look like you've seen a ghost."

He gave her a long, troubled look as if he hadn't decided if he could confide in her. Emily moved closer to him and touched his arm. "You know you have my confidence, Doug. Anything we talk about stays between us, okay?"

His dark lashes dropped to cover the pain in his eyes. His reluctance to speak about his worries showed in his gaunt expression.

"Oh, shit I'm losing it. I need to talk to someone, and you are the only person I can trust. Jock had confidence in you, and I have great faith in his judgement. I've got to know you, and you're as honest as the day is long." Doug dragged in a few ragged breaths. "I'm really struggling to keep focused, so give me a second. Shock tends to push my buttons and causes flashbacks, so bear with me, love."

Emily squeezed his arm and stared into an expression marked with tragedy. She smiled and lowered her voice to just above a whisper. "Take your time. Whatever is wrong we'll face it together. You're not alone, Doug, not anymore."

"I don't want to involve the others — not yet. Not until you've heard me out. I might be hallucinating." He dragged a hand over his face and grimaced. "It happens, *has happened* a lot since Afghanistan."

She cupped his cheek. "Tell me what brought this on and I'll work through it with you."

Doug waved a trembling hand towards his desk, and a tremor skidded through him.

"I rang the assay office, and they confirmed the results could only be collected by a person with a driver's licence or passport, and they hold a photocopy. I had to email them a photo of my driver's licence to prove my identity before they would discuss anything. I explained the results were missing and mentioned the deaths in the family. I requested the number on the licence to discover who had collected the results and they gave it to me." He sucked in a deep breath and shuddered. "I went through my dad's stuff, he always kept his expired licences, and found an old one — it's the same damn number. None of them are missing." He dashed a hand through his thick black hair. "Don't you understand what this means, Em'?" He took a deep breath in an obvious attempt to keep calm and grasped her by the shoulders. "Someone resembling my dad collected the results *with* his current driver's licence. We know my dad didn't collect the paperwork because you mentioned Jock wrote about the trip in his diary and said my dad intended on going to the assay office *after* the picnic with my mom. This means someone must have been at the accident site before the car caught fire and took the licence out of my dad's wallet." He swallowed. "Maybe they set fire to the car to destroy evidence of foul play."

She grasped his waist and stared into his eyes. "Not necessarily, they may have stolen the licence out of his wallet from the motel room. It is possible. If it was a hot day, I bet he went for a swim in the pool, all the motels have pools here, don't they?" She had to keep him calm and rubbed soothing circles on his damp back. "I'm sure you don't bother to check the contents of your wallet all the time. It's normal not to constantly look for things that are normally safe inside. He might have even left his wallet behind on purpose too if he was going on a picnic with your mother the day he died."

He pressed his hot chest against her and her flesh quivered under his racing heart.

"It's unlikely because we are required by law to carry our licences at all times when we're driving." He stared at the door. "We can check and see if it's missing from his belongings. Robbie would know. He collected my parents' bags from the motel, and the police released any personal items that survived the accident." The pain etched in Doug's face made her heart ache. "Problem is, love, Robbie was in Darwin just like me. I *know* I didn't murder my parents and like Ian, and me, Robbie is also a spitting image of my dad. I know Ian was in university when the accident happened so we can count him out." A tremor went through him. "I don't want to — no. I *refuse* to believe Robbie is involved."

Emily held him close, and the shudders racking him broke her heart. "No, I'm sure it's *not* Robbie. First of all, what would he have to gain? I assume he is quite comfortably off with the profit share from Winnawarra and his practice. No, it makes no sense." She drew a deep breath and hoped she sounded convincing. "Secondly, I have great instincts, and I feel safe with him. In any case, he is a doctor and has a million of undetectable ways to kill people without staging a car accident." She lifted her chin and gazed up at him. "It's *not* Robbie or Ian, and I *know* it's not *you*." She sighed. "If you're correct about someone stealing your father's ID then we are ahead of the game. We are looking for someone between thirty and fifty with black hair, about six feet tall. At least we have a clear description to go on."

"Jock was right, wasn't he? Some bastard murdered my parents." Doug buried his face in her neck, and his warm breath brushed her skin. All the tension seemed to drain from him. "I must be going crazy to blame Robbie. He's a gentle person, and my parents' death hit him hard. It proves how unbalanced I am to consider such a thing. You'll have to make sure I'm not losing it, Em'. Everything you say makes sense and breaks through the panic. I *need* you, Em'. Help me keep my head straight."

When he pressed kisses along her chin, nothing else mattered. She slid both hands around his neck and buried her fingers in his thick hair. Emotion choked her, and she hardly recognised her throaty voice. "I'm here for you and for as long as you need me, I promise."

"You have no idea how good that makes me feel." Doug brushed a tender kiss across her lips then lifted his head and stared into her eyes. "I'm so glad you're not scared of me. I'll never hurt you."

Emily swallowed the lump in her throat. Weak at the knees from his embrace, she would have walked on fire for one more kiss. "I'm counting on it — I mean *you*. I trust you, Doug, and I don't for one second believe you're crazy."

He gave her a crooked grin. "Jeez, Em', how could you trust a broken-down soldier?"

She went on tiptoe and swiped a lick across his bottom lip. "I trust you with my heart too, Doug."

"I'm so glad you do because you keep me sane and I *love* kissing you." He nuzzled a damp path down her neck.

He took her breath away. "Then don't stop."

He kissed her again, tasting of peppermint, and she kissed him back wanting so much more. Their tongues tangled in a now familiar dance and she breathed him in bathing in his delicious musky scent. When his hands cupped her bottom and squeezed, she moaned with delight. She pressed her hips against the front of his jeans grinding against his arousal. When he deepened the kiss, demanding more of her, she wrapped one leg around his hips opening for him.

He lifted his head on a low feral growl, his eyes filled with passion. "I want you, Em', I want you so bad." He lifted her shirt, and his warm hands moved up her chest.

She moaned as he slid his fingers under her lacy bra lifting it away from her breasts. When he moved back and stared at her with tenderness in his eyes, she wanted to pull him to her.

"You are so beautiful." He bent his head and nuzzled her aching breasts.

When his hot wet mouth closed over her nipple, she arched into him. Sizzles of erotic delight surged through her. He teased one then the other then returned to claim her mouth in a demanding kiss.

The sharp knock on the door had him lifting his head, annoyance crossing his face.

"Go away."

Emily righted her clothes and cupped his face. "It might be important."

"More than this?" He groaned and squeezed her bottom.

Ian's voice came through the door.

"I need to speak to you."

"What is it now?" Doug opened the door and glared at him.

When Ian poked his head around the door, his gaze slid over her, and he raised one dark eyebrow and grinned.

"You look awfully flushed, Emily. My brother isn't making a pig of himself, is he?"

She straightened her shirt and had the urge to run a hand through her hair. "Don't be silly. We've been discussing a few extremely traumatic facts concerning your parents' accident. I'm sure Doug will bring you up to speed."

"Is Robbie home yet?" Doug slid one hand around her waist and drew her against him in a possessive claiming.

"Yeah, he's in the kitchen, why?"

"Do you have any idea where he stored our parents' personal effects from the accident?" Doug held her close.

Emily inhaled his unique scent of aftershave and male musk and tried to make her voice come out normal as if she allowed handsome hunks to cuddle her on a daily basis. "We need to see if your father's driver's licence is in his wallet." She had a sudden thought. "Oh, and are their bags here from the motel — because if your father *did* pick up the results, they would likely be inside his suitcase. Being important documents, he would hardly risk leaving them in a hire car."

"You *do* know, if there are no documents and his licence is missing, we have to face the fact some bastard murdered them?" Doug grimaced.

Ian paled and swallowed. "Oh, shit." He rubbed the back of his neck and narrowed his gaze. "I think, Jock told Johnno to bring the bags back with him from Darwin. As far as I remember, you were in hospital and Robbie was still working." He moved around uncomfortably. "Robbie didn't come home straight away after the accident because he had to tie up loose ends in Darwin and apply to join the Royal Flying Doctor Service. After Jock died, he was the first of us to arrive home. You probably don't know, but at the time of Jock's accident, I was in Thailand with some of my mates." He shrugged. "After getting my degree, I wanted a break before I returned to Winnawarra."

"I didn't know you went overseas." Doug smiled at him. "I'm real proud of you though, you know that, right?"

"Yeah, I know." Ian jerked his thumb towards the door. "I guess Jock would have told Johnno to put our parents' stuff in the storage barn. I believe the police gave Jock a list of their personal items from the accident, but I don't think any of us would have been inclined to go through anything the cops released from the accident. It's still too painful and seeing their personal things all burned up would do my head in."

Emily wanted to hug him. He looked so desolate. "I'm afraid someone has to check through them and see if your father's wallet and the documents are there."

"I can't." Doug straightened.

"Me either. We keep the barn locked but if you want it opened let me know. You'll have a big job on your hands because the place is full of junk." Ian met her gaze. "Will you take a look for us? If not, Robbie would be the best person, he isn't squeamish."

"I'll ask him." She stepped reluctantly from Doug's embrace missing the contact immediately and smiled at Ian. "Can you ask Johnno if he remembers where he stored their personal effects in the barn?"

"No worries." Ian indicated with his chin the door. "Do you want to come with me?"

"No, she doesn't." Doug glowered at his brother. "I don't want her anywhere near him."

Emily stepped between the men and smiled. "Do you want me to explain our theory to Robbie as well?"

"Yeah, but can you omit my impressions about him, I wasn't thinking straight." Doug gave her an apologetic smile. "It wouldn't hurt to let him know how suspicious he looks though."

"Who looks suspicious?" A nerve ticked in Ian's cheek. "Don't talk as if I'm not here. I want the details. Are you speaking about Robbie?"

"Yeah. Someone picked up the assay results using Dad's driver's licence. Jock didn't mention anything about Dad picking up the results. It wasn't me, and you were in Thailand, so I had one of my crazy episodes and thought it must have been Robbie." Doug held up one hand to stop the stream of abuse threatening to spill from Ian's mouth. "I know, I'm an idiot but Em' put me straight. Problem is someone had Dad's licence and must resemble him to have convinced the clerk at the assay office."

"Just wait here, both of you." Ian stormed out the door, and his footsteps pounded on the wooden floor.

Moments later Robbie walked in with Ian on his heels. He stood hands on hips, and his blue eyes flashed with concern.

"Did you by any chance get a date when those results were picked up?"

"Sure did. They took a photocopy of the licence so we have a date and time." Doug moved to the desk and handed a piece of paper to Robbie. "See for yourself. That is Dad's licence number. I have his old one here — see it's the same number." He held out the plastic covered card.

"Pass me my journal. It has a five-year calendar inside." Robbie took the paper from Doug and checked the date. He gave him a long considering stare. "You know, I'm hurt you'd even think I'm capable of murder, but I'm putting it down to your condition. Next time, I won't be so forgiving." He pointed to the date on the calendar. "The date the results were picked up is a Tuesday afternoon and my regular date for surgery. I would have been at the hospital for twelve hours or more and on call until ten for any postoperative problems. It is easy to check if you want to put your mind at rest. I'll call the hospital in the morning on speaker and ask for confirmation."

"There's no need." Doug slapped him on the back. "I lost it for a moment after I spoke to the assay office. It's all good."

"Oh, I insist." Robbie scowled at him. "I don't want *any* doubt not ever."

Emily eased towards the door, needing to escape the overpowering scent of angry men. "I'll go and chat with Glady. Can you ask Johnno about those things, Ian?"

"Yeah, I'm on my way." He followed her from the room.

* * * *

The following morning, the men spent the day settling the new ringers and overseeing the final travel arrangements for the muster. The tourists would arrive late Friday, and they would head to the muster at sunrise on Saturday. Emily pushed her clothes and necessities into saddlebags then removed her satellite phone from the charger. Excitement thrummed through her at the thought of joining Doug in the chopper and herding the cattle from the outlying areas to the ringers on horseback or trail bike.

She heard footsteps, and Doug appeared at her door.

"Hey, Ian unlocked the storage barn, and Johnno found the box containing my parents' personal effects and two suitcases. The lighting is good inside, so if you are ready, you can take a look. Robbie is already there, making sure no one has tampered with the seals."

A cloak of dread dropped over her happiness, and she nodded. "Yes, I'm all packed. Lead the way."

"Have you covered this type of investigation in your studies?"

"Yes, I was only one term from finishing my degree. It can be very interesting when I'm not involved with the family." She met his stride as they walked towards a building set apart at the back of the homestead. "It's like solving a puzzle. I keep my head away from the tragedy, although I always have respect for the victims. If I wasn't detached, I couldn't do it." She held up a white box with a large red X on one side. "I have everything I need in this medical box. Robbie gave it to me earlier."

The barn had a musty smell, and a light coating of dust spread over the rows of shelves containing a surprisingly wide array of objects, from lamps to car parts all neatly arranged and labelled. Plastic wrapped items sat beside metal trunks painted with large white letters. On a long bench in the middle of the barn, Robbie was guarding a large cardboard box wrapped in plastic with an official looking seal, plus two similarly protected suitcases. The light above the table spilled down over the scene sparkling with dust motes. Johnno leant against the entrance with a smirk on his face. Emily smiled at him. "Thanks for your help. We don't want to keep you from your work. Robbie will return these to storage."

"Sure thing, sweetheart." Johnno wet his lips and sauntered away.

She stared after him. "He thinks he's all that."

"He is an asshole." Doug brushed a kiss on her cheek. "I'll leave you to it. Robbie will make sure you get back to the homestead without being harassed."

Emily squeezed his arm. "Thank you." She watched him walk away then entered the huge building.

Robbie glanced around as if checking to see if they were alone then lowered his voice to just above a whisper.

"This seal has been tampered with and whoever opened the box did a great job of resealing it. Look at the stamp, it's been removed with a sharp knife and re-attached." He pulled the phone from his pocket and took a photograph of the box and both suitcases wrapped in plastic. "Give me a pair of gloves. I don't want to contaminate anything. I'll search the bags, I need to do something to help." He pulled on the gloves and reached for the suitcases.

Emily moved closer and watched him search each bag. When he completed the examination with no sign of the test results, a wave of panic rushed through her. The day had become suffocating as if someone had pushed her inside a small dark room with no escape. She swallowed her rising fear and met his eyes. "What now?"

"Now we look for the driver's licence. If it's damaged, we'll have to hope some part of it will be recognisable." After breaking the seal on the carton and spreading the bags of charred remains on the table, he stepped back. "Take a look, you're the expert. What do you see?"

"The plastic bags are all sealed except one. You know very well, when police collect evidence at a crime scene it's placed in a bag and sealed immediately, so this evidence was never considered for the inquest. I wonder why?" She chewed on her bottom lip and bent to examine the bags. "Take photographs of everything before we proceed. If we find anything suspicious, we don't want anyone thinking we've tampered with the evidence, so keep clicking away. Get pics of everything I do, a step by step record."

"I have a better idea." Robbie picked up his phone. "I'll record the entire process. We can download it when we get back to the house."

"Brilliant!" Emily took a pair of latex gloves from her pocket. "I'll do a commentary." She donned the gloves and waited for him to start recording. "This is Emily Perkins, with me is Dr. Robert Macgregor." She gave the date and time then reached for the first bag; examined it briefly and moved to the next. "We are looking for Mr. Macgregor's wallet to discover if his driver's licence is inside as we have proof from the Darwin assay office that it was used to collect privileged information."

Emily waited for him to pan over the evidence bags and then went through each bag of fire-damaged remains.

"I've found the wallet." She held up the bag, and Robbie moved in to film the seal. "As you can plainly see this bag *has* been opened." She pulled open the plastic wrapper and tipped the charred black leather wallet onto the bench. Taking a pair of long-nosed forceps, she teased the billfold open. "As you can see the interior of the wallet is only slightly damaged. This is consistent with a lower ignition point fire rather than the burn pattern of a petrol fire." She sniffed the inside of the bag then checked all the bags on the table and frowned. "Something is terribly wrong here. These all smell the same and not consistent with the smell from a petrol fire. I would expect similar damage from a different accelerant, for example, *methylated spirits*." With care, she removed the credit cards and examined each one. "The edges of each of the cards have melted and are consistent with minor fire damage." She frowned. "This in itself is suspicious. If the car exploded on impact, as stated in the report, the wallet would have been incinerated."

"Ah, here it is." As she eased out the driver's licence, Emily held her breath then nausea gripped her. The licence dropped on the bench was untouched by fire. Heart pounding, she gaped at Robbie's pale face.

"Read it." Robbie moved closer.

"The name on the licence is Mr. James Macgregor's, and it appears to be untouched, yet it was found between two damaged cards of the same dimensions." She held up the card. "I would conclude by the overall fire damage to the wallet and contents that the driver's licence was placed inside the wallet *after* the fire. The licence shows no indication of damage by heat or smoke." Sick inside, she turned to Robbie. "Open a specimen bag, please. This may need to be dusted for fingerprints." She looked into the camera. "This concludes my investigation at this time."

"Okay." Robbie turned off the phone and complied. "This is not what I expected."

Her head spun with the idea of someone rifling through Jamie's pockets, as he lay dead or dying in a wrecked car. The dread of informing Doug of their findings lay like a heavy weight across her shoulders. "This means they were murdered, doesn't it?"

"It's not conclusive, but it sends up a red flag that's for sure." Robbie's eyes narrowed. "You haven't had the time to go over all the coronal enquiry documents. The local mortician may have removed the wallet, and cleaned the licence to read it." He offered her a small patient smile. "My mum's handbag looks like it wasn't burned, so she may have had ID inside too."

"I'll take a look." Emily reached for a large plastic bag containing a brown handbag. "Take a few pics." She displayed the bag then opened it and removed the handbag.

The soot-streaked bag had a metal clip at the opening, and it sprung open. Inside a purse, untouched by fire, contained a driver's licence and credit cards plus a substantial amount of cash. She drew in a deep breath. "Well, it wasn't robbery." She chewed on her bottom lip running the case through her mind, her attention fixed on the wallet. "Why wasn't your dad carrying cash? All men carry cash."

"I have no idea. I guess the cops returned it to Jock. There will be a list of items removed from the scene and the personal items from the mortuary in the safe." Robbie cleared his throat. "After seeing this, I'll be interested in what you find in the post-mortem report. Up to now, the cause of death hasn't been an issue." He waved a hand at the scorched items. "This tells a different story. It's not looking good, is it?"

"No, it's not, not at all." Emily glanced at the charred remnants of two people's lives. Tears pricked the backs of her eyes at the sight of a small bag of soot-covered gold jewellery containing a number of rings and a watch. "I think those items should be cleaned and put in the safe too."

"I agree, but make a list of each item with a short description and give it to me for the file, so I can compare it to the original list. If someone has tampered with this evidence, I want to know." Robbie snapped photographs of the bag then handed it to her. "They are a constant reminder of tragedy."

Sadness engulfed her, and she took the bag holding it reverently as if it contained memories of her own parents. She stood beside the bench and watched him replace every item inside the carton, seal it with tape then sign his name in three places before carrying the items back to the shelves.

Emily took in Robbie's serious expression. "Going on what we've seen here today, especially the use of an accelerant for the fire. I'm sure that would be enough evidence to reopen the case."

"I guess." Robbie removed his gloves with a snap and rolled them into a ball. "I don't recall the medical examiner mentioning the burn pattern. This in itself is significant. Add the suspicion, the killer used the victim's identity, and we have to face the fact Jock may have been correct."

"I'll write a report and get Doug to send it to the lawyer. He can start the process with the coroner."

"After the muster." Robbie sighed and stretched. "We'll need time to make sure we have all the evidence we need. I think sending a sample of the burnt items for testing to determine the accelerant would bolster our case."

"Good idea. They can't dispute a laboratory's findings, but they could mine." Relieved the harrowing experience was over Emily gripped the bag of jewellery to her chest and followed him to the barn door. She started at the sight of Johnno leaning casually against the wall chewing a piece of grass. If he overheard their discussion, their findings would take off like a bush fire across the station.

She rolled her eyes and mouthed "Oh, shit" to Robbie.

"We'll wait for you to lock up." Robbie straightened his wide shoulders and glared at him. "We wouldn't want you to get the blame if anything goes missing."

"Me?" Johnno slid the metal door shut and snapped the padlock. "I'm not the one snooping into things best left alone. Dead is dead, and she shouldn't be stirring up trouble. You know damn well all this shit will push Doug off the rails again. He doesn't know what he's doing when he has a flashback and believes everyone is the enemy."

"Doug's mental state is none of your concern unless you've recently become his psychiatrist." Robbie glared at him. "Get back to work."

"Emily will be right in his firing line." Johnno gave her a cocky smile. "Best you remember that, sweetheart." He pulled on the front of his cowboy hat in a mock salute then strolled away towards the stables.

Emily stared after him frowning. "I trust him about as far as I can throw him." She sighed. "I'm a little overwhelmed with what we've discovered. I hope I don't overlook a vital clue in the forensic documents, so far what we've found is pretty damning." She glanced at him. "I'll take a rest then look at them later."

"You'll need your wits about you. There is so much evidence to digest."

CHAPTER FOURTEEN

Emily scanned the files collected from the Broome police. She tried to distance herself from the photographs laid out across the desk and thought about the muster. Soon, she would be in the chopper with Doug and flying off to the far reaches of Winnawarra to move the cattle towards the homestead. A day away from the investigation would be heaven.

Unfortunately, she had to examine the images of the charred remains of the bodies. She would make sure none of the Macgregor boys accidentally opened the file. One glance at the horrific images of their parents would haunt them for the rest of their lives. She would need a couple more days to look through all the documents, but so far, her first impressions were the same. The car ran down an embankment and hit a tree, but it didn't burst into flames or explode. There was no indication of the fuel line rupturing in the accident. The fire came afterwards and from the post-mortem report, Jamie and his wife were alive at the time. Both victim's lungs displayed smoke inhalation.

She massaged her temples. Both were pinned inside the car, possibly unconscious but the airbags had deployed, and their skeletal damage was minimal. This would suggest they survived the impact which led her to suspect a third party was involved in their deaths. From the coroner's report, all indications told her the fire killed them. She examined the position of Jamie's body and believed it would be possible for someone to remove his wallet, assuming he kept it in the back pocket of his jeans.

In the photograph, he had turned his body at an angle towards his wife as if he was trying to protect her. She was convinced a third party removed the wallet then set fire to the car using a type of alcohol as an accelerant. She shook her head. *Next, I'll have to check out the report of Jock's accident.*

She gathered up the paperwork, pushed it into a leather case, and zipped it shut then attached a small lock. She picked up the cash and the package containing the jewellery, and a shiver ran up her arm leaving a trail of goose bumps. She would have to speak to Doug about the jewellery but worried about the effect seeing his parents' personal items would have on him. She had cleaned and polished each item. Taking a pen from a cracked cup, she went down the list Robbie had given her. "All correct and accounted for."

"What is?" Doug grinned at her from the open doorway.

The world closed in around her, and she sucked in a deep breath. Dear God, he appeared so relaxed and happy. Now she had to ruin his day by showing him the jewellery. She lifted her chin ready for the backlash. "There is no way to say this gently, Doug. I have your parents' jewellery. I was just checking to make sure nothing was missing before I gave it to you. There is a bundle of cash too."

The reaction she expected didn't happen. Doug flicked a deep blue gaze over her then moved towards her and wrapped her in his arms. She inhaled freshly showered man and all the tension bottled inside her flowed away. He placed a tender kiss on her cheek and lifted her chin to gaze into her eyes.

"That must have been very difficult for you, Em', but don't worry you don't have to tread softly around me." He brushed a whisper of a kiss over her lips and smiled. "Show me."

Doug stared at the small pile of gold and forced his emotions down. With tender care, he lifted his mother's earrings and placed them reverently in the palm of his hand. He glanced at Emily. The poor kid was as pale as a ghost. She cared for him, and he refused to let her down by going apeshit. "Did you find a locket?"

"No, that is everything on the list from the police." Emily moved to his side. "Are you sure it wasn't left here?"

His mother never removed the locket. It had a small photograph of her three sons inside and was a gift from his father.

"No, it wasn't in their room. She never took it off, and it was precious to her. You know, I'd wondered what happened to their things. It's strange, Mum's locket and Jock's rabbit's foot are missing, and both were treasured items." He collected up the small pile and gazed at her. "I'll put these in the safe."

"Oh, here's the cash we found and can you lock up these files too. They're the documents Detective Standish gave us." Emily handed him a leather container and an envelope stuffed with notes.

Cold crept around his heart, his in-built defence against feeling and he pushed the folder under one arm. "No worries. Are you ready to muster some cattle? We'll grab a bite to eat then head off. Robbie is due to take off in about fifteen minutes, he will be covering the south pasture, and we'll go north."

"That sounds like fun. I can't wait to see more of Winnawarra's fantastic scenery." Emily leaned against the desk. "When will the rest of the muster team join in?"

He opened the safe, stowed the items and shut the door. "They'll be moving out at sunup. We'll take the chopper up and drive the cattle towards them." He strolled out into the hall and led the way to the kitchen. "But tonight, we're having one hell of a party. Can you dance?"

"Not if you mean boot-scooting or the Texas two-step, no, not a chance, I'm a rock and roll or waltzing type of girl."

He slid an arm around her waist and chuckled. "Ah well, nobody is perfect." He grinned at her disillusioned face. "I'm only kidding. I'll teach you how to enjoy yourself cowgirl style in no time."

In the kitchen, he pulled out a chair for Emily and dropped into one beside her. Before he could say a word, Glady had pushed a plate of food under his nose and filled a mug with coffee. "Thanks, Glady."

"So what happens at a muster?" Emily sipped her coffee, and her beautiful eyes scanned his face. Dear God, he wanted to kiss her and never stop. He swallowed the food in his mouth and tried to get his mind from the pink tongue flicking across her full lips. "Oh, ah . . . well, we bring the cattle down from the outlying areas and move them into the paddocks closer to the station. We sort them out, steers, calves, breeding stock and the like. We drench them, tag the calves, and band the males. Then we sort them into export and local market, what we are keeping, those we need to fatten and what is ready for sale."

"That sounds like a lot of work." Emily lifted one-half of a sandwich and peered inside. "I can't believe people actually pay you to work their backsides off."

Doug allowed the hilarity to bubble up and he grinned at her. "Nope, no figuring city folk but if they *want* to pay me to work on my cattle station who am I to refuse?"

"They are a pain in the arse." Ian strolled into the kitchen and dropped into a chair. "Half of them have never ridden a horse in their lives, and I end up leading them. How can I do my job properly if I'm spending all my time teaching a couple of inexperienced women how to enjoy themselves?"

Explicit images conjured in Doug's mind, and he cleared his throat. "Maybe you should rephrase that, little brother."

"I mean, I need to work, cut out the steers, and work the herd." Ian snorted in disgust. "I can't do my job leading women who can't ride a damn horse." He flicked a glance at Doug. "I'm not doing it again this year, so take that smirk off your face. Give the nursemaid's job to someone else."

"I'm going to be in the chopper this year and so is Robbie, for the most part, so you're the boss. Delegate." Doug pushed food into his mouth and sighed at the taste of sliced turkey.

"Sweet!" Ian grinned. "You going to the dance tonight, Em? It will be a good night, we usually have a before and after muster dance. Tomorrow we leave at dawn but the next shindig goes into the wee hours, and we get to sleep in. The tourists have Saturday to get over the party, and they leave on the busses Sunday morning."

"I wouldn't miss it." Emily giggled. "Watching sex-starved men chasing after the tourists will be a hoot."

Doug stared at her. *Sex-starved doesn't come close.*

* * * *

Inside the chopper, Emily peered through a dusty cloud whirling like a giant orange will-o'-the-wisp to a group of men on horseback all riding hell for leather towards the herd of cattle Doug had collected from the far reaches of Winnawarra. The chopper swooped down behind the stampeding cows to head them towards an open gate in a fenced pasture. The ringers, all experienced Aboriginal stockmen rode alongside the herd guiding them expertly through the gate. The chopper rose high in the air hovering above the red dust cloud. She turned and smiled at Doug. "Wow! That was incredible. What happens now?"

"This is when the muster begins for the tourists. They ride here and help the ringers move the cattle through a series of fenced pastures. We make camp along the way, and it takes a week to bring the cattle back to the yards for us to sort. Most leave after the muster, but some ask to be put on as staff." He grinned at her. "We can head home now, and I suggest you have a rest before I dance your legs off tonight."

She laughed, but his smile warmed her heart. "You wish."

"Oh, I don't wish, Em', *I know.* Once a city girl dances with a cowboy there is no turning back." He turned the chopper for home. "We'll be leaving on horseback with the others in the morning. Robbie picked up all the strays, and all the cattle are in the paddocks. Our next job is to help Ian move the herd and entertain the tourists."

"Do you teach the tourists how to move the cattle?"

"No, it is too much of a risk, and our cattle are far too precious to allow untrained people too close. The ringers do most of the work. The tourists usually tag along behind, but I'll be staying with you the entire time."

"Good. I must admit sleeping rough isn't one of my most favourite things to do for entertainment." She shuddered at the thought of sharing her sleeping bag with a snake or huge spider. "Is it safe? I mean with all the creepy crawlies?"

"Yeah, nothing will get inside your tent. They are zipped up all the time." He chuckled deep in his chest. "You'll have a tent and me to protect you . . . unless you'd prefer not to share?" He met her gaze with a smile. "Don't worry, Em', I won't jump your bones *unless* you want me to but if you're uncomfortable with me so close say the word and I'll share with someone else."

She swallowed hard at the delicious thought of sharing a tent with him. "I would love to share with you, Doug."

He flashed her a grin, and his gaze lingered on her mouth. "*Sweeeet.*"

CHAPTER FIFTEEN

The evening came clear and with a cooling breeze. Humming with excitement, Emily stepped out of her bedroom dressed in jeans, a new western shirt complete with fringe, and soft leather cowboy boots. She hoped Doug would not think she looked like a complete idiot then she caught sight of the Macgregor men waiting on the veranda. All dressed in black with tight jeans and boots polished to a high shine, the sight of them made her stomach drop to the floor and run out the door.

When Doug turned to her and flashed his perfect smile her bones melted. She allowed herself the pleasure of scanning him in intimate detail from the boots up. Her gaze lingered on his tight jeans and to the silver buckle at his waist embossed with a huge DM. His black cotton embroidered dress shirt was unbuttoned at the neck to expose a vee of hard muscular flesh. She dragged her attention up to his freshly shaved jaw and clenched her fingers to prevent the urge to caress the errant curl falling from under the brim of his cowboy hat. He moved his deep blue gaze over her, and beside him, Ian let out a long whistle.

"Wow! You scrub up good, Emily." Ian winced from the elbow Doug dug into his ribs. "What? That's a compliment. She looks amazing and here I thought we'd never take the city out of her."

She gave them each a considering stare, before lingering on Doug's face. "You all . . . er . . . 'scrub up' pretty good too."

"We have to make a good impression. It's expected." Doug moved to her side. "I'm afraid I'll have to move around and chat with the visitors tonight and dance with a couple of the women. Two max, I promise, and the rest of the time I'll be at your side." He met her gaze and shrugged apologetically. "As the head of the family, I don't really have a choice. I want you to promise to stay with one of us and not wander off on your own. I don't want to give your stalker a chance to bother you." His gaze flicked over her face. "Will you be okay?"

A wave of jealousy hit her like a truck. She pushed down the "we're not married" retort threatening to leap from her mouth and smiled. "I'll be fine and make sure I'm not alone. I'll enjoy watching you strutting your stuff. I can't dance anyway."

"Oh, you'll dance." Doug grinned. "I've made it my mission in life."

"Then you'll be sorely disappointed." She giggled and leant into the arm he slipped around her waist.

"Never." Doug bent so close his warm breath brushed her ear sending goose bumps down both arms. His deep voice dropped to a seductive whisper. "I can't wait to hold you in my arms again." He pulled her against him. "Ready to meet the tourists?"

"Yes. I thought the dance would be in the hangar, but Glady said they had set up in the cookhouse."

"Yes, we have visitor's choppers, so we needed the hangar." Doug led the way down the front steps and took her hand. "This is the meet and greet. When the visitors arrived, Brian and Johnno went to welcome them. Glady and the Jillaroos had them all settled in the bunkhouses and fed by six. Tonight, we celebrate their arrival, and next weekend we celebrate them leaving." He chuckled.

They strolled along the pathway lit by small solar lanterns to the cookhouse and Emily noticed lights highlighted every path and fairy lights hung in the trees. The Winnawarra staff had made so many changes she hardly recognised the yards. People milled around dressed in their finest and Country and Western music thumped from the open cookhouse doors. They strolled into a wide beam of light streaming from inside, and the people congregated around the doorway separated to allow them to enter. Behind her, she could hear Ian and Robbie talking ten to the dozen. As they moved to the front of the crowd, the three Macgregor boys stood in a line all smiling and waving at friends.

By the friendly shouts, the annual muster dance attracted people from the neighbouring stations.

Doug raised both hands to quieten the crowd and returned the smiles of a few attractive women in the front row. Normally he would have welcomed their advances but did not intend to spoil the fragile relationship with Emily. He would select a couple of the married women and ask them to dance, then his heart sank at the sight of a pretty redhead. Julie or maybe Jan, he spent time with her at a dance a few months ago in Broome. He worried about the scar on his chin and acted like a fool. Glancing at Emily, he wondered if she was the jealous type because as sure as the sun would rise in the morning, the redhead would be all over him like a rash. He cleared his throat, introduced his brothers and grinned at the crowd. "Welcome to the Winnawarra muster. Let's get this party started. Turn up the music."

The people whooped, whistled and took to the floor whirling around to the latest Country and Western chart-topper. He glanced over at Emily and winked. Her cheeks pinked and she backed against the wall then grinned at him. He pushed down the need to go to her and drag her into his arms. He loved the way she looked after kissing her, and ached for her. Instead, he gave her an apologetic shrug. *Don't worry darling, you won't be a wallflower for long.*

"I thought you would have called me after our weekend together." The curvaceous redhead moved in front of him and slowly wet her lips in an invitation as old as Adam. "Did you lose my number?" She flung her arms around his neck. "I've been looking forward to seeing you again, Dougy."

Her heavy perfume filled his nostrils, and he flicked a glance at Emily over the woman's shoulder to see her turn her back on him and strike up a conversation with a tall bloke in a white cowboy hat. He glanced down at Jan or was it Julie? Smothering his annoyance with a smile, he shook his head. "Yeah, I lost your number, love. Sorry about that, but these things happen." He untangled her from his neck. "I'm not here to party. The muster is part of our business, and I have to go and chat to the tourists."

"*One* dance and I'll let you go, but I want to talk to you later — in private." She pouted glossy pink lips and gripped his arm. "Pretty please with sugar on top."

Rather than make a scene, he led her into the twirling dancers and cursed as a slow song came over the loudspeakers. He took her in his arms and caught sight of a necklace with "Julie" spelt out in nursery letters strung on a thin chain around her neck. "Okay, Julie, one dance but then I'll have to go. I will be too busy to meet with you later. If you have something to say to me, say it now."

"I've put my name on the list to be in your group at the muster." She slipped one arm around his waist and pressed against him. "We can ride together. Do you want to share my tent?"

I am in so much trouble. He cleared his throat and tried to make a space between them. The day he met her had slipped into oblivion, and he had no recollection of spending a night of drunken lust with her, but it was possible. Bloody hell, he couldn't recall her name, let alone that particular weekend of self-pity binging. How could he let her down gently? "I'm already sharing, sorry, love." He moved her along to the music ignoring the disapproving looks from his brothers as they danced by.

When she fitted herself against him, he groaned. Shit, he could feel every inch of her rubbing against him. He was getting aroused, and by the way her voice turned into a purr, she knew what she was doing to him. Their intimate movements were becoming more of a sex act than a dance. He pushed her away, but she stuck like glue.

"Well, you don't have to share *all* night." Julie pressed her full breasts against him. "Do you? We were so good together."

He cleared his throat wishing the floor would open up and swallow him. "Things have changed since we met." He decided to consign his welfare to the Almighty. Hoping she wouldn't knee him and ruin his ability to sire children, he stared into her confused eyes. "I'm seeing someone."

"No, you're *not*." She curled her lip in a most unflattering gesture. "I asked Brian, and he said you haven't dated."

"Well, I'm afraid he's wrong." Not wanting to give her any details, he offered her a reassuring smile. "We can still be friends, can't we?" The song finished and he stepped away with the need to run for the hills twitching at his legs.

"Friends? Hmm, we'll see." She turned and in a swirl of skirts made her way towards a group of men.

Doug turned at once to scan the room for Emily. He hoped she hadn't seen him with Julie. The little show Julie had put on had been more an act of possession than a simple dance and Emily would see him as another man betraying her trust. He stood more than a head higher than most on the dance floor but couldn't pick out Emily in the masses. *Where is she?* Worried one of the men may have cornered her, he did a slow three-sixty-degree turn, but his beautiful blonde was nowhere in sight. Panic gripped him and images of a stranger forcing his intentions on her filled his mind. Pushing through the line of people at the bar, he headed towards the long queue at the refreshment table. His racing heart returned to normal at the sight of her chatting to Glady.

Emily sensed Doug behind her and kept her concentration on Glady's complaints about the current bunch of tourists. When he moved to her side reeking of cheap perfume instead of his delicious aftershave, she wanted to slap him. His dancing exhibition with the redhead had embarrassed her and by the number of people snickering within earshot was his usual style on the dance floor. She tried to keep calm. The small shows of affection he had offered her, paled into existence after seeing his hips grinding into the buxom redhead. When he touched her arm, she gripped the lemon squash tight enough to shatter the glass.

"Would you like to come with me to speak to some of our visitors?" Doug smiled down at her and jerked a thumb over one shoulder. "The next slow dance is ours."

She wrinkled her nose and stared at him in her best innocent expression. "I don't think so."

"Why?" His hands went to his hips, and his dazzling blue eyes narrowed. "I know I asked *you* to the dance, but I did explain I'd have to dance with some of the girls. It's good for business." He frowned. "I didn't ask Julie to dance by the way, she kind of forced me."

Emily rubbed a finger under her nose. "Oh, it's not . . . what's her name . . . ah yes, *Julie*, I'm worried about *Dougeee*." She emphasized the pet name the redhead used. "It's her cheap perfume. It must be like skunk. Once you go near one, you can't wash off the stink, and I don't want *eau de* slut all over me, thank you very much." She placed the glass on the table, turned and escaped into the crowd. She didn't need to discuss his reasons for dancing so intimately with Julie. *I've had enough excuses from unfaithful men in my life to fill a book.*

On the opposite side of the hall, she noticed a small group of women heading for the toilet block. Needing to be alone, she walked swiftly to catch up with them, and once she'd reached them, she walked past the brick building and continued along the pathway skirting the barn. Seeing the way ahead well lit, she headed for the stables. Everyone would be at the dance, and she had a chance to visit Dolly, the mare Doug had chosen for her to ride on the muster.

She strolled inside then ran her hand down the wall searching for the bank of light switches and flicked on one hoping she wouldn't disturb the horses' sleep. The smell of straw, leather and warm horse filled her nose. Soft wickers of greeting met her as she moved into the light. She made her way along the rows of stalls. Filled to capacity with horses brought in from the pasture for the visitors to use, the temperature inside was humid. She made her way between the stalls to look for her mare. Each horse had its name printed on a small chalkboard on the front of the stall, and she found the chestnut mare with the white blaze in no time. "Hello, girl." She rubbed the horse's nose and up to her ears.

Glancing around the stall for any sign of snakes, she inched open the gate and slipped inside. Yes, spending a few minutes getting to know her mount wouldn't hurt and she would have a chance to remove the stink of Julie from her nose. She ran one hand down the horse's neck, and the mare rewarded her with a huff of breath then nuzzled at her pocket. "I will bring you a pocketful of treats tomorrow."

Impressed, she moved around the mare, running one hand down her wide back. Doug had certainly picked a good mount for her to ride. A warm feeling curled in the pit of her stomach at the thought of him. His kisses still tingled on her lips. She had fallen for him and sharing him with the tourists would drive her insane. Considering the situation, she chewed on her bottom lip. Could she share him once a year at the muster? She closed her eyes. Maybe two nights a year, he would dance with other women. Oh yes, she would be jealous, but something deep down inside told her he would always keep the last dance for her.

* * * *

"You know, I thought you were the one with brains." Ian shot a look of bewilderment at Doug. "Crikey! Get a room if you plan to dance with Julie again. That was plain embarrassing. I thought we were supposed to set the standard here now you're in charge. Does this mean you've changed your mind about Emily?"

Doug had seen Emily head off towards the toilets with a group of women, or he would have chased after her to try to make her understand. He shrugged acting as nonchalant as possible but inside his stomach ached with worry. "No, everything is sweet with Em' she understands. I told her, I have to dance with some of the tourists."

"You call that dancing?" Ian rubbed his chin and stared in the direction Emily had taken. "Emily didn't look too happy to me. Since when did you and Julie become an item anyway?"

He turned to Ian and grimaced. "S'truth, I don't remember sleeping with Julie, but I gather we spent the night together after the auction. She was going to make a scene, so I agreed to dance with her. The slow song was just bad luck."

"Right." Ian snorted. "So, was grinding into her part of that *bad* luck too?"

"That was more *her* than me." Doug rubbed one hand over his face. Damn, he could still smell her. "It was like dancing with a boa constrictor." He moved closer to Ian. "Do I stink? Em' said I smelt like a skunk."

Ian gave an exaggerated sniff and gagged.

"Yeah, skunk comes close." He shook his head slowly. "I think you should take another shower. You've heaps of flash clothes, and it would be better to change if you plan to dance with Emily later."

Doug stared at him. His brother had lost his mind, but he took in his dismayed expression and swallowed his pride. "Is the smell that bad?"

"I don't really care if you smell like cheap perfume, but I'm sure Emily won't appreciate being reminded of Julie every time you get close to her." Ian shuddered. "My guess it would kill the mood."

"Fine. I'll take a damn shower." Doug glanced towards the doorway noticing a few of the women had returned without Emily. "Keep an eye out for Em'. I'll be back in five minutes." He headed for the door.

Outside the cookhouse, he hadn't taken two steps towards the homestead before Julie had him by the arm. He glared down at her. "Look, love, I'm sorry but my girl is very special to me and having you hanging around me just isn't right, so I'll say goodnight. You have a great time. There are heaps of blokes inside waiting to dance with you."

"I've been very patient waiting for you to call, Dougy." She moved closer blocking his path. "You said you loved me and wanted to see me again. I came all this way to see you, so what made you change your mind?"

Doug stared at her in disbelief. He usually didn't look twice at a girl who put on her makeup with a trowel, and he couldn't believe he'd been stupid enough to sleep with her. He cleared his throat and lied. "I say that to all the girls. I had a lot to drink that night, and since the accident, my memory isn't what it used to be. Why don't you tell me about our weekend together to jog my recollection?"

"We met at the party after the auction and danced together all night then one of the ringers insisted he take you to the motel. I would have stayed with you but you'd had too much to drink, and when you told me you loved me, I wrote my number on your hand. You said we would get together the next day. Do you remember?"

Relief flooded over him, and he smiled. "I remember dancing with you, the rest is a blur. I woke up with one hell of a hangover and took a shower. I must have washed off your number. Sorry, love, nothing is going to happen between us, I have someone now, and I'm not interested in a relationship with you. If I led you to believe something different, I apologise." He pulled away from her clutches. "I have to go, my girl is waiting for me." He jogged towards the homestead. *Thank you, God.*

* * * *

After giving Dolly one last pat, Emily headed back towards the toilet block intent on freshening up before returning to the dance. She giggled. Turning up smelling of horse after complaining about Doug's *eau de femme fatal* wouldn't do. She inhaled the night air, filled with the aroma of barbecued sausages and onions. The fairy lights and music made Winnawarra Station appear magical against the clear night sky. Above the buildings, a full moon lit up the blackness of night, and a cool breeze blew in from the direction of the river. In the distance, she could just make out the howl of dingoes calling to each other.

She sighed contented with her life, and if she could square things with Doug, it would be perfect. The idea of having him in her life made her stomach squeeze, but he attracted women like bees to honey. Would she be able to cope with the amount of women who openly flirted with him? His words crept into her head. He had promised she could trust him and would never hurt her, yet seeing him with the redhead plastered to his body had made her as mad as hell. *It was only one dance, and he did come back to me. You're overreacting, Perkins.*

Midway between the barn and the stables, the pathway lights went out plunging her into total darkness. She stopped mid-stride blinking to break through the wall of black in front of her. She turned slowly squinting and made out the homestead in the distance in the other direction, with light streaming from the front door. She would have to negotiate the bullpens before she reached the house. Slowly her eyesight adjusted but the path and everything around her had slid into obscurity. She needed to get to the barn first, once there she could walk around the walls if necessary to get back to the toilet block. Using the fairy lights in the trees near the cookhouse as her guide, she edged forwards slowly.

A rustle in the dry grass sped her heart. She glanced around. A soft crunch of gravel underfoot nearby. Someone had moved onto the pathway. The hairs on the back of her neck stood to attention. She spun around peering into the darkness. "Hello. Is somebody there?"

No one replied.

The sound came again closer this time, and her heart picked up its pace. With her pulse thundering in her ears, she turned again trying to penetrate the cloak of shadows. If someone was out to get her, she had to get to safety and took a few steps in the direction of the lights around the cookhouse. Pain shot up her shins and reaching out, her palms met smooth rock. She had collided with one of the boulders lining the pathway. Biting back a sob of fear, she went for the phone attached to her belt and found it missing. She had left it in her bedroom believing Doug would keep her safe. Cursing her stupidity, she glanced behind her and heard the whisper of a low chuckle.

In terror, she used the line of boulders to gain a general direction and throwing caution to the wind, ran for her life. Branches from an overhanging bush tore at her hair then she tripped over and crashed to the ground. Air rushed from her lungs, and she gasped short, painful breaths. She rolled onto her back, and gripped the shooting-hot agony in her chest and moaned. *Get up. Get up.*

After peering in all directions, she crawled on hands and knees feeling her way. Ahead, the solar panels on a pitched roof reflected a sliver of moonlight and beneath she made out a dark building. *The barn.*

With a groan, she pushed to her feet then froze at the sound of footsteps crunching on the gravel path. "Who's there?"

The footfalls stopped, and the chuckle came again. She strained her eyes to search the path behind her but could see no one lurking in the darkness. Pain surged through her ribs, but she forced her legs into action and ran towards the barn. She gasped for air, as she reached the large open door and seeing a tiny fairy light glistening on the other side ran through the centre pathway and barrelled out the other side. She hit something hard and screamed. Someone big and very strong had her arms, and she kicked out using the tips of her boots aiming for the man's shins.

"Em', settle down it's me, Doug. You're safe."

The familiar voice broke through the barrier of fear, and she fell against him gasping.

"What the hell happened?" Doug pulled her to his solid chest and stroked her hair. "Why are you out here alone?"

She couldn't speak and clung to him with relief. With her face buried in his shoulder, she sobbed. Under her cheek, his muscles tensed and his chin rose. He moved his head back and forth as if scanning the immediate area then bent and in one swift movement lifted her into his strong arms.

"I'm taking you back to the homestead." He marched past the toilet block and took the path to the front door. Once inside he carried her to her bedroom and lowered her gently to the ground. "Do you have your key?" A long feral growl escaped his lips the moment he examined her face. "Bloody hell, did someone attack you?"

Emily pushed a hand inside the pocket of her jeans and pulled out the key. She handed it to him with a shake of her head. "N–no. I w–went to see the horses and on the way back the lights w–went out. I heard someone f–following me. I panicked and fell over."

"You have cuts on your cheek that need tending." He took the key from her and opened the door then examined her face with a tender expression. "This is my fault. I shouldn't have left to get changed, but I needed a shower to get rid of Julie's perfume." He opened the door, swung her into his arms and carried her as if she weighed nothing then placed her on the bed. "I'll grab the first aid kit. Are you hurt anywhere else?"

She nodded and rubbed her ribs. "I'm afraid I hurt my ribs and shins but I'm sure nothing is broken."

"I'll call Robbie." Doug reached for his phone and explained the situation in a few words. He pushed the phone back into the carrier on his belt then eyed her critically. "Who do you think was following you?"

She pushed her hair behind both ears and gazed at his concerned face. Her heart gave a little twist. She gathered her thoughts and tried to make sense of what had occurred. "I'm not certain, but someone turned out the lights, so it wasn't a visitor, and apart from footsteps on the gravel, I heard a man chuckle. It made my skin crawl. I thought he was going to attack me." She sucked in deep breaths in an attempt to stop the tears. "I tried to run and fell over the boulders along the path, but then I saw the barn and ran towards it."

"The lights are on a timer and went off at nine to prevent the tourists sneaking into the stables and disturbing the horses." Doug lifted her chin and examined the scratches with tender care. "It must have been one of the ringers playing a joke on you."

Footsteps in the hall heralded Robbie's arrival. He poked his head in the door and frowned at Doug.

"I'll grab my bag. Best you leave and allow Emily to undress so I can examine the damage." He gave Doug a long meaningful stare. "You don't need to be here. Why don't you get back to the dance, I think the redhead is looking for you?"

"I'm staying, and I don't give a damn what the redhead wants, I already told her I have a girlfriend." Doug's fists balled at his waist and electricity sparked between the brothers. He touched her cheek with a feather-like stroke. "You want me here, don't you, Em'?"

His girlfriend? Confused, she gaped up at him. "Yes, I feel safe with you here."

"See?" Doug gave his brother a boyish "I won" grin then turned back to her. "Do you need any help undressing or should I step outside?"

"Ah . . . no. I'll pop into the bathroom. I want to wash my hands and face." She held up her dirt-streaked palms. "Please wait here. I won't be long."

"No worries, I'll be here, love."

Doug considered her sheet-white complexion and waited until she'd closed the bathroom door before turning to Robbie. "Is she in shock?"

"Someone frightened her, but she's not pallid and sweating. I think she will be okay, but I'll give her a full examination then maybe give her something to make her rest. I'll get my bag."

Robbie met his gaze, and a smile twitched at his lips. "*Girlfriend*? So you've staked your claim then?"

Doug straightened, he did not intend to blush in front of Robbie but his cheeks heated in an uncontrollable surge of acute embarrassment. *Damn!* His brother could always humiliate him with a few well-chosen words. "Yeah, it sure looks that way."

"Sweet!" Robbie turned away and strolled down the hallway whistling a tuneless melody.

Twenty minutes after Robbie had banished him from Emily's bedroom, the door finally opened, and his brother waved him inside. His attention went to Emily propped up in bed her eyelids heavy and her gaze slightly unfocused.

"She's fine. A few bumps on her shins and the scratches on her cheek. They'll heal up nicely and won't leave a scar." Robbie slapped him on the back. "It would be best if you sat with her for a while. I'm heading back to the party."

"Will she be able to come with us on the muster?"

"I can't see why not but you'll have to ask her in the morning and if she refuses be gracious." Robbie rubbed his chin. "You *do* know she believes someone was following her out near the stables?"

Doug nodded. "With the suspicion surrounding Mum and Dad's accident, she has serial killers on the mind. When she ran into me, I took a long look behind her and couldn't see anyone lurking around the barn."

"Okay." Robbie smiled. "I'll ask the staff to keep a look out just in case."

Doug turned to speak to Emily, but she had fallen asleep. "I'll make sure she stays with me from now on, and I'll keep her safe."

"See that you do." Robbie picked up his bag and met his gaze. "Grab the spare key to her room, so you can lock her door if you have to leave her alone. Put her key on the bedside table so she can find it." He cleared his throat. "I don't think she has a vivid imagination. I believe someone is causing her strife, for what reason I have no idea but until we get to the bottom of it, I suggest you take what she says very seriously indeed." He turned away and strode from the room closing the door behind him.

Doug sat on the edge of Emily's bed and pushed her spare pillow behind his head. He took her hand and rolled her snug against his shoulder. If she woke, he would be there for her, and if anyone dared to break into her room, he would deal with them, Doug style.

CHAPTER SIXTEEN

Late the next morning, Emily joined Doug in the chopper for a final check on the stock. She tingled with excitement as the chopper landed. As the spotter on the short chopper trip circling over the holding pastures, her job was to make sure none of the cattle had escaped the enclosures. With everything in order, they returned to Winnawarra. Her thoughts turned to waking wrapped in his arms. Seeing how much he cared had been a welcome surprise. Although, the moment she moved, he had offered a mumbled apology for falling asleep with his boots on and left the room. His crumpled and weary appearance had not stopped him from grinning from ear to ear at her before he left.

She went over the horrifying experience from the previous night trying to make sense of everything that had happened. Her ribs ached, but a hot shower put paid to most of the soreness. In fact, she felt rather foolish and wondered if she'd allowed her imagination to run away with her. So many creatures roamed the night, any one of them could have sounded like a man chuckling and if someone *had* wanted to harm her why hadn't they when they had the chance.

"When do we leave?"

"Ah, I'm not sure if you should come on the muster, Em', not after last night. It will be a hard ride. I know you have sore ribs." Doug cut the engine and spoke into the radio informing the air traffic control he had landed.

"I'm fine, yes a bit sore but Robbie told me I'd be okay." She lifted her chin and took in his hesitant expression. He was unusually quiet, and she put his silence down to the concentration needed for the dips and turns necessary during the trip.

"Okay, but I want you to tell me straight away if you're feeling ill." He turned giving her a long considering stare. "We need to talk about last night."

Heat crept into her cheeks, and she dropped her attention to her hands. She expected him to question her sanity after running around like a chicken without a head but wished he'd let the incident drop. She swallowed the lump in her throat and nodded. "Yes, I guess we do."

"When I came home from hospital, apart from being a little crazy, I thought I'd never pull a good-looking woman because of the scar on my face." He rubbed the ragged red line along the side of his jaw. "I kind of went a bit overboard. I drank too much, got into a lot of fights and slept with too many women most of who I don't remember." He cupped her chin in his warm palm and lifted her head to meet his gaze. "I'm not proud of that time. If Ian and Robbie hadn't dragged me back to Winnawarra, I would probably be dead by now. I didn't care, I entered rodeos and rode the toughest bulls in the hope one of them would trample me to death." He dropped his hand.

She took in his troubled expression, and her heart squeezed. She wanted to offer him something, anything to console him. "I gather that's a symptom of PTSD. I'm glad you're feeling better now."

"Well, bad behaviour has consequences, and Julie is one of them." He grimaced and glanced away as if not able to look at her.

Her stomach rolled. This was far too much personal information even though he'd called her his *girlfriend* in front of Robbie. She didn't want to hear about his sexual exploits with the redhead. "Who you shared your affection with is really none of my business, Doug."

"I need to explain because I know I hurt you and even if you tell me it doesn't matter, I owe you the truth." He closed his long work-roughened fingers around her hand. "I met Julie at a dance, and I'd had way too much to drink. I don't remember what happened, but apparently, I told her I loved her, so she came to the muster to see me." He heaved a long sigh. "I didn't sleep with her. The dance with her was to avoid a scene, and I made it very clear I wasn't interested." His deep blue gaze settled on her face. "I have to tell you, I still have the odd flashbacks from my time in Afghanistan, so taking all this into consideration. Will *you* be my girl, Em'? I'll be true and never like the mongrel in England, cross my heart."

She stared at him gobsmacked and tried to breathe to calm her racing heart. Gathering her wits, she moved saliva around her suddenly dry mouth and tried desperately to think of a reply. Of course, she wanted to scream, "Yes! Yes!" but she had to explain her worries to him. "I'm not sure if I could cope with women grinding all over you, or watching you flirting with the tourists — even if it's good for business." She rubbed her temple with an index finger. "I'm afraid I'm the jealous type, and my trust level is sitting just above zero."

"That's my fault. I shouldn't have danced with Julie." He ran the tip of one finger down her cheek in a soft caress. "If you agree, it will be you and me. I *promise*, there will be no flirting and I'll only dance with the old married ladies." His eyes had darkened, and he dropped his lashes moving his attention to her mouth. "We'll take it one day at a time until you trust me."

Oh, my God! He is so out of my league. She could not form words to reply and just nodded her head like an automaton. When his hot lips caressed her mouth, she slipped one hand around him and pulled him closer. His strong arms enclosed her, he deepened the kiss, and she opened to him falling bonelessly into the erotic delirium of the spell woven around her. He moved his hands, caressing her back and used his delicious mouth to drive her crazy with need. The way he nibbled a path down her neck and pushed her tee shirt down to flick his tongue over the top of each breast drove her wild with desire. When he lifted his head and gazed at her with passion, her heart leapt with joy.

"I won't let you down, Em'."

He ran the pad of one calloused thumb over her bottom lip, and she could not resist flicking her tongue out to taste him. She wanted more of his kisses, more of his touch. He sighed and leant back examining her with a gleam in his eye as if he could read her mind. He probably could, being a player in the world of love. Giving herself a mental shake, she smiled. "I guess we'd better get going."

"Yeah, we will if we plan to make the camp before dark." He reached behind him for his black cowboy hat, slid it on his head and grinned at her. "Wait there. I'll come around and lift you down. I don't want you to jar your sore ribs." He jumped down to the ground and bending to avoid the still moving chopper blades ran around to her side. "You go and freshen up, and I'll meet you back here in five minutes."

"Thanks."

A short time later, she followed him to the stables. She could not believe she would be with him twenty-four hours a day for the next entire week. When they returned to Winnawarra, she would have to return to the task of working on the suspected murder investigation. Although, out of her depth in the legal points of view and disturbed by the gruesome images, to some degree the process of eliminating suspects and searching for clues intrigued her. To put aside her accounting skills and concentrate on a new career as part of a detective agency would be an invigorating change and if they could work in the rainy season, the job would not conflict with the running of Winnawarra. She chewed on her bottom lip, and the small action caught Doug's immediate attention.

"What's wrong, love?"

She offered him her best bright "nothing is wrong" smile and shrugged. "Nothing. Will it take us long to catch up with the others?"

"Nah, we'll be there by the time Glady has dinner ready." He waved to one of his men to bring up the horses. "I've packed food for our lunch, and we'll head out via Rainbow Gulley. It's on the way, and I'm anxious to take a look to see where the mining company took core samples. If they've done any damage, there'll be hell to pay." He went to a chalkboard and added the time of their departure to the destination beside their names.

She moved to his side and read down the long list of names. A team leader was responsible for each group of tourists and ringers. "Why is that necessary?"

"To keep track of everyone's movements." Doug cupped his hands and boosted her into the mare's saddle. He mounted his black stallion with ease and smiled. "Team leaders and singles check in to a nominated person. If we don't check in, someone will be out searching for us. Jack is handling the board today, so when we arrive at Rainbow Gulley, I'll call him. When we leave, I'll call him again, and tell him our next stop. He writes our destination and ETA on the board. If we don't check in within two hours, the first thing Jack does is try and call. If we don't reply then they'll send the chopper out." He smiled at her. "We don't take chances at Winnawarra, and if I had my way, everyone working here would have a satellite beacon attached to them." He grinned and with a click of his tongue urged his horse forwards to lead the way out the stable.

They rode in compatible silence across the open plains in an easy pace and headed towards a huge red rock formation in the distance. The confident way Doug sat low in his saddle and moved as if one with his prancing black stallion told her he had ridden most of his life. Unable to take her eyes from his wide shoulders and the bunched muscles trapped beneath his stretched tee shirt, she swallowed hard and allowed her attention to drift to his long legs clad in tight jeans. *Oh my, you are one delicious cowboy.* She smiled into the sunshine. To think that less than a month ago, she had planned to give up men for life and now all she could think about was Doug. Waking up wrapped around his muscular body as if they were lovers and his promise not to stray gave her hope she could trust him with her heart.

Two hours later, the sun had climbed high in the sky, and the ground ahead shimmered in a heat mirage. Vast numbers of kangaroos sat in mobs in the few shady spots, lounging on their sides with their ears flicking at flies while others bounded in groups across the open plains. She sighed with relief as they entered a sheltered gully with a small rock pool so beautiful in its magnificence it astounded her. In this remote place sat a hidden paradise. Tall ferns lined the sandy pathway, and lizards the size of small dogs basked in the sun on massive boulders. The strange trees in the shape of fat bottles intrigued her, and the amount of wildlife astounded her. She pointed towards one of the giant lizards. "I've never seen anything like that before in my life."

"That's a goanna." He smiled at her. "They don't like people very much so keep away from them. Once we climb up the top of the gorge, you will probably see a few Mertens' water monitors, they are much like goannas or monitor lizards but with a longer neck and they usually stick to the water's edge — they won't hurt you. Don't forget there's a lot of snakes too so keep your wits about you and watch your step."

She shuddered. "Is there anything nice here at all?"

He gave her a slow smile, and his blue eyes flashed with mischief.

"You mean apart from me?" He chuckled. "Oh, there are some nice green tree frogs, and once we get to the rock pool, the varieties of birds are pretty spectacular." He pointed to a small wallaby feeding on a green bush. "Then there are the rock wallabies, they're pretty cute, and if we stayed here overnight, you might see a sugar glider."

"What about dingoes, they're like wolves, aren't they?"

"Nah, they're native dogs, but they don't bark like dogs. They will keep their distance most times but they are scavengers, and we don't feed them because it encourages them to hang around the camps. They'll take down calves and raid the chicken coop if we let them." He gave her a long considering stare. "Oh, don't think they'll go hungry and starve, we have a rabbit problem, so they're well catered for."

As they rounded the rock formation, he pointed to mounds of disturbed earth. The dark brown soil stood out against the rust coloured sand. "Bloody hell, that's where they took the samples. Only three boreholes, but they did enough damage the arseholes." He scrubbed a hand over his face. "I'm glad Jock didn't live to see this." He shot her a pleading glance. "We'll have to find out who is behind this desecration of Winnawarra. Some of our land contains sacred sites, and we want to protect them from the outside world."

She squeezed his arm. "I know you do. We'll find out who is behind this, I promise."

"Thanks." He covered her hand. "I'm so glad you came here."

"So am I. Now I understand why Jock wanted to conserve this area at all costs." Her attention moved up a jagged deep orange rock face standing out against a brilliantly clear blue sky. The gulley had the most exotic species of trees and plants she had ever seen in her life. The temperature had dropped considerably in the dappled sunlight, and she shivered. "Wow! This place is amazing. It's so wonderfully cool here in the shade."

"Wait until we climb to the top. We might be able to see the first campsite in the distance, or rather the orange dust cloud from the movement of the cattle." He grinned. "This little pool is nothing. There is a spectacular waterfall on the other side fed by an artesian well. It spills into a deep rock pool then falls down to join the river running past the homestead. We can take a swim there if you like. It's safe, crocs can't climb this high." He dismounted and took a pair of leather straps from his saddlebag. "I'll hobble the horses. They'll be safe here for an hour or so and will appreciate a drink."

She dismounted and unhitched her backpack from the saddle. If he planned to go for a swim, she would need her towel at least and her toiletries. She did not intend to ride in the afternoon heat without her sunblock. Arriving at base camp looking like a lobster was not going to happen. She had not forgotten the jokes about her lily-white skin, and although she now sported a great tan, even burnished skin turned to sunburn in this climate. She flapped her tee shirt to cool her flesh. "Does it get much hotter than this in summer?"

"Oh yeah, we couldn't risk riding this far in summer. The horses would drop dead. The temperature can be another fifteen to twenty degrees higher not to mention the storms. It rains so hard, *when* it rains it's dangerous. The place can flood in minutes." He hitched his backpack over one shoulder and picked up his rifle. "Yell out if you need a rest." He moved up the sandy path.

The walk to the top of the gorge took all her concentration. She followed Doug's steps placing her feet in his footprints and keeping a watchful eye for anything waiting to bite her. A few snakes of the bright green variety moved away, and she noticed a large number of cobwebs hanging like lace curtains between tree branches. She shuddered wondering how big a spider would be to make such huge webs. The sound of rushing water reached her before they made the summit. The path opened into a clearing, and she squinted at the reflection of sunlight on a massive rock pool. The stretch of blue, clear water moved slowly between huge boulders to disappear into what must be the waterfall.

"See the reddish hue in the distance?" Doug pointed to the west. "That's the ringers bringing the cattle down to the first campsite."

"So really the ringers not the tourists move the cattle?" She shielded her eyes and peered into the distance.

"Mostly, but from the first camp, we take a casual pace back to the homestead. So they become involved on the trip back." He removed his sunglasses and smiled at her. "We have to move slowly because of the calves. We don't need to lose any along the way."

"I'm surprised they survive at all in this heat. I can't believe how hot it is on this rock."

"I have the perfect cure for overheating." Doug removed his backpack and dropped it on a rock. "Feel like a swim?"

The idea of submerging her dusty body in the cool, clear water was too good to refuse, but the moving water worried her. "We won't be sucked over the edge, will we?"

"No." He chuckled, and his gaze drifted over her. "You're different to every girl I've brought up here. Most say, 'I haven't got a swimming costume'."

She returned his smile. "And what do you say, Mr. Macgregor?"

"*Mr. Macgregor* is it now?" He pulled her against him and nuzzled her neck. "I say, 'neither have I'. Everyone skinny dips here it's a kind of tradition."

"Hmm, and if I remember you promised me you wouldn't try to jump my bones." She lifted her chin and took in the amusement in his eyes.

"I'm not that kind of guy, Em', but you like kissing me, right?" He pressed small kisses to her neck sending a line of goose bumps marching down both arms.

"Yes, very much." She tipped back her head to give him access and almost purred under his caresses. "You do it so well."

"Well, then get undressed and slip in. I'll turn my back and go over there to undress." He waved towards a rock formation. "I'll call Jack and tell him we've arrived safely." He wandered away leaving her behind a clump of bushes.

Should she? *Why not?* She pulled her tee shirt over her head and disposed of her clothes swiftly then made a dash to the sandy bank and slid into the blissfully cool water. The pool fell away a few paces from the edge, and bitterly cold water hit her heated flesh. Teeth chattering, she swam a few strokes then trod water. The sound of the waterfall was deafening and looking out for Doug, she moved back towards the bank. The next moment he appeared from behind a tree and dived into the pool in a flash of tanned nakedness. He vanished into the depths. When he didn't emerge after some moments, she feared for his safety. She moved slowly towards the last place she'd seen him. Something cold touched her back. Screaming, she turned to see Doug grinning, his dark hair plastered to his face.

"Sorry, love, I didn't mean to scare you." He spread out his arms. "I'll race you to the other side." He took off like a seal moving without a ripple through the water before she had a chance to reply.

She stared after him, conscious of her nakedness then dived beneath the surface enjoying the cool water over her head. Surfacing in deep ice-cold water, she spotted a shadow moving between the boulders. Fearing a dingo, she stared around frantically for Doug. He had reached the far bank and turned to wave at her. She beckoned him, and when he turned and cut through the water at speed towards her, she glanced back to the hillside. The shadow moved again, and by the time Doug had reached her side, she had imagined a great slobbering beast swooping down and eating them.

"What's wrong, love? Is the pool too cold for you?" Doug bounced in the water beside her a concerned expression on his face. "Your lips are turning blue. It's time we dried off I think."

She pointed towards the soaring red rock formation. "I'm sure I saw a shadow moving up there as if something is watching us."

His gaze narrowed and he scanned the area.

"Nah, I can't see anything. It's probably a wallaby they move around, and their shadows look quite big." He smiled and pressed a cold kiss to her cheek. "Off you go, I'll turn my back so you can get out. Not that I don't appreciate watching a wet, curvy woman but I plan on keeping my word." He waved her towards the bank and flicked a shock of black hair from his eyes. "You sure are pretty. I like a natural woman, one who doesn't need layers of makeup to look spectacular."

"You could charm the shoes off a horse." She giggled. "Don't ever stop."

"I don't plan to." He reached for her and lowered his dark head.

With her hard nipples pressed against his smooth chest, his soft lips moulded to her mouth, she rested both hands on his shoulders and enjoyed. No man had ever kissed her like Doug, the way he teased her lips and touched her made her feel beautiful. He broke the kiss and lifted her out of the water, then captured one cold nipple in his hot mouth. She moaned, tipping her head back, wanting more. When he moved to the other breast, she gasped in delight with each flick of his tongue.

"You are so beautiful." Doug kissed each breast then lowered her to take her mouth in a long passionate kiss.

Aching with need, she complained when he broke the kiss and opened her eyes to see him watching her from below his lashes. Trying to gain some form of composure, she smiled at him. "You make me feel beautiful."

"I'm falling in love with you, Em'." He sighed. "Shit, I shouldn't have said the 'L' word, should I?"

She giggled. "Yes, because I'm falling for you too."

"That's a relief. Now get back on dry land before I forget I'm a gentleman." He turned her around and gave her a gentle push towards the bank.

She reached the edge of the pool then turned and true to his word, he had his back to her. "Hmm, a hot cowboy and a gentleman, I must be in heaven."

Hidden behind the bushes, she dried and dressed quickly then reached for her bag. She moved to a rock half in the shade and brushed out her long hair. By the time Doug appeared, she had applied sunblock and made ready to leave.

"Come and eat." He took her backpack and led her into the shade. "We have cake for later too. It's about an hour maybe more to the camp. We'll rest the horses halfway at a waterhole and eat again. Trust me after riding and swimming you will be famished."

"I am." She sat down on his bedroll and dug into the packet of sandwiches. "I've never eaten so much food in my life. If I told my friends in the UK how much I eat they'd never believe me."

"You work hard, so you need more food, we all do." Doug leant back on his elbows and his intent gaze settled on her. "I want to kiss you again so bad, but if I do, I'll get carried away, and we'll be making out all afternoon then we'll never make the campsite by sundown. I don't plan to sleep here overnight. It's not safe."

She swallowed the food in her mouth, and a surge of need rushed over her. Unconsciously she touched her lips. The stroke of his kisses still tingled, and she wanted more but cleared her throat. "Don't you believe I'm capable of stopping you going too far?"

The slow seductive smile tugging at his lips made her nerve endings quiver. She wanted to look away, but his magnetic presence dragged her attention to his mouth. His white teeth flashed, and he chuckled.

"Maybe we'll put that notion to the test soon."

A *crack* from a rifle echoed close by. Terror slammed into her, and she dived behind a rock and crawled under the canopy of boulders. The loud noise made her ears ring, and for some moments, fear immobilised her. Trembling, she edged her way around the boulder. "Doug?"

Silence.

CHAPTER SEVENTEEN

Heart hammering and with every muscle taut with shock, Emily wormed along the ground keeping in the shadows to take a quick peek into the clearing. Nausea hit at the sight before her, and her teeth chattered so hard they hurt. *Oh, my God!* Doug sprawled on the ground with a sheet of blood covering one side of his face and running over one ear to pool in the sand. "Doug. Doug. Wake up!"

He didn't respond, and shadows obscured him. She couldn't see if his chest was moving. Neck stretched to look across the rock pool, she searched the area for the shooter and seeing nothing she inched ahead. The rock by her ear exploded. Pain ricocheted through her as shards of stone shot into her scalp and shoulder. She slumped onto the ground and the peaceful beauty around her crinkled at the edges of her vision.

She tried to breathe, to make sense of what had happened but fear had her by the throat. Agony ripped through her head and her shoulder burned at the slightest attempt to move. Out the corner of one eye, she could see a crimson patch spreading on the ground. *I've been shot.* The information drifted into her mind in a matter-of-fact way as if taking bullets happened to her every day. One part of her mind told her to run, and the other insisted she should fade into blissful oblivion. The memory of Doug covered in blood came back to her in a rush of horror. *Oh, my God, Doug.*

She went for the phone at her waist and came up empty. Damn, she'd left it in the saddlebags with the horses, but Doug had his with him all the time. Trying to push through the shock, she took inventory of body parts, moving toes, legs then arms. Sharp searing pain smashed into her shoulder, and she sobbed in agony then ground her teeth to gain control. Okay, so one arm worked. With care, she edged backwards into the alcove of rocks.

She glanced around. In this position, the boulders would protect her unless the shooter climbed to this side of the gorge. Acutely aware of the minutes ticking by, she remembered how long it had taken them to climb to the top of the gorge. She would have to get to Doug's rifle before the shooter finished the job.

With her jaw clamped against the pain, she pushed into a dizzying sitting position and gingerly touched her head. Dust and gravel fell into her lap. She moved her fingers carefully, she located two shards of stone and pulled them from her scalp. "Bloody hell."

Next, she ran one hand over her shoulder and winced as she hit another splinter. Blood coated her fingers, and the uncontrollable shaking made grasping the slippery rock difficult. She sucked in a deep breath and counted to three then yanked. Red-hot torment sent shudders through her and to her dismay, the sliver refused to move. A wave of giddiness washed over her and fighting the terrifying idea of passing out and being at the gunman's mercy, she shook her head. A voice inside her mind insisted women could survive in situations where men perished. If she planned to live, she must dig deep and use the fear induced adrenaline rush to her advantage.

The image of Doug in a pool of blood slammed into her brain. If he was alive, he needed her. He had no one else so she'd have to woman up and protect him because there was no way she would allow him to bleed to death. Suddenly her mind slotted back into rationality and time seemed to slow. As if an inbuilt instinct to survive kicked her brain into overdrive, she glanced around plotting an alternate course in the shadows towards Doug's position.

She chewed on her bottom lip and moved in the opposite direction keeping to the deepest shadows then wiggled across the sand to circle behind him. She bit down the urge to call out again and pushed on using her good arm to drag her forwards. Something moved close to her face, and she froze biting back a scream. Her heart pounded so hard she thought it might burst through her chest. In the damp shade, a snake slithered by its forked tongue flicking out tasting the ground. She wanted to squeeze her eyes shut, run away, scream, but the overpowering need to help Doug forced her to move.

The snake moved away, and she gasped in a few steadying breaths. Ahead she could make out the top of Doug's head and the pool of congealing blood. Her pulse raced, and her chest tightened with fear. The backpack and rifle would be close by but might as well be a mile away. She peered towards the head of the path, but the only movement came from a flock of brightly coloured birds, hanging upside down to feed from the flowers high in the trees. It had taken her too long to get this far, and the maniac with the gun could be moments away.

With every small movement sending waves of torment down her left arm, she edged closer until she reached the boulder beside Doug. She peered around and gaped at his ashen face, stark against black hair matted with blood. His cowboy hat had fallen from his head and sat upturned near his body. He lay so still, and the sight of his cadaverous appearance unnerved her, but she had to discover if he was alive. She would have to expose part of her body to touch him but keeping as concealed as possible, she reached out and pressed her fingers to his jugular. A strong beat pulsed against her skin.

He was alive.

She prodded him and called his name in an urgent whisper. His eyelids twitched, but he remained as still as death. Not knowing what to do next, she sat back and sucked in a few long breaths. If the gunman had reached the top of the pathway, going into the open would be suicide, but she had to revive Doug. She did a visual search of the area then broke a branch from a bush. She hung Doug's hat from one end, waved the hat over the edge of the rock and waited. When no shots rang out, she ignored the throbbing in her shoulder and belly crawled closer to Doug. She examined him and found a cut across his right temple. The bullet had skimmed his head and knocked him unconscious. *I have to get help.*

She reached for the backpacks then dragged them painfully slowly, one by one into the shelter of the boulder beside him. She searched the pockets for Doug's phone but could not find it. He had called Jack when they arrived, so it had to be here somewhere, perhaps it was on his belt, and he was lying on it. She slipped her hand under him, located the empty phone holder on the clip at his waist. *Damn! Where is the phone?* The rifle was propped against a boulder, and she carefully retrieved it but having no idea how to use a weapon, placed it within reach. Doug's backpack held water, and a substantial first aid kit. With one eye on the path at the top of the gorge, she stared at Doug's motionless body. She needed him alert, or they would die, and no one would find them.

Her own injuries could wait. She used the antiseptic to clean Doug's wound. It had stopped bleeding, and she dabbed at the deep graze with care. She shook him again. "Doug, come on wake up. We can't stay here. He may come back to finish us off. You have to wake up."

If only he would regain consciousness, they could hide behind the rock. Desperation gripped her. In her state, she'd had trouble opening the bottle of antiseptic let alone dragging his heavy body to safety. She shook him again and slapped his face, but he remained unconscious with only the slight rise and fall of his chest as indication of life. In furtive glances, she checked out the area and wished her pulse would stop beating in her ears so she could hear if anyone was coming up the trail. The crushed rocks along the path would make it difficult for anyone to sneak up on her but if the maniac with the rifle marched into the clearing, she would be defenceless.

Maybe not. She hid in the shadows and examined the rifle. If she pointed the weapon at the gunman maybe he would have second thoughts about shooting her. A trickle of blood ran into her eye reminding her of her injuries. The adrenaline rush had numbed the agony for a short time but now the pain throbbed in relentless tandem with her heartbeat. She wiped her face on her shirt and listened intently for the crunch of boots on the gravel trail but heard nothing but birdsong. If she intended to fight, she should tend to her head wounds and take a handful of painkillers, but she would have a long wait before attempting to remove the splinter from her shoulder.

For now, no threat approached her position, so she would take a few precious minutes to wrap a bandage around her head. She could not fight with blood trickling in her eyes. Her attention moved to the backpack, and she noticed something glistened in the sun on the other side of the clearing and recognized Doug's satellite phone, sitting beside his boots. After a long look at the pathway, she pushed to her feet and grabbing the rifle dashed across the clearing. She scooped up the phone then hid in the bushes and searched the contacts for Jack's number. Cursing her trembling fingers, she found the number and pressed connect.

"Are you leaving Rainbow Gully already?" A man's voice came through the earpiece.

"Jack, this is Emily. We are at the top of the gorge. Doug has been shot. There's a maniac up here, send help."

"Are you on the top of Rainbow Gully? How bad is he can you put him on?"

Exasperated by his nonchalance, she grit her teeth. "He's unconscious. Stop wasting time, or you'll find two corpses up here. I'll contact Robbie. Send out a chopper, anything, and hurry."

"Right you are." Jack hung up.

She stared at the phone and tears threatened to spill. Through blurred vision, she located Robbie's number and called him to explain the situation but before he had time to reply she heard the sound of boots crunching on the gravel path. "God help us, he's here."

"Don't hang up. I'll get a chopper, and I'll be there as soon as possible." Robbie's anxious voice did nothing to calm her. *"Don't hang up."*

She placed the phone on the ground beside her, she lifted the rifle. The heavy weapon dragged at her sore shoulder, and she gasped at the burn. Words like, "safety" and "kickback" ran through her mind from watching old cowboy movies. What chance would she have to fire the damn thing let alone hit someone?

The footsteps grew louder making the hair on the back of her neck stand to attention. The walk was in confident long strides, and she shrank back trying to control her breathing before her wheezing gave away her position. The birds fell silent as if they recognised the threat entering the clearing and then she saw him.

Johnno.

When he glanced around, Emily held her breath hoping he could not see her. The metal tips of his boots glistened in the sunlight, and his spurs jingled with each chilling step. As he moved past, she let her breath out very slowly but when he raised his rifle and aimed at Doug's prone body self-preservation fled. "D–don't you d–dare shoot him."

Johnno lowered his rifle and turned with a smirk on his face to look at her in amusement.

"Oh, darling, I thought you were dead. Never mind. I have plenty of time to kill you." He licked his lips. "But first, we'll have some fun."

Anger rushed through her like a hurricane of mad. "You bastard."

A torrent of anger welling up inside her burst. She let out a banshee's scream, raised the heavy rifle above her head, and charged at him. Using all the strength she possessed, she swung the rifle at his head. A flash blinded her, and the kick from the discharged weapon threw her on her back. She blinked rapidly and gasping for air, rolled on her side in time to see Johnno stagger to the edge of the gully and tumble gracefully over the edge. The soft thump of his body hitting the rocks filled her with a grotesque relief. She ignored the screaming noise in her head and the red-hot agony in her shoulder, and crawled sobbing towards Doug and fell over his chest.

When his arm came around her back, she lifted her aching head and stared at him. "Oh, thank God." She could not control the tears of relief at seeing him awake. "How do you feel?"

"What in God's name happened? My head is killing me, and you have blood all over your face. Was it a rock fall?" Doug eased her from his chest examining her face critically. "Bloody hell, you have a piece of rock as thick as my finger sticking out your back. Oh shit, the world is spinning." He sat up slowly, then turned away and vomited on the ground.

"Johnno shot you."

"Johnno? Why would he try and shoot me?" He scanned the bushes. "Where is he?"

She dashed at her eyes then pointed. "Over there. I think I killed him."

"You what?"

Emily shuddered. "The gun went off when I tried to hit him over the head with it."

Doug patted the ground next to him and smiled. "Tell me what happened. Take it nice and slow."

She recounted the incident and Doug turned to examine the boulder behind him.

"My guess is when the rifle went off the bullet ricocheted and hit him. Where did he fall?"

She wished her teeth would stop chattering and waved in the general direction. "He staggered that way then disappeared. I think I heard him hit the ground, but my ears are ringing so loud I could have been mistaken."

"It's not a long drop on that side, so he may be alive. There is a plateau and a walkway below. I'll check him as soon as I can stand." He touched her face then used his warm fingers to wipe away her tears. "It's going to be okay, but we'll need to call for help."

Emily sucked in a long breath. "I called Robbie. He's on his way."

"Thank God." Doug waved towards the backpacks. "Can you reach the first aid box? I will need to look at your head and try to pull that spike out of your back. Where is my phone?"

"I'll get it, stay here." She struggled to stand and staggered to the bushes. After retrieving the phone, she pressed it to her ear. "Are you still there, Robbie?"

"Yes. I heard everything. Hang tight, my ETA is ten minutes." The phone went dead, and she handed it to Doug. "Robbie will be here soon. I called him straight away."

"I'm so proud of you. Let me take a look at you. Unless you'd rather wait for Robbie?"

She sat before him and tried to prepare for the agony to come by taking deep breaths. "No, it's fine you do—"

Behind her, Doug cursed and sprang to his feet. She turned to look up at him, but his deadpan ice-cold expression froze her words. He had changed in an instant, and she did not recognise the empty-eyed man standing feet apart in a fighting stance. The grass rustled a few feet from them, and she turned in horror to gape at Johnno staggering through the bushes, hunting knife in hand.

"How sweet." Johnno glared at her, his thin lips twisting with menace. "That bitch tried to kill me, boss." He waved the hand with the knife towards a wound in the top of his left arm. "What are you going to do about her? You need to make sure she doesn't inherit Winnawarra. We can play with her a bit then toss her over the waterfall. No one will hear her from up here." He licked his lips and grinned. "The crocs will cover any evidence, and I'll be your witness to say she swum too close to the edge." His gaze went to Doug, and he lifted both eyebrows in question. "I'll let you go first."

Oh, my God, Johnno murdered Doug's parents. The sick realisation crept into her mind like a flickering 1930's mono silent horror movie chilling her to the bone. Johnno had been in every location the murders had occurred and had access to their belongings, but his motive remained a mystery.

She forced her attention back to Doug. His handsome features had formed an unreadable mask, and his deep blue eyes had hardened into unseeing sapphire orbs. The man who had held her so gently and promised to protect her had left the building and in his place stood a trained killer.

Inside her head she screamed, but dread grabbed her throat, and the sound came out in a wheeze. Trapped in a dream-like state of shock, her legs refused to move, and gasping for air, she wormed her way into a fissure in the rock face then turned to face the men. Whatever happened she would fight until her last breath.

Johnno lurched towards her, a sickly grin on his face.

"Cat got your tongue, boss?"

She caught a flash of movement and Doug had Johnno on his knees with one arm twisted behind his back. The knife dropped to the ground and spun slowly in the red soil the tip moving in her direction like a marker on a wheel of fortune. Doug lifted his arm and in one sickening punch drove his huge fist into the back of Johnno's head then stood back as the unconscious man fell on his face. Ignoring her, he removed the carry strap from the rifle and hog-tied Johnno's hands and feet. Terrified and sick to the stomach, Emily stared at him.

Doug fought to push his head back into the now. When Johnno advanced with a knife, he triggered a flashback so powerful he'd been sent back in the hot shimmering desert, guns blazing and the smell of blood in his nose. His programmed instinct to survive against all the odds had kicked in and blocked out emotion. The doctors instructed him not to dwell on the enemies he'd killed or the fact they were men, human beings like him with families and people who loved them but he would never forget. He remembered the faces of every man he had killed in battle. Their sightless eyes never left his dreams.

He shook his head to clear the images from his disorientated mind and gazed down at Johnno wondering why he was hog-tied and bloody. Spotting the knife with Johnno's initials, he figured something bad had happened.

Emily's ashen face flashed into his mind and the events of the day drifted back into place. A roar of fear clenched his gut, and he spun around to look for her. He had probably frightened the hell out of her during his flashback. The last one had put the fear of God into his brothers, so it had not been pretty, and Emily's confidence in him would be shattered beyond repair. A shadow moved close by, and he lowered his voice into what he hoped would be a coaxing tone. "Emily, where are you? I had a flashback, but I'm okay now."

He hardly recognised the scratchy voice coming from his throat and coughed. The movement sent a wave of nauseous pain into his temple. "Oh Jeez, Em', I hope you're okay because I feel like shit. Did someone hit me on the head?"

"Doug?" Emily's pale blood-splattered face peered around a boulder. "Are you okay?"

He went to her in four paces, lifted her stiff resisting body into his arms, and she cried out in pain. With a gentle touch, he carried her to a rock shelf and sat down. He stared at her face, and the petrified expression in her eyes startled him. Dear God, she was terrified of him. *Did I hurt her? Oh, please God, no.* "You're hurt. What happened, Em', I had a flashback. Everything is kind of fuzzy after we had a swim."

She gazed up at him, eyes brimming with tears and shook her head as if unable to speak. He heard a chopper circling overhead and by the sound of the motor it had landed. "Did you call someone?"

"R–Robbie."

He stroked the damp hair from her eyes. "It's okay. It sounds like he is coming. You're safe now, love."

"J–Johnno tried to kill us, and I thought you were dead—" She gasped and shook so much her teeth chattered.

He brushed a kiss on her cheek. "Don't try to speak. You can tell me later when we're home."

His phone rang, and he balanced Emily on one arm to answer. Robbie's voice came through the speaker.

"Thank God you're conscious. Where are you?"

Doug sighed with relief. "I'm fine. We're on top, in the clearing by the rock pool. Bring your med kit, Emily is injured, and Johnno isn't looking too good either, but I gather he deserved it. I hope you brought help."

"Yeah, I did. We're on our way."

CHAPTER EIGHTEEN

The next half hour seemed to move in slow motion while they waited for the men to climb to the top of the ranges. Emily, wrapped in towels to stop her going into shock waited for Doug to call the police and explain the situation. He dropped onto the sand beside her and gave her a worried stare.

"They've dispatched a police chopper to meet us at Winnawarra." Doug flicked a glance at Johnno, who had regained consciousness and was scowling up at him. "You have a lot of explaining to do, mate."

"I'm not your mate." Johnno turned his face away and snorted sending up a puff of sand by his nose. "You don't know me at all, do you?"

Emily glared at him. "We know you tried to kill us and I bet I will be able to tie you in with Jamie's accident."

"I should have killed you when I had the chance." Johnno turned to face her. "Meddling little bitch."

"Watch your mouth." Doug started to rise, and Emily put a hand on his arm.

"Don't waste your energy with him." She examined Doug's face and frowned. "How are you doing?"

"Me?" Doug took her hand and linked fingers. "I'm good, you though look like shit." He glanced at the entrance to the clearing and let out a long sigh. "Thank God, there's Robbie."

After an examination, Robbie decided Emily would require an X-ray before removal of the shard from her shoulder. She accepted the offer of a pain relieving injection, and they made their way down the ravine with the ringers in charge of Johnno. At the bottom, Doug sent his men back to Winnawarra with their horses and loaded Johnno into the chopper.

Emily sank into the seat oblivious to pain. With Robbie at the controls and Doug in the seat behind to keep an eye on Johnno, they headed for the homestead. With a large white dressing on his temple and a bruise forming under one eye, Doug's expression was grim. When he spoke, she could hear him clearly through her earphones over the noise of the engine.

"Why did you try to kill us, Johnno?"

Emily turned in her seat. She did not intend to miss his explanation. "Yes, I'd like to know that too."

"What a bunch of wankers." Johnno shook his head and looked away. "I'm ashamed to have your blood running through my veins. None of you deserve Winnawarra."

"What the hell do you mean by that?" Doug glared at him, and the nerve in his cheek twitched with annoyance. "You're not a relative."

"That's where you're wrong." Johnno turned to scowl at him. "My mother was Annie Brewster. Does the name ring a bell?"

"Nah. The only Brewster I know is the accountant." Doug rolled his shoulders in an agitated move, but his attention remained on his prisoner. "There's no one with the name 'Brewster' in our family tree."

"Oh, yes there is." Johnno snorted then chuckled as if he did not have a care in the world.

Emily stared at him wondering if he was exhibiting the unfeeling persona of a psychopath. He flicked a cold, unemotional glance her way and her flesh pebbled.

"My mother worked on Winnawarra as a Jillaroo when she was about sixteen, that's how she knew Jock. After her parents died, her brother sent her to the UK to live with relatives. That's when my uncle set up the accounting firm in Broome." Johnno shrugged then shot Doug a look of pure hatred. "That was around the time Jock's wife died, and he went on this jaunt around the world. He ran into my mother and took advantage of a young woman alone, and I'm the result." He lifted his chin belligerently. "Before she died, I promised to get even for Jock leaving her to bring me up in shame. I came back here and waited. Yeah, I waited so damn patiently, saying 'yes boss, no boss' to my own father then taking shit from the three of you." He gave them a savage smile. "You should be calling me 'boss' boys. I'm your uncle."

"Bullshit!" Robbie manoeuvred the chopper over a rocky outcrop. "Your name is John Williamson, not Brewster."

"That's what I call myself, but my name is John William Macgregor, and Jock is named on my birth certificate as my father." Johnno's lips twitched as if he had just delivered the punchline to a joke. "I couldn't give you my real name now, could I?"

Emily needed more information and fought the painkiller fuzziness to question him. "Did you kill Jock?"

Johnno gave her a long stare as if weighing up his reply. "Well, darlin', what do *you* think? You are so damn good at solving mysteries."

Emily shuddered and tried to push words over the lump in her throat. Having Johnno so close frightened her. She dragged a dry tongue over cracked lips. "I *know* you tried to kill me and Doug so, *yes*, I do believe you're capable of murder."

"I had a good reason. Jock treated me no better than a dog. I could never be the son he doted on. He treated Jamie as if he'd crawled out of God's arse. Killing him and Jenny was the best thing I've done in my life." Johnno moved around in the seat and his gaze flicked to the cabin door.

She caught the flash of pure evil in his eyes and flinched. "I'll do everything I can to make sure you're put away for a very long time, and I'm sure I will find evidence to implicate you in both murders."

"It will never happen. I'm far from getting even with the Macgregor brothers." Johnno unlocked his seat belt, laughed in a maniacal chuckle and launched towards the opening of the cabin. "If I'm going down for murder you're all coming straight to hell with me."

"What do you think you're doing? Have you lost your mind, you'll kill us all." Doug moved to grab him but trapped in the seat belt Johnno easily slipped his grasp.

"That's the plan. For a military bloke you're not that smart, are you?"

To her horror, Johnno gripped the handle inside the cabin and lowered his feet to the skid. His headphones ripped from the plug, and although his mouth moved, she couldn't hear him over the noise of the rotor blades. With his weight on the right landing leg of the chopper, he bounced up and down, his face twisted in a horrific grin. As the chopper lurched under his assault, terror gripped her and pain shot through every nerve ending in her damaged shoulder. "*Aaaarh.*"

The beautiful scenery blurred into a mass of colour as Robbie fought to keep control of the bucking chopper. Hot dusty wind rushed into the cabin swirling her hair over her eyes. *We're all going to die.*

"For Christ's sake, get back inside." Doug unlatched his seat belt and wiggled across the back seat on his stomach to peer down at Johnno.

Stiff with fear, she faced forwards unable to watch Doug's heroics behind her. As the horizon tilted back and forth in a sickening haze of orange and green, she gripped the seat convinced the chopper would crash. When Robbie's controlled voice came through the earpiece like a calming balm, she gazed at him.

"It's going to be okay. Johnno thinks he can bring us down, but he has no chance. It's going to be a rough ride, but I've been through worse." Robbie flicked a glance at her. "This baby has plenty of power to get us out of trouble."

The engines roared, and the chopper tilted sharply making a sweeping turn but rather than landing, Robbie took the bird higher. She chanced a look over one shoulder to see Doug laying across the back seat, hair whipping in the wind with a death grip on Johnno's wrist.

"The lunatic is doing everything he can to make us crash." Doug's voice came out in a grunt of effort. "I can't hold him much longer."

"Let him go and get back into your seat. You're only making things worse." Robbie's voice boomed through the earpiece. "Strap in. I'm going to try and land her on Devil's Peak before the idiot falls and breaks his stupid neck."

Emily stared in horror at the wall of red rock directly in front of them. The chopper spun then swayed and tilted to one side as Robbie wrestled with the controls with the calm expertise of a veteran. The chopper jerked wildly, and the craft came so close to the rock face, she fought to breathe. As the plateau came into view, the pitching stopped, and the chopper straightened hovering close to a flat mountain peak. Through the headphones came Doug's voice in a string of curses then he let out a long sigh.

"We don't have to worry about Johnno anymore." His voice dropped into a serious tone. "He jumped and could not have survived the fall."

Bile rushed up the back of Emily's throat, and she gagged. *He jumped. Oh. My. God.*

"Bloody fool." Doug peered out the window. "Log the coordinates with Search and Rescue then head home."

"Roger that. I'll do a sweep by to make sure." Robbie spoke into the radio explaining the situation then turned to her. "Eyes front, Emily, some things you don't need to see." He took the chopper in a slow turn down towards the valley then headed west. "We'll be home in ten minutes. How are you holding up?"

Pain shuddered through her. She leant back in the seat and closed her eyes. Rather than sickened by Johnno's suicide, she felt numb. "I've been better."

"I'll have your shoulder X-rayed the moment we get home." Robbie's soothing voice came through her headset as if watching a man fall to his death happened every day. "You'll be fixed up in no time."

She wanted to run away and hide. Her mind refused to allow her to shut out the last terrifying hour and replayed each detail in slow motion like reruns of a bad horror movie with her in the lead role. In an effort to move her thoughts on to another topic, she turned carefully in her seat to look at Doug. The pain in her shoulder had calmed a little, but any movement sent flames of agony searing down one arm. "What about Ian? He'll want to know what's happened."

"I told Jack to send a chopper for him, and I've arranged for some of the hands to take over the tourist groups. They'll be safe enough with twenty men with rifles keeping an eye on them." Doug smiled at her. "The other chopper should be home by now."

Emily frowned. "What about the muster?"

"It practically runs itself." Doug reached out to squeeze her hand. "The crew have done this many times before. They won't miss us." His concerned gaze moved over her. "Right now, my priority is making sure you're okay." He shook his head. "I wanted our date to be memorable but this memory we don't need."

She grimaced and leant back in her chair. "Trust me. This is one date I'll never forget."

* * * *

The following afternoon, Doug sat on the edge of Emily's bed regarding her with bemusement. The girl was feisty and keeping her in bed resting would be as impossible as toilet training a bull. "The cops are back again. Apparently, they plan to search Johnno's room first, and now you're feeling better they'll be taking statements about what happened at Rainbow Gulley and in the chopper."

"Okay. Ian dropped by to tell me the cops emailed the airline passenger lists we requested. I should be going over the police reports from your parents' accident and Jock's fall again to see if they can tie Johnno into the murders." Emily gave him a belligerent look. "It's not fair. I have to sit here doing nothing when I'm perfectly fine. Have they said anything to you about Johnno being involved?"

"No, not a word." He took her hand and brushed a kiss over her fingertips. "Right now you have to wait here. You can't get involved, love."

"Why the hell not?" Anger flashed in her eyes, and he bit back a smile.

"Em', in case it slipped your mind, Johnno tried to murder us, and we just happened to be in the chopper when he committed suicide." Doug cleared his throat. "You also have to inform the cops about the stalker."

"Yes, but it's hard to believe it was Johnno stalking me." Emily swallowed. "He tried to scare me off, just like we thought."

"Obviously, and the cops know you're my girlfriend and might believe we had it in for him. They only have our word to say he committed suicide by jumping out the chopper. For all the cops know, we pushed him to his death." He sighed. "Especially if you start blaming him for my family's deaths too."

"That's not fair. I didn't try to pin anything on him." She let out a long weary sigh and flicked a lock of blonde hair over one shoulder. "It's a bit late for the cops to take statements from us now. We could have killed him and made up the suicide story." She gave a little snort of disgust. "They should have kept us apart and questioned us separately."

He squeezed her hand and frowned. "That would have been a bit difficult with us all in the chopper when it happened. Let's face it we could have easily made up a story before we called in the suicide. Although, I'm sure Robbie's name is above reproach in the district and I don't have a criminal record so why would the cops doubt our word?" He wiggled his eyebrows at her. "*Unless* you're a black widow or something?"

"Oh doh!" She slapped his arm. "I saved *you*, didn't I?"

A knock on the door stopped the conversation, and Doug turned to see Ian. His brother's pale expression had him on his feet. "What's happened now?"

"You need to come to the kitchen." Ian gripped the door frame with both hands as if for support. "The cops have found something in Johnno's things, and they need to speak to us." He turned his attention to Emily. "You'd better come too."

Emily threw back the covers. "I'll be right behind you."

She closed the door and discarded her nightgown then dressed. Hurrying down the passageway, she met Robbie. "What's happening?"

"I checked out Johnno's whereabouts at the time of the accidents. He was in Darwin when Jamie died but nothing so far on his movements around the time of Jock's accident." He held up a sheaf of papers. "I informed Detective Standish and brought him up to date. After what Johnno said in the chopper, it's reasonable to believe he could have been involved in our parents' and Jock's deaths.

"Detective Standish has a team here searching Johnno's belongings." Robbie shrugged. "I guess they found something."

A sombre mood met them in the kitchen. The brothers with expressions of dread gaped down at the long kitchen table. Detective Standish waved Emily forwards, and they edged closer. In the centre of the table sat a small wooden box.

"Good, you're all present." Detective Standish turned to his constable. "Record the findings, Smith." He turned his attention to the drawn expressions of the men. "I've found a few items, one of which I think belongs to Jock. I've seen him with one similar many a time." He donned a pair of latex gloves then lifted the lid. "I need confirmation this porcelain rabbit's foot belonged to Jock. He had it hanging from his keys if I remember. It's not like any rabbit's foot I've seen before." He held up the figurine.

"It's Jock's." Doug's expression had changed into a blank mask and Emily moved to his side taking his hand. His mouth turned down at the corners, and a shudder went through him. "Our grandmother made it for him, and he treasured it. I know it was with him in Perth because I remember seeing it when he visited me in the hospital." He lifted his chin and stared blankly at Detective Standish. "How did Johnno get hold of it?"

"It seems Johnno liked to keep trophies." Detective Standish grimaced. "It is the classic behaviour of a serial killer."

"Wait just a minute." Ian held up his hand to stop the conversation. "What do you mean by 'serial killer' are you saying a monster has been living at Winnawarra for the last four years?"

Emily's heart raced, and she gripped Doug's hand waiting for Detective Standish's reply. *A serial killer?*

Detective Standish dropped his gaze to the box, and his shoulders slumped as if the subject weighed heavy.

"From the evidence we've discovered, I think Johnno was a busy boy." He hesitated, and his hand trembled slightly as he reached inside the box again then held up a locket.

The moans of disbelief from the three brothers made Emily's heart ache. Beside her, tremors ripped through Doug, and his chest heaved. He removed his hand from her grip, slipped it around her shoulders, and pulled her close against his side. She hugged him and waited for the axe to fall. Doug was losing it big time, and she had to keep him stable.

"That belongs to our mother. She never removed it not even when she showered. It contains photographs of us as babies." Robbie took the pair of latex gloves Detective Standish offered him and pulled them on before examining the necklace. "Yes, I can confirm it was my mother's." His face drained of colour and he turned to look at her. "This puts him at the scene of the accident, doesn't it?"

"I'm afraid so." Emily squeezed his arm. "I'm so sorry."

Detective Standish cleared his throat with authority, and everyone moved their attention back in his direction.

"After discovering your father's driver's licence had survived unscathed from the fire I had it dusted for fingerprints. They came up as a match for Johnno. Luckily he was in the database for a drunk and disorderly charge, but as he had access to your parents' property after they died, it was plausible to believe he'd snooped through their things before he stored them. So we had reason to discount him as a suspect." He raised his chin and took a deep breath. "There's more, you'll have to see. He took photographs of the crime scene with his phone." He reached into the box and removed a phone, a belt buckle with the initials, JM, a number of pairs of panties, a women's wristwatch and a necklace with gold capital R."

"That's my dad's belt buckle." Ian's voice quivered a little, and his Adam's apple moved rapidly up and down. "I don't recognise any of the other items."

"I do." Doug's face paled. "Sally Miller gave me that wristwatch to keep in the safe during the muster. It was her mother's. I gave it back to her when she left. The gold chain belonged to Rosa Mortisse." He flicked a worried look at Emily. "I can't believe we had a serial killer living here."

"Obviously, your parents weren't his only victims, and he was your stalker, Miss Perkins." Detective Standish held the phone and flipped through the photographs.

Emily stared at him in disbelief. "You have proof?"

"Yes." The detective narrowed his gaze. "I'm warning you, you'll need a strong stomach if you plan to look at the entire file."

"Just show me the one concerning me for now."

Emily stared at the images of her sleeping and bile rushed up the back of her throat. She bit back a gasp of despair and covered her mouth. When Doug turned her around and buried her face in his chest, she closed her eyes to shut out the horror. She had escaped Johnno by the skin of her teeth. Gathering her thoughts, she lifted her head. "Johnno told us he was Jock's son and planned to inherit Winnawarra. He mentioned Mr. Brewster, the accountant, was his uncle. Do you think he is involved?"

"That remains to be seen, and I've already been advised of the connection." Detective Standish cleared his throat. "Brewster is in custody being questioned. I'll contact the station shortly." He let out a long-suffering sigh. "It may come out that Jock was right about him after all."

She glanced up at Doug's face. His eyes had filled with unshed tears, but he held his head high.

"I've never believed Jock fell down those damn stairs." Doug shook his head slowly. "I wish Johnno was alive. I'd tear him apart with my bare hands." He glared at Detective Standish. "Why the hell didn't you believe Jock about my parents' murder?"

"There was no evidence of foul play." Detective Standish opened his hands wide. "I'm sorry, but I have to go on the coroner's verdict."

Doug's full mouth turned down at the edges, and a frustrated growl came from deep in his chest.

"Until now. Call the station. We have a right to know if Brewster was involved, and I want to know what he has to say for himself."

"He is the least of my worries." Detective Standish straightened and gave the items on the table a sweeping look. "I'm hoping Miss Perkins will give me her opinion."

Emily prayed Doug would not explode and held him tight. He stiffened in her arms every muscle on high alert and ready to spring. She went on tiptoes and dropped her voice to a whisper. "Hold on for just a few moments longer."

"It won't make any difference what conclusion you offer." Doug closed his eyes, and his expression of anguish tore at her heart. "He'll never pay for what he's done. I hope he rots in hell."

She turned to Detective Standish. "Right now, I don't have any conclusions."

Doug held Emily's trembling body close to his chest and bathed in the glow of her comfort. She kept him sane and right now, if she let go he would shatter into a million pieces. He clamped his jaw shut to prevent anger bursting out. He had never suspected anything was wrong until Jock died. Johnno had been a reliable worker albeit a wolf in sheep's clothing when it came to women. He should have recognised something was wrong with him. After all, he had trained to pick up unusual behaviour. *I've been such a damn fool. I didn't deserve to survive the crash. I'm not capable to look after myself let alone care for Emily and run Winnawarra.*

As if she'd read his thoughts, Emily lifted her soft blue gaze and frowned at him.

"I hope you're not blaming yourself for this? First, you didn't live here when Johnno went psycho, and secondly, after he started stalking me, I couldn't identify him." She let out an exasperated sigh. "None of us thought he was capable of murder."

"I can't believe he murdered Jock as well. He treated him like a son." Doug sighed. "I had no idea he hated us all so much." He pushed his hands into the front pockets of his jeans. "What else do you need to prove Johnno murdered my parents and Jock? You obviously have photographs you're not showing us."

"Not of Jock, no." Detective Standish pulled on one ear as if trying to remember something important. "We have proof Johnno arrived in Broome from Perth. He took the red-eye back the night Jock died. We don't have an exact time of death for Jock. According to the Winnawarra flight records, Jock flew Johnno to Broome three days before he died. We can put Johnno in Perth before Jock's death, but we can't prove he was in the same suburb so unless he had an accomplice we have no idea how Jock's rabbit's foot came into his possession."

"We still have a lot of records to look through, so we'll keep checking his name against the passenger lists." Emily scratched her head and sighed. "I guess we'd better check the lists for Mr. Brewster as well." She shot a look at Standish. "Can we get both men's credit card records? If we can prove Johnno was in the area, we'll have proof."

"Yes, Johnno's won't be a problem, but we'll need a court order for Brewster's unless he gives his permission. I'll get my sergeant onto that straight away. Right you are then." Detective Standish collected up the evidence and placed it back into the box. "I'll take your statements and get back to the station. I'll call Doug later to keep you informed." He took a large notepad out of a briefcase by his feet and sat down at the table. "Who wants to go first?"

CHAPTER NINETEEN

After dinner, Doug remained at the table and pulled Emily onto his lap. He wrapped one arm around her and stared in bewilderment at the pile of documents she had dropped onto the table. He reached for his coffee, but nothing would stop his stomach churning or the taste of bile in the back of his throat. Getting his mind around the fact Johnno had murdered his family would take some time. To think his parents had taken him off the damn street and treated him like a son. He thought back to when Johnno arrived. Now in hindsight, his arrival had been opportunistic considering he and his brothers were away at the time. No doubt, Mr. Brewster had greased his way using his friendship with Jock to get Johnno the position of assistant manager. His parents would have missed their sons and taking in strays was one of his mother's downfalls. She had a huge heart and never turned away a man prepared to do an honest day's work, but with Johnno, it had been different. He worked alongside them daily and was a trusted member of the staff. Yes, Johnno had ingratiated himself into his parents' and Jock's trust then murdered them. *I know he murdered Jock. If it takes forever, I'll find out the truth.*

He sipped his drink, glad to have Emily's comforting heat against his chest. He loved her, he had no doubt, and she completed him in so many ways. He wondered if she would ever be confident enough to become his wife. Perhaps when life got back to normal, and she started the detective agency, she'd be happy for him to move their relationship to the next level.

"What are you thinking?" Emily turned to look at him. "Have you remembered anything relevant?"

"Not really." He placed his mug on the table and sighed. "No doubt the forensic team will keep the case tied up forever."

"I was thinking." Emily ran the tip of one finger around the top of her cup. "Does every member of your family keep a journal? Is it sort of a tradition?"

"Yeah, we all keep them." Robbie's chair scraped as he pushed it back to stand. "Although, we're a bit lazy at completing them regularly we have bound volumes with our names on each year." He brought the coffee pot to the table and refilled the mugs. "Why?"

An image of Johnno scribbling in a book flashed into Doug's mind. He swallowed hard and tried to remember exactly what he had seen. "Oh, shit. If Johnno thought he was our uncle, do you think he kept a diary too? I can remember seeing him writing in a fancy book just before you arrived." He glanced at Ian sifting through documents on the table and cleared his throat to get his attention. "Do you remember Detective Standish finding a diary in Johnno's personal effects?"

"Can't say that I do." Ian sipped his coffee. "I'm sure Detective Standish would have mentioned if he'd found anything of the sort. A diary would be very significant."

"Which means, he may have it hidden somewhere close at hand." Emily glanced around the faces at the table. "Any ideas *where* he may have hidden it? I'm sure you know every nook and cranny in Winnawarra."

"Up to the time Emily arrived, he had access to all areas." Ian scrubbed both hands down his face then shook his head like a wet dog. "It could be anywhere."

"Not likely." Emily drummed her fingers on the table and stared into space. "He believed he had the same rights as you, so where do you keep yours?" She turned to smile at Ian. "In Jock's office, right? I've seen the bookcases stuffed full of journals, all leather bound with names on the spine. It makes sense he would keep it in there, hidden maybe but it was his symbol of belonging to the family."

"You went through the journals, well my parents' and Jock's." Doug squeezed her gently. "Did you notice anything out of order?"

"No, but I wasn't looking." Emily chewed on her bottom lip. "I had enough problems reading Jock's diary let alone snooping through all the shelves."

Doug rubbed his chin, trying to bring the image of Johnno writing at Jock's desk. He'd thought nothing of seeing him in the room. It was an office, and Johnno did order supplies, so it had not seemed out of place. The memory slipped back into focus. "The book had a black cover with gold lettering. I remember when I spoke to him he shut the book."

"That's a start." Emily smiled at him. "Why don't we go and take a look in Jock's office. Robbie and Ian can keep going through these documents."

Ian shook his dark head and waved one hand absently towards the window.

"I'll go and speak to Brian. He might remember seeing Johnno with the book, especially during the time they moved from here into the bunkhouse." He pushed to his feet then strode towards the door.

"I can look on my own if you'd prefer." Emily slipped off Doug's lap and touched his shoulder. "Unless you'd rather help here?"

"I'm fine." He stood and laced his fingers with hers. "If it's in Jock's office we'll find it."

After searching for two hours, Emily dropped into Jock's office chair and sighed with defeat. "Well, it's not in here."

"I've even checked for loose floorboards." Doug stretched and let out a big yawn. "It's late. I guess we'd better get some sleep. I'll tell the others to call it a night. The diary will still be here tomorrow." He cast a concerned look in her direction. "You should be taking it easy, Em'. I think you've been through enough since you arrived here and your shoulder hasn't had time to heal."

She gaped at him. "I'm fine, my shoulder hardly hurts at all, and I'm part of the team."

"Okay, no worries, love." Doug held out his hand to her. "Come outside for a walk in the moonlight with me." He lowered his dark lashes and heat rushed into her cheeks. "We both need time to unwind before we hit the sack."

"I'd like that very much." She took his hand and walked with him to the cool veranda. "It's such a shame Johnno ruined the beauty of this place. It is so peaceful in the moonlight."

"This land is ancient with a tribal tradition instilled in every grain of sand. If you asked the mobs that live here, they'd tell you that one bad man is not able to unbalance the beauty of nature. Winnawarra goes through time like changes in the seasons, each one seeing death and rebirth every year. The land continues, and nothing can steal its beauty. We're only passengers on a very short ride and here to ensure it remains untouched." He pulled her into his arms. "Like you, Em', you can't allow one man to destroy your life." He nuzzled her neck sending goose bumps down both of her arms. "Give me the chance to make you happy."

Her eye's misted, and she found it hard to catch her breath, he spoke so beautifully, and his accent slid over her like warm honey. With her arms wrapped around his waist, she leant back to look at him. "I've already said I'd be your girl. It's only been a couple of days since you asked me, Doug."

"I need you, Em', as in *forever*. I want to take care of you." He lowered his head, and his warm, dry lips caressed her mouth. He licked a path along her chin and moaned. "Stay with me tonight. I don't want to be alone." He lowered his head, and his long tender kisses demanded a reply.

She melted against him, lost in him. He stroked her back and kissed a path up her neck to nibble at her earlobe. Falling in love had not been in her game plan, but he'd attracted her from the moment she set eyes on him. In truth, she feared the nightmares the last few days would generate and welcomed his company. She kissed him back and pressed against his wonderfully hard muscular body in a silent demand. When he finally lifted his head and gazed down at her, she nodded. "I don't want to be alone either."

He slid one large hand around her waist and led her inside. Nerves shivered down her spine combined with a strange feeling of belonging. She leant into him inhaling his now familiar scent. When they stopped outside his bedroom, her heart raced in anticipation.

"My bed is bigger." He smiled down at her and turned the handle then in one swift movement lifted her into his arms.

His gentle kisses pushed away any doubts, and when her back hit the sheets, her love for him spilled over her in a waterfall of desire. She wanted to touch him and tugged at his shirt dragging it over his head then running her palms over his bronzed muscular chest. Under her hands, his flesh pebbled and his flat nipples hardened. She gazed at him and her mouth watered. Leaning forwards she used her mouth to tease him, nipping at his hard, brown nipples and making him groan with desire.

"I want to see you too."

Doug undressed her with gentle care then looked at her with such tenderness she wanted to cry. He cupped her breasts weighing them in his hands then rubbed his rough thumbs over the throbbing tips. She arched into him, and he lowered his head and captured one aching tip in his hot, wet mouth. The way he used his tongue made her squirm, heat pooled between her thighs in carnal delight. She held his head urging him to give pleasure to her other breast and sighed when he complied. "You do that so well."

"You taste like sin." He lifted his head and grinned at her. "Undo my jeans. I want to be skin on skin with you."

She ran her fingers up his thigh and his muscles tensed under her touch. His arousal pressed hard against the front of his jeans, and she fumbled with the zipper. She heard him chuckle and his hand covered hers guiding her. Against her palm, his flesh, hard hot and so alive, throbbed a welcome. She stroked taking in his length and girth and smiling at her fortune. Wriggling down the bed, she bent to taste him, enjoying the slide of silken flesh over her tongue, the flavour of the man she loved burst across her taste buds. She feasted taking him deep, then pulling back to flick the solid tip.

"Oh, darlin'." So close to ecstasy, Doug lifted her away from him. He needed protection and a five-second break to gain control. "Your mouth is so delicious, but I want all of you." He dragged off his jeans and tossed them and his boots on the floor. "One second." He rolled toward his bedside table and pulled open the drawer.

He heard her chuckle and turned to look at her beautiful face. "What's so funny?" He grinned. "Do I look like a gorilla?"

"I don't like condoms." She moved closer and ran the tip of her tongue from buttock to his earlobe. "I'm on the pill, and I want to feel every delicious inch of you."

He rolled her onto her back and stared down at her. "You are so beautiful. Perfect."

"You need glasses." She giggled and buried her long fingers in his hair dragging him to her lips.

He took her mouth in a savage claiming, kissing her until she begged him to take her. *Not yet.* Wanting so much more he nibbled his way to her breasts, teasing the hard nipples, enjoying her small pants of desire. He moved over her belly to her slick centre and lapped. When she cried out and jerked her hips, he held her hovering on the edge, flicking and swirling his tongue, gorging on her sweetness.

"Please, Doug, I can't take anymore."

He pressed one last kiss on her mound then moved between her thighs. When she arched, he suckled her hard nipples and nibbled her neck. He wanted their lovemaking to last forever and gazed at her flushed face. He licked her bottom lip, and she moaned but kept her eyes shut. "Tell me you want me."

"I want you so bad, don't keep me waiting. We have all night to practice." She wrapped her long legs around his waist

"So I need practice, huh?" He chuckled. "Look at me, Em'."

Her eyes opened, and unfocused blue orbs settled on his face. He rolled his hips and plunged into paradise. So wet and so hot, she held him tight and destroyed his control. He moved taking them on a ride of sweet discovery. She raked his back lifting to meet him, and her sweet moans of pleasure drove him mad with lust. Flames of passion curled in his groin sending waves of bliss up his length, and when she quickened around him, he thrust deep riding over the erotic precipice with her with a shout of triumph. He wanted to stay inside her and never leave, but when the last tremors of her climax slowed, he reluctantly withdrew. Spent and heart racing, he rolled to one side, worried he might hurt her ribs. When she reached for him, and her soft lips brushed his mouth, he kissed her tenderly.

"I love a man who cuddles after sex." She pressed kisses down his neck. "You are one of the rare ones, Doug Macgregor, and trust me, you don't need practice."

He pulled her close. "Why do I feel a 'but' coming on?"

"But" — she giggled and nipped at his chin — "I think with a man like you, once is never enough."

He pushed the hair from her eyes and kissed her forehead. Had he died and gone to heaven? He'd fallen for a woman who matched his sex-drive, and what a woman. She was perfect with a capital P. "I want you again too."

"That's good." She let out a long sigh and snuggled closer.

He stroked her back as she lay naked across his chest. Her long hair tickled his chin, and by her even breathing, she had fallen asleep. He closed his eyes. For once, everything was right in his world.

CHAPTER TWENTY

The following morning after a luxurious breakfast, Doug led Emily onto the veranda. A cool breeze moved her hair sending blonde wisps across her beautiful face. He could not stop looking at her. Her cheeks held the glow from their spectacular dawn shower sex, and her eyes still sparkled with passion, passion for him. He wanted to shout out his love for her.

He linked fingers with her and drew her closer, glad of her comforting presence. They were a match made in heaven, and he planned to ask her to marry him. Holding her close in the night, he'd made his intentions abundantly clear but hadn't said the words. He wanted to have an engagement ring ready to slip on her finger. His father had taught him to treat women with respect, and he wanted to make life perfect for Emily. He would ensure their engagement was special with wonderful memories to replace the terrible experiences she had suffered. When she snuggled into him, he squeezed her gently and gazed into her eyes. He wanted to reinforce his love for her and be the man she needed. "You are so beautiful. I can't believe you're my girl. I'm a very lucky man."

"I'm the lucky one." Emily's cheeks pinked, and she sighed. "I feel guilty about being so happy in the middle of such tragedy, but it keeps on bubbling up and popping out like a cork from a champagne bottle." She shook her head slowly. "I must have been grinning like an idiot at breakfast. Did you see the look Robbie gave me?"

"Well, he was talking about the other murders Johnno might have committed." He cleared his throat pushing down the need to kiss her and changed the subject. "I wonder how the muster is going. Ian headed back this morning to give the visitors the impression we are taking part. Robbie will meet them tomorrow. The ringers will bring the herd down and do the sorting, drenching and the like. The tourists enjoy this part of the experience as well, mainly I think because they get to sleep in a bed after sleeping rough for a few days."

"I'm looking forward to being involved next year." Emily wet her full lips and stared into the distance. "I like doing the chores with you. The accounts are a breeze but getting my teeth into investigating cold cases and being involved as a consultant for the police would be exciting." She sighed. "Do you think before we set this all up I could finish my last term in forensic science? I'm sure the universities in Australia will accept what I've done so far?"

"We'll enquire. Most likely you'll be able to finish most of your degree online."

"I hope so. I've always been a natural investigator, and the forensic science degree was my first choice, but my mum wanted me to be an accountant. It was difficult trying to work on stuffy books when I wanted to be solving crimes using forensic science. I compromised and did both." Emily giggled. "I just need one more semester, and I'm done."

"I'm sure they'll accept your previous studies. Heaps of people from overseas finish their degrees here." He tucked a lock of long blonde hair behind her ear. "You seem to be a natural when it comes to digging for information, but I'm worried about this part of the job. The crime scenes will be very disturbing. Will you be able to cope?"

"Of course." Emily lifted her chin with a confident air. "I've been taught to look past the graphic horror for clues." She gazed up at him. "That doesn't mean I should disregard the fact a person has died or been murdered. Everyone deserves to be treated with respect, that's why I insist on using the victim's names as often as possible to make sure everyone remembers they are someone's loved one."

"That's a good idea." Doug shrugged. "Right now, we need to concentrate on discovering if Brewster was Johnno's accomplice."

"We must find Johnno's diary. He was so sure of himself I wouldn't mind betting he recorded every detail." Emily grimaced. "If Mr. Brewster was involved, Johnno might have implicated him or made mention of his visit to Perth. That can't be coincidental. From what he said in the chopper he wanted to wipe out the Macgregor family and probably me as well." She sighed. "I'd like to know why he didn't tell Jock he was his son."

Doug slid one arm around her shoulder. "Jock would have welcomed him. He always told us he wanted more children."

"There you are." Robbie joined them on the veranda coffee in hand.

"We were trying to understand why Johnno went crazy." Emily shrugged. "Do you think his hatred built up over the last four years?"

"You can't rationalise the mind of a psychopath." Robbie wrinkled his nose. "Killing Jock surprised me because I gather at one time he craved to be accepted as one of the family. I guess he thought with our dad gone he could take his place. Maybe he planned to tell Jock he was his son but his plan backfired. Jock was inconsolable and whatever triggered Johnno's psychosis escalated."

"What do you mean?"

"From what I know about mental health, Johnno fits a psychopath profile in some respects but not in others, which means he was probably at the beginning of his murdering rampage. Most get off on the thrill of killing strangers, but once they extinguish life, the victims are no more use to them than a burger wrapper. Hence leaving victims in plain sight and taking trophies to relive the moment. Not many psychopaths kill their immediate family or friends, but we don't know what influence Brewster had on him. He could have fuelled the fire so to speak." He offered Emily a small smile. "You were very lucky not to become one of his victims."

Doug pulled Emily against his chest. "I had no idea, and I can usually read blokes pretty well." He tipped back his hat and stared at the sky. "I blame myself."

"You're not to blame, and sooner or later he would have acted the same regardless." Robbie frowned. "Psychopaths can convince a fly to jump into a spider's web. They don't look any different to anyone else, and smooth talking seems to be part of their charm."

"He was certainly charming." Emily glanced up at Doug. "I think we need to find his diary."

* * * *

Emily brushed the dust from her blue cotton shirt and rubbed her hands together. "It's been three days and no one has found a thing." She stretched her aching back and sighed. "This is a massive homestead. Johnno could have hidden his diary in a thousand different places."

"We might have to face the fact we'll never find it, if it exists at all." Doug glanced at his watch. "Perhaps we'll have another look in the storage barn once the tourists have left." He smiled at her. "I'm sorry you've missed the chopper tour of the Kimberley. I'll take you myself as soon as we have a moment to spare."

She frowned and rubbed her itchy nose. "Oh, I didn't want to go with Robbie and all those strangers. I'm not going anywhere until we've found the diary, and you'll have plenty of time to show me the sights another time." She jerked her chin towards the noisy crowd walking past the homestead and grinned. "I hope you're not planning on dumping me at the dance again tonight?"

"I didn't *dump* you, and this time I'm not leaving your side." He chuckled and cupped her cheek. "I'm only dancing with *my* girl."

"Ah, excuse me." Ian stood in the doorway dressed to charm and dangling a gold bracelet from between his finger and thumb. "I found this in the barn. It's solid gold and worth a pretty penny.

Can you put it in the safe?" He dropped the jewellery into Doug's open palm. "You can ask tonight if anyone has lost an item of jewellery." He swept a gaze over Emily then grinned. "You going to the dance dressed like that?"

Her face heated and she glanced down at her dusty clothes. "No, of course not, I'm heading for the shower now." She smiled at Doug. "I won't take long. I'll meet you in the kitchen in half an hour." She headed out of Jock's office and jogged towards her room.

Doug prodded the bracelet in his hand. "I can't imagine why women risk wearing such a delicate thing to muster cattle." He strolled to the landscape painting covering the safe. After twirling the dial in the outdated but substantial strongbox, he depressed the handle and pulled open the door. He scanned the familiar interior. The box of cash and the small pouch containing his parents' jewellery he had placed inside recently sat beside the files Emily had given him for safekeeping. At the back, he made out a dark leather-bound book. His chest tightened, and after dropping the bracelet inside, he reached for the hardcover. Apprehension gripped him as he turned the volume to read the spine and stared at the gold initials J.W.M. *John William Macgregor.* He called after Ian. "I've found Johnno's diary."

"I'll get everyone." Ian snapped his fingers under Doug's nose and glared at him. "Pull yourself together and lock the safe. Don't you dare read a page of that book until we're all present."

"Maybe we should call Detective Standish?"

"He said he wanted a word with Emily, so I've invited him to the dance. He'll be arriving soon in the police chopper." Ian ran from the room his boots clattering along the hallway.

Doug stared at the book turning it over in his hands. Would they discover the disturbed mind of a serial killer within these pages? Had Johnno always planned to kill his family or had something triggered his madness? He placed the book in the middle of the desk and wiped his hands on his jeans in an effort to remove Johnno's touch. When footsteps came from outside the office, he dropped into Jock's chair, and the smell of his grandfather surrounded him. He glanced over one shoulder convinced he stood behind him. "Have you come to seek justice, Jock?"

"What did you say?" Emily moved into the room dressed in a white bathrobe, her feet bare, and glanced around.

Doug leant back in the squeaky office chair and shook his head. "Nothing, love. I thought I could smell Jock's aftershave and thought maybe he'd come back to seek justice."

"I can always smell him in here." Ian strolled into the room and dropped into a seat by the window. "If a man sits in a leather chair for thirty years, it's going to carry his scent."

Robbie joined them, and they took seats and stared at him with expectant expressions. Doug ran a hand over his face and decided he had to man up and face the fact Johnno murdered his parents and Jock. He had been in hospital at the time and refused to take the blame another minute. His gaze moved to Emily and seeing the love for him shining in her eyes bolstered his resolve. He opened the cover and thumbed through the pages. "It's a five-year diary, four years in and will take some time to read. After what's happened recently, we have to make an appearance at the dance. Any suggestions?"

"If it goes back as far as you say then the first entry often sets the scene. He would have just arrived and might have written some insight into his motive for being at Winnawarra." Emily cleared her throat. "Take a look then jump forward to the days before your parents died then forward to the day Jock died."

"Good idea." Ian leant forward in the seat as if itching to grab the book from him and read it himself.

I wish someone else would read the damn thing. Doug opened the cover and glanced down the first few pages. He shook his head. "Nothing here but being excited about meeting his father. I gather he means Jock." He moved on and found the date of his parents' death. His skin crawled at the graphic detail contained on each page, and he swallowed the bile creeping up the back of his throat. He lifted his gaze to the concerned faces. "Yeah, he planned every detail of our parents' accident. He'd failed at an attempt to shoot them on a visit to Rainbow Gulley." He gave Emily a long look. "He must have refined his plans for us." His attention went back to the book. "He made an excuse to go with my parents to Darwin and knowing they would be having a picnic in the usual place, he cut the brake lines just enough to leak slowly. He followed their car some way back and waited for the accident to happen. The road is very steep there, and the path is tree lined. It's an isolated place only known by the locals. He took the driver's licence from my dad's wallet then doused them in methylated spirits." He looked at Emily. "That's just like you said." Grinding his teeth, he moved on. "The bastard set them on fire and watched them burn alive trapped in the car. It's all here — every detail."

"Do you want me to read the rest?" Emily offered him a sympathetic smile.

He straightened with determination. "Nope. I'm a big boy." He flicked through the diary and found an entry about Jock's murder. The horrific details had him reaching for a glass of whisky. He poured the drink with shaking hands, took a gulp then lifted his attention to the room. "The arsehole pushed Jock down the stairs." He closed the book unable to read another word, it was as if Johnno was invading his mind.

Suddenly Emily shot to her feet and moved to his side.

"There is a very good reason the cops keep this information from family members." She held out her hand. "Give me the diary. I'll take it from here."

Reluctantly he handed her the book, and she sat down. She turned the pages back and forth, for what seemed like an hour before lifting her chin.

"I'll make this as brief as possible. Jock was correct, Brewster was involved, but there is nothing here so far to implicate him in the murders. He did manage to get Jock to sign the papers to allow the mining company to do the core samples and filtered money into dummy accounts including one for Johnno." Emily wet her lips. "This is the proof we needed for Brewster's involvement."

"I can't wait to get my hands on him, the bastard." Doug flicked a gaze at Robbie. "I wish Jock had confided in us. We might have prevented Johnno's killing spree." He moved his attention back to Emily. "I can't imagine why Johnno didn't tell Jock he was his son. He spent all those years with anger gnawing away at him when Jock would have recognised him. I refuse to believe Jock turned his back on a pregnant woman. It wasn't his style. What else does it say, Em'?"

"There's a lot to sift through, and we'll have to give the diary to the police as evidence. He gives a clear account of why he came to Winnawarra and his intentions. Johnno was born in England, and when his mother died, he came to live with Brewster. He'd promised his mother he would find Jock and claim his rightful inheritance. Brewster arranged a job for him at Winnawarra but decided to keep Johnno's identity a secret. He thought if Johnno made a good impression on Jock he'd be proud to call him his son." She lifted her gaze to Doug. "Did you know Johnno had access to the safe?"

He shrugged. "Yeah, he was the assistant manager. He needed access to the cash box for the bar at the weekends. Jock never mentioned any money missing."

"He decided to kill your father after discovering Jock's will. So, I gather it's kept in the safe." Emily gave him a tight smile. "In the first copy, Jock had left everything to Jamie. Johnno had the crazy idea if he killed your father and Jock, he would come forward as Jock's son and inherit Winnawarra."

"He didn't factor us into the equation." Ian pulled a face. "What an idiot."

"We were added to Johnno's hit list after the reading of Jock's will." Emily straightened and her gaze swept over them. "I gather you told Johnno, Jock had changed his will to include all of us?"

"It was discussed." Ian frowned. "We had no idea what he was up to."

"Does he mention murdering anyone else?" Robbie raised one dark eyebrow in question. "My reason being, psychopaths usually start off slowly."

Emily cleared her throat, and her mouth turned down at the corners.

"Oh yeah, he started quite young. He hated the shame his mother had forced on him. He wanted to make women of easy virtue pay for his mother's affair with Jock." She rubbed both index fingers on her temples in slow circles. "He mentions a string of victims in the UK. Seems he left the country before the police implicated him. He drove a delivery truck, so spread his victims from one end of the country to the other." She held up the diary. "He has a detailed list on the inside of the back cover. I found descriptions of the murders as if he re-lived them on the anniversaries."

Disbelief shook Doug to the core. He swallowed trying to ease the lump in his throat. To think he'd worked beside a serial killer, slept under the same roof, and not had a clue. He sucked in a deep breath and took in the shocked expressions on the faces of his brothers. "This is very hard to believe. I mean, Johnno was a ladies' man. I would never pick him as someone capable of murder. He did his job, and we treated him like one of the family."

"The diary is the ramblings of a very sick but smart man." Emily lifted her chin. "Robbie mentioned psychopaths can have an incredibly high intellect and can outwit most people. They act like your best friend and on the outside appear to be a wonderful person. They don't have the 'dirty old man' or 'dangerous' persona and blend in very well. That's why they are so hard to find."

Anger raged in him. Johnno had fooled them all. "What else did you discover about Brewster and why did Johnno need the core samples?"

"Once he inherited Winnawarra, he planned to sell the property to a mining company. He tried to field the calls from prospective buyers before Jock's death. Your grandfather was disturbed about a call from a mining company and mentioned it in his diary. Detective Standish recalls the same thing in a complaint." Emily took a drink from a bottle of water then levelled her gaze on him. "Johnno needed Brewster to con Jock into signing the sample request forms and offered him a share in Winnawarra. He convinced him to syphon money from Winnawarra into dummy accounts in case his plan backfired. Johnno doesn't mention discussing murdering the family with Brewster but misrepresenting documents to a client is very underhanded for a man in a position of trust."

"I think that's everything we need to know." Robbie got to his feet. "It's getting late, and we need to put in an appearance at the dance." He held out his hand for the diary. "This needs to be in police hands. I'm sure the coroner will include the contents in his investigation." He looked from face to face and narrowed his gaze. "It's over folks. We have proved Johnno and Brewster's guilt beyond reasonable doubt. What happens next is out of our hands. We need to put this behind us and move on."

Doug pushed to his feet and nodded in agreement. "Yes, one day at a time. I'm not looking forward to the inquest, but I'm sure we can put up a united front for the tourists." He smiled at Emily. "Off you go, I'm not taking you to the dance wearing a bathrobe."

"Give me ten minutes." Emily ran out the door, the bathrobe billowing out behind her.

"Looks like just us blokes." He held up a bottle of Jock's fifty-year-old Scotch whisky. "I think a toast is in order." He poured the golden liquid into three shot glasses and passed them around. "To Mum, Dad, and Jock. Always in our hearts and never forgotten."

The glasses clinked together, and Doug blinked back the tears pricking the backs of his eyes. He offered his brothers a small smile. "Now this is over, I'm going to ask Em' to marry me. I know it has only been a few weeks, but I don't plan to marry her tomorrow, maybe in a couple of months."

"Are you sure?" Robbie eyed him critically.

"He is." Ian grinned like a monkey. "Haven't you seen the way they look at each other?"

"She'll be good for you." Robbie slapped him on the back. "One piece of advice. Keep away from redheads."

* * * *

With the immense weight lifted from her shoulders, Emily strolled beside Doug on the way to the dance. The magic of Winnawarra surrounded her like a warm hug as if the wild and unpredictable yet magnificently beautiful landscape was thanking her. Inside her bones, she understood why she never found peace in her life. Her home had not been in England, it was *here* in the magnificent Australian Outback with Doug. She sighed when he linked fingers with her, and his rough thumb stroked her flesh in an intimate caress.

On her walk towards the jostling crowd, she reflected on her future. She wanted to be useful and handling the station's books and helping with the chores was one thing but having the chance to do more, solve crimes made her quiver with excitement. Beside her, Doug cleared his throat, and she looked up into his handsome face. "Did you say something?

"Oh, no. I'm sorry I was away with the pixies."

His white grin lit up his face, and he turned her around to face him. They'd stopped under a tree covered in fairy lights winking in a rainbow of colours.

"I think tonight is the first time I've seen you relax." He slipped both large hands on her waist. "Are you happy at Winnawarra, Em'?"

She gazed up at him, his cowboy hat cast a shadow over his eyes, and she could not see his expression. "You are starting to read my mind. I was thinking how lucky I am to be here. I *love* Winnawarra and feel I've found my niche in life at last."

"And me?" He pulled her closer and her nostrils filled with his enticing scent. "Do I fit into your niche?"

She pressed her hands to his broad chest, she nodded. "Yes, you are a very special part."

The way he stared into the distance for long minutes made her stomach drop. Surely, after their blissful nights together, he wasn't planning to dump her? When he nuzzled her neck, she relaxed and sucked in a deep breath.

He lifted his head, and the reflection of a dozen fairy lights twinkled in his eyes.

"You know I'm broken. Out at Rainbow Gulley, I had a flashback, and I can never be sure they won't happen again." He cleared his throat. "You calm me. When I'm with you, the images stay away. I think it's because the love I have for you is stronger than the memories of the past." He rubbed her arms in long, slow strokes. "I want you beside me, to grow old with me, and watch our kids grow up strong and healthy here at Winnawarra. I want you for my wife, Em'. Will you have a broken soldier?"

Tears pricked the backs of her eyes. The unimaginable had happened. The magic of the Kimberley had woven a spell to keep them together. She cupped his face and kissed a path along the jagged scar on his chin, then brushed his lips. "Yes, I want you in my life too."

"Hang on." He pushed one hand into the front pocket of his jeans and pulled out a diamond ring. "This was my grandmother's, and I know she would want you to wear it. She was English like you." He cleared his throat. "It might not be the right size, and if you'd rather a new ring, I'll understand." He reached for her hand.

As the warm gold ring slipped over her knuckle and perfectly into place, Emily blinked back tears. She lifted her chin and smiled at him. "It's perfect, and I'd be honoured to wear it."

She melted against him, and he sealed their promise with a slow, delicious kiss. She moaned when he pulled away and chuckled. The sound came like a purr from deep in his chest.

"Come on, I want to tell the world." He took her hand and led her towards the noisy party.

Inside, he swept her onto the dance floor for a slow number. He held her close, and she fell easily into step with him. As she gazed into his eyes, the scene became surreal, wonderful. He kissed her possessively bringing snorts and chuckles from the people beside them. The song did not last long enough, and she wanted it to go on forever. When the music stopped, and a boot-scooting number screamed out the speakers, Doug grasped her hand and led her across the room towards the DJ. He motioned to the young man to stop the music and grabbed the microphone. Everyone turned to stare.

"Ladies and Cowboys, I would like to announce, my girl, Emily Perkins has given me the honour of accepting my proposal." He grinned widely. "We're engaged!"

Whoops and hollers followed, and the men dragging Doug to the bar made her laugh. They did everything differently in the Outback. She grinned at the merriment then noticed Glady at her side.

"Congratulations and for God's sake show me the ring. I can't wait another second." She grinned at Emily's outstretched hand. "Oh. My. God. That is one hell of a diamond." She glanced at the crowd jostling around Doug, but he broke away and moved to her side.

"What's up, Glady?"

"Can you slip away for a moment? Detective Standish wants a word, he is waiting outside."

"Of course." She smiled and followed Doug through the crowd. Outside she caught sight of Detective Standish standing a few feet away. He greeted them, and she waited expectantly for the detective to speak.

"First, I'd like to send the Police Commissioner's thanks to you for the many hours of tedious work you put in uncovering Johnno's crimes." Detective Standish swept a gaze over her and cleared his throat. "Of course, there is a deal more work to do before the coroner hands down his decisions on the deaths, but you have certainly given him enough evidence to re-open the cases." He met Emily's gaze. "The public prosecutor found you and the Macgregor boys have no case to answer in the death of Johnno."

Emily sucked in a deep breath and smiled. "That is wonderful news. Not that we were worried."

Detective Standish rubbed his chin thoughtfully then cleared his throat.

"My request to use your talents was approved with the proviso Miss Perkins finishes her degree, but we can help with that. Apparently, one term will satisfy the requirements. You'll be paid a consultancy fee for solving these crimes." He raised both eyebrows to his hairline. "Also, the consultancy job is ongoing. We have at least twenty cases for you to work on during the rainy season if you're interested?"

Emily gaped at him in disbelief then turned to Doug. "What do you say?"

"It will make life interesting." Doug grinned. "My brothers will be part of the team. We'll need Robbie's expertise."

"It will be your business, to run as you see fit. Now all you need is a business name." Detective Standish rubbed his chin. "I'm sure Emily can handle the paperwork necessary to register a business once her permanent status is verified."

"That won't be a problem, we are getting married." Doug pulled her into his strong arms and kissed her soundly.

"Congratulations." Detective Standish grinned. "Well then, you let me know when you have everything up and running. I'll leave you two lovebirds alone." He wandered toward the dance.

As they stared into the darkness, Emily snuggled in Doug's arms, and they turned towards the last rays of the setting sun. The spectacular sunset had been her first taste of the beauty of Winnawarra. How could she have possibly known when she arrived in this mystical place she would find her soulmate amid so much chaos. She pointed at the red and gold hues clinging to the darkening sky. "What about Red Skies Detective Agency."

"Sweet." He looked down at her, his expression intent. "I promise to make you happy, Em', *forever*."

She tipped back her head and looked into his eyes. "I know you will."

At that moment, a shooting star cut a silver path through the Outback sky and for the first time in her life Emily knew she had found true love.

THE END

AUTHOR BIOGRAPHY

Romance One Word at a Time

Born in London, England and now living in Australia, Elizabeth spent twenty years in a small rural town before moving to the coast. She enjoys the thrill of writing romance and creates stories that will remain with the reader long after the final page.

Connect with Elizabeth

http://www.elizabethmdarcy.com/

ELIZABETH M. DARCY

LUMINOSITY
PUBLISHING

CPSIA information can be obtained
at www.ICGtesting.com
Printed in the USA
LVHW090148240619
622128LV00001B/10/P